THE
GATE
OF
ALEPH

J.H. Ellis

To the Rev. Cheryl Daniels—
you wrote what you heard.

Lift up your heads,
O ye gates; even lift them up, ye everlasting doors;
And the King of glory shall come in.

Psalm 24:9

(King James Version)

Chapter One

STARRY GOODBYES

The moon was rising over the Gardens of Destiny when Shammah overheard two palace slaves muttering prayers to Livnath. One begged for healing from an infected leg wound, the other pleaded for a lover to return. While Shammah refused to worship the goddess, the slaves' woeful petitions to her made him remember that disastrous feast.

Shammah had been standing on the temple platform. The full moon blazed ivory and throngs of people cheered from below. The high priest Haran gestured to Aikah to drop coals into a large, fiery bowl. After that, the king was expected to recite a prayer.

Stalking to the bowl like a tiger, Aikah gripped the priest's tongs. He tossed the coals into the fire. "Forever, you are patroness of Seth, my Livnath!"

The coals sizzled as Aikah waited for Shammah to join him and Haran. As Shammah calculated how to dodge the priest and his tongs, light fled from the fiery bowl.

Haran swung around in agitation to see what had doused the flames. The turn was awkward, and the priest pivoted on his ankle, slipped on the train of his robe, singed his fingers, and dropped the tongs. As the younger acolytes tended to the embarrassed high priest, Aikah threw a punishing glare at Shammah.

The message was unmistakable. Aikah believed Shammah used the night arts to instigate Haran's mishap. When Haran howled in pain and couldn't continue the ritual, Aikah called an end to the ceremony.

The clouds shuttered the moon, and the people went home. Shammah knew the reprieve wouldn't last. One day, he would stand in his father's place as the savior-king of Seth, the Proud Lord of the Seven Gates, forcing Shammah to follow every king before him and grope and wail at Livnath's altar.

The path in the Gardens of Destiny curved gently to the left. Shammah could no longer hear the slaves' voices near the Ten Pillars etched with the name of each savior-king. A few steps beyond the canopy of pillars sat a large crystal lens held together with uncut stone and bronze plates. He peered into the lens and glimpsed the grainy image of the moon. The seven clustered stars twinkled before him as he studied them.

"Ah." Chazon settled his lanky frame on a bench, palming bony knees. "The *kimah* on the shoulder of the bull enthralls you again. The stars continue to mystify you."

"Of course." Shammah faced him.

Chazon studied the sheer clouds. "What you seek is not far from you."

"Will your answer satisfy the needs of the poor and judge those who divert them from justice? Shammah asked. Will your answer explain the origins of life and overturn the grief of death? Those are my questions when the *kimah* blink at me with the gaze of an unfathomable king."

Chazon's heavy black brows clung together in thought, but he remained silent.

"You offer me answers from the gloomy Aleph," Shammah continued. "The other gods sparkle in the sky. Their overfed priests preen in bright robes in their temples. But your Aleph, where you serve as priest, hides out on a mountain that's drab on a sun-drenched day."

"Ask Aleph for vision, and it will come," Chazon said.

"I offer an observation and you respond with a riddle." Shammah sighed as the glittering *kimah* faded into the sky.

Chazon folded his arms. "I am playing your childhood tutor again, and this time, on the early morning of your departure. You set a trap for me. I tumbled into it."

Fondness rose on Shammah's face. "I will miss our debates."

"Yet you persist in rejecting Aleph."

"I reject all gods. Even your mountain. I have always wondered why my father, the spirit-slave of Livnath, allowed you to tutor me."

"We were boyhood friends."

"No. He thinks Livnath is more powerful than Aleph. He tolerates you."

Chazon raised a brow. "Perhaps. Whatever Aikah thinks of me, your father tests you."

"I followed your lessons," Shammah said.

"Your father's lessons. My lessons will yet test you."

Shammah groaned. "This feels like a day with you and the scribes. How my heart pants for your tutelage, priest."

"When you understand who you are, you will turn away from the roads that do not reach the gate of Aleph," Chazon said.

"If I can count the stars, I can number the times you've said that to me."

"You remembered it, did you not?"

Shammah laughed. "A tutor's torments never fade."

Aikah walked toward them. "What did Shammah remember?"

Shammah stiffened. His bantering mood slipped away as Aikah joined them. "Chazon's lessons, Father. Old age must be upon him. The priest repeats himself."

"Men anticipate war and victory, love and sorrow, old age and death," Aikah said. "In our youth, we race toward them all. As old men, we fail trying to outrun them. Chazon and I act on our wishes for you—to sit on the throne of Seth."

Chazon grunted. "And upon whom has old age fallen? Aikah sounds like he addresses the overfed nobles—the ones more intrigued by barley prices than war. Laugh with us Aikah, and I promise not to tell Shammah how on one starry night you tricked Haran into getting a beating."

"You weren't that kind to Haran, either," Aikah said.

"I was not. I bullied him with you..." Chazon paused. "But he did not envy me. Your mother nurtured you. Haran's mother humiliated him. Your father taught you to fish and use a knife. They found Haran's father dead after a brawl over a woman. Haran yearned for what you had, what you were."

"Haran is the high priest, and he hasn't forgiven me—nearly thirty years since. I thought Livnath's privileges had atoned for my childhood insults."

"He does not realize that many covet the freedom you give him," Chazon said.

Aikah didn't reply to Chazon's light, but direct rebuke. Only the priest of Aleph spoke plainly to the king. For a moment, Shammah wondered whether Chazon's words were too sharpened by truth. Aikah demanded loyalty and obedience from everyone—from servant to soldier and all in between.

"Perhaps," Aikah said. "My actions lie in the hands of Livnath, whose moon shines on us. My heir will lead Seth to new territories."

"I hope so, Father."

"You are my son. You do not doubt."

"But I have questions."

"Your expedition into the marshes will answer them. Find out the Mikana's movements. They have hovered near Nifla for weeks. I expect an attack. Do not engage them if you don't have to. Kill immediately if you are forced to."

Aikah's voice relaxed as he continued. "Have you bid goodbye to Mahalath and her family?"

Shammah flexed his shoulders. His father ordered war and love for him, and Shammah pushed the bile of resentment down his throat. "I met with Lord E-ven and reassured him that I would set the marriage date upon my return."

"Good. You'll be the envy of many young men, not just because you will be king, but because of Mahalath. Her loveliness rivals anyone in Seth."

Shammah didn't reply, but his face loosened into a sweeter expression as he observed Gila walking toward them: an elegant queen in the smallest details with her gold robes, fiery hair, and skin the color of nutmeg.

She fixed her attention on Shammah. "The Mikana thirst for war. I thirst for your life."

She pulled a seal from her robes. "I know you have the one that you crafted for yourself years ago, but I wanted you to have this to carry with you, in case you're lost, in case you have to prove—or remember—that you are beloved by the kingdom of Seth. And by me."

The carved seal bore the face of a man with the body of a four-winged hawk.

"Your mother spoils you," Aikah said. "I daresay she paid an artisan handsomely."

Shammah suspected that Gila's gift moved Aikah. Like no one else, Aikah understood that every expedition that involved the Mikana carried risks.

"The queen reminds Lord Shammah of his destiny," Chazon said. "It is something your mother would have done, Aikah."

The king gazed at the moon before he replied. "Mother gave me love without limits."

Shammah focused on Gila. He closed his right hand over the ivory seal and kissed Gila's cheek.

"Expect me," Shammah said.

She gripped his arm. "Hurry."

Everything was burning. White, hissing flames emanated from the bodies of the Mikana and spewed from farm to farm. Human cries soared over the chaos in the fields surrounding the city gates. The soldiers protecting the city of Nifla remained armed and unmoved on the great walls.

"Restraint from the Proud Lord of the Seven Gates. See how the savior-king veils his intent," Commander Ciycera murmured. His half-dog, half-man face shifted in the moonlight. With a clawed forefinger, he caressed his gold and amethyst necklace.

"Commander?" The lieutenant standing near Ciycera arched his massive neck. Salvia bubbled between his bared teeth. Ciycera understood the young lieutenant's thirst. He lusted for mortal bones to chew, a delicacy the Mikana could enjoy once the battle ended.

Ciycera grunted. "Expect a place at my table."

The promise of feasting overrode the lieutenant's disappointment, and he barked a signal to the other warriors. "Warriors, we're going home," the lieutenant said.

The Mikana warriors grumbled in surprise as the embers beneath their skin vanished. Lifting their spears and swords high, the Mikana retreated.

Ciycera held back, letting the gleeful lieutenant lead the warriors from Nifla without him. They had fulfilled their mission to harass Nifla's people and killed a few mortals.

While they hadn't penetrated the city's walls, the Mikana had identified a weakness in Nifla's military. The soldiers appeared to be disciplined, but King Aikah hadn't led his army into battle in about twenty years. Ciycera also noticed that many of the soldiers guarding the wall were younger and appeared untested; they could disobey orders and break from the wall if they heard death loudly enough.

Ciycera leaned on his sword and watched the dying flames. Wails of men and women entering the realms of death pealed through the night, and he cherished the sound.

The lieutenant led the warriors yelping through a forest of gnarled date palms and scattered rocks. Some of the men pulled out waterskins bulging with Mikana wine and the essence of poppies. Ciycera forbade drinking during military campaigns, but the lieutenant was in charge now, and the warriors were returning home to the City of Knowledge.

The sixty-six-member contingent took turns imbibing, even forcing their riding beasts to slurp wine. The warriors' cackles became louder as the night deepened.

Regaling the troops with war tales, the lieutenant froze in mid-sentence to sniff the air with his large nostrils. Dead animals. Recently killed. He couldn't detect a human scent, but he suspected enemies surrounded them.

The lieutenant signaled the Mikana warriors with him and they assembled in a disjointed formation. Too drunk to stand, or to leap on their beasts, the warriors crawled on the ground, looking for enemy prey. They reached a ridge. Shadows crossed before them.

Anxiety rushed through the lieutenant like cold water. "Attack!"

He shouted the command as spears and arrows showered on them. The Mikana warriors stumbled on the rocks, too drugged to fight back. An arrow pierced the lieutenant in his jaw. His skin sizzled. Poison.

As the lieutenant lay there, Nifla soldiers emerged from the forest, covered in bloody animal skins. He tried to focus. He now understood. Not every Nifla soldier had guarded the wall. Some of them had hid in the date forest to entrap the Mikana as they returned home.

The lieutenant growled as someone stabbed his right hoof. He stomped back with his left hoof and punched the soldier's thigh.

As he did, the lieutenant glimpsed one of his younger Mikana warriors rolling away on the ground. He was escaping.

The lieutenant wanted to rejoice and rise, but he couldn't. Another Nifla soldier pointed his sword at his throat, then tore off the lieutenant's gold and amethyst necklace, the prize given to every Mikana warrior at birth identifying them as Zuzim offspring.

"Defeated by mere men." The lieutenant muttered in disbelief as he slipped into darkness.

Shammah's feet sank in the mud. He had stopped calculating how long they had followed the lone Mikana warrior from Nifla. Like his men, while focused on capturing the warrior, his face bore less worry. The expedition was almost over. Their ruse with the men from Nifla defeated the bulk of the Mikana contingent. Capturing the warrior who escaped would sweeten their homecoming.

Gripping their bows, Shammah and his men dodged through the thick date palm forest. The hooves of the Mikana warrior charged ahead as he tore dead fronds from his path.

Shammah joined the young soldier and kneeled to examine the shiny skin, the expandable rib cage, and the glowing gold and amethyst necklace that encircled the warrior's neck.

The warrior fell.

Sweat poured down Shammah's back. The warrior's scaly, glowing skin and shifting features mesmerized him. The smell of burnt, rotten flesh sickened him.

"We must cut off his head. If he survives, we die." The commander who spoke to him was one of Aikah's most trusted men, a witness to decades of war.

"My lord. You defy the orders of the savior-king," the commander continued. "Every Mikana dies at once. Allow me to use my sword."

"Bind the beast." Shammah paused. "For now."

"My lord?" The commander's face turned pomegranate-red. Shammah didn't reply.

The commander relented. "Bind the beast!"

The soldiers approached the unconscious warrior as he lay facedown in the mud. Air scratched through the warrior's nostrils and the noise penetrated the width of the marsh. The warrior was nearly the length of a young cedar tree.

The soldiers wound ropes around the warrior's arms and hooves and bound his mouth and claws. When they finished, they stepped back, poised to flee.

"You!" shouted the commander to a frowning young soldier gripping his bow with a steady left hand. "Stand watch first."

Shammah joined the young soldier and kneeled by the Mikana examining the shiny skin, the expandable rib cage, and the glowing amethyst necklace that circled the warrior's neck.

She'iya clung to Aikah, human nectar for his honeycomb of power. This was how she loved him. Seduce, then possess. Swallow his soul until they ruled the kingdom of Seth as one; until he cried out only for her.

She screamed that desire within her heart, yet she forbade her lips to say it, for the king could banish her and Aikah's furies surpassed her own. Many of the maimed in the City of Kings and the dead in the tombs suffered because of his rages. She'iya wanted to be his queen, not his victim.

She tangled her tapered fingers between his heavy locks. The two were relaxing on his palace balcony, but he ignored her caresses. The moonlit Gardens of Destiny held his attention. She knew Aikah worried needlessly about Shammah. No one cared about the boy Aikah kidnapped after pillaging Nifla. Many believed that Aikah should have left Shammah in the North Country instead of bringing him to the palace, adopting him as his son, and naming him heir.

Surely Livnath hadn't destined Shammah to be king. He was handsome and scholarly enough, but he wasn't Dahv—the son She'iya had with Aikah. Dahv embodied military genius and an image of Aikah in his youth, but a concubine's son couldn't become king, unless Aikah overturned the law, which he refused to do. She'iya felt snubbed and avoided challenging Aikah openly. She picked at Shammah, nibbling at his abilities and character like a strangling vine that sought to dominate quietly.

Aikah had pushed Shammah toward war, but She'iya warned him that he wasn't the battle type. Against her counsel, he'd sent Shammah to the outskirts of Nifla to track a Mikana contingent. The last word they had received from Shammah was two months ago. Meanwhile, Aikah's worries had grown. She'iya was certain the Mikana had devoured Shammah and his men.

The temptation to have her way drove her from the boundaries of self-control. She'iya tugged another one of Aikah's curls and twisted it into a tight coil between her fingers.

With a grunt, Aikah pulled away. "I feel your claws tonight."

He studied her for a moment, then buried his hands in her heavy hair, set with polished stones of lapis lazuli. "My touch is fiercer than yours, my cheetah. Beware of me."

She lifted her face so that he could roam her dark eyes. "My king, please forgive me. I, too, worry about the whereabouts of the king's heir. We should have had word days ago. Let me help you bear your sorrow."

"Kindness toward my heir? No. You believe Dahv languishes while I prepare Shammah for the throne," Aikah said. "You're a mix of childish arguments and happiness. You excite my blood. But kindness? Generosity of spirit drowned in the river of your childhood wishes. The gods scorched your heart and mine before we understood their burning. They captured you with beauty and lust. They overcame me with promises of power. You do not care for Shammah and you don't care for your son. As Dahv satisfies your ambitions, you release affection like a stingy water pot."

"Then pretend I care about the whereabouts of your heir," She'iya said, "and kiss me before the dawn comes."

He brought his lips near to hers but paused. His hands flexed beneath her hair. His cruel words and harsh grip didn't wound her. But his unwillingness to kiss her did.

She pressed her face to his. "What is it? Do you need reassurances of my love? If I'm bound to no one else, even my son, surely I'm lovesick over the king."

He breathed in the scent of wine and dates. From the first time she had seen him enter the gate of the City of Kings, leading his army after defeating the Mikana, she wanted him. The tempest within him called out to her, although she knew one day it would cost her.

Aikah wrapped his arms around her. "Can uncontrolled fire and flooding waters reassure me?"

He kissed her, and she relaxed.

The doors to Aikah's chambers flung open, and Queen Gila rushed in. Slender as a reed, regal as one of the founding mothers of Seth, Gila was She'iya's rival and, here, she was in command. The woman she could never unseat from Aikah's side.

Aikah didn't release She'iya, but he turned his attention to the queen. "What's wrong?"

Gila walked right up to them, focusing on Aikah and ignoring She'iya, the insect crawling on a leaf.

The king shoved She'iya away.

Panting with impatience, She'iya retreated a few steps, but refused to show any sign of guilt or embarrassment; she stood proudly with her tousled hair and robes.

"He has returned," Gila said.

"But that's good," Aikah said. "Let us thank Livnath."

"Only in part. There were many losses."

Aikah waited for Gila to say more. She clamped her lips.

"Where is he?" Aikah demanded.

"In his quarters. In the Gardens."

"But I didn't see him."

"Perhaps someone stole your attention." The queen threw a glance of full-blown disgust at She'iya, who felt every drop of Gila's bile.

She'iya tightened her stare, longing to return Gila's distaste with hatred. A concubine could seduce a king, but she couldn't defy a queen's authority.

"We should go to him in the morning," Gila said to Aikah. "After he has slept and eaten."

"Of course," the king replied.

Gila left the chambers, and Aikah walked to the balcony. She'iya followed his gaze to a small structure not far from the crystal lens. Lamps were lit. Slaves bustled in and out of the building with fresh water, clothes, and platters of food.

Aikah's heir was home.

Aikah didn't come to She'iya's chambers that night, and menacing dreams filled her sleep. Aikah was right. Livnath had already taken so much from her.

She was a child at Livnath's first visit. Her people were poor farmers who lived outside the gates of the City of Kings. They had few expectations for their ten children. Survival robbed them of lofty desires. They often murmured "work and live" to She'iya and her siblings as they went to sleep.

When Livnath came to her during the harvest, the goddess enticed her with promises of riches and fame; she promised a higher social status for She'iya if she committed to her in blood. She'iya made the vow.

The girl started accompanying her father when he brought his produce to the City of Kings to sell. She soon learned that a lingering caress on the hand sold more vegetables. From there, she graduated to higher ambitions. Outwitting a prominent nobleman during a street game earned her a place in his house. She eventually met Aikah while being escorted by another noble at a royal feast.

Her family didn't weep when she left her parents' shabby mud home. Nor did they seek her help when they spotted her with wealthy nobles or even the king. Pride, or fear of Livnath's wrath, barred them from approaching her.

Tonight, she didn't seek Dahv to console her with a son's love because she didn't have a mother's affection to offer in return. She balled up her body and cried out for Livnath to shatter the bond between Aikah and Shammah. Their estrangement would make her happy because Aikah's heart would belong to her.

Content with her petition, she reconsidered the preparation of a private feast for Dahv. She could let him taste one of Aikah's special wines. Her greedy son would be grateful for every cup she gave him.

CHAPTER TWO

UNEXPECTED WINDS

With a grunt, Shammah tossed two clay tablets that cracked on the mud brick hearth. Reading about the battles generations ago deepened his sorrow about his thirteen men in Nifla. Earlier in the day he had gone to the homes of their families in the City of Kings and declared his condolences and responsibility for the failed mission. Several families spat at him. A few never opened their doors. Only the father of the young man who had guarded the camp at the first watch embraced Shammah. The man's silent greeting had wounded Shammah the most.

The second tablet contained a hymn about the romantically ruined, and the narrative was a comical piece. If he could remember who insisted he read it, Shammah would send the tablet back with a few biting words about a banal effort that lacked meaningful proverbs and even hope.

Shammah ran his fingers on another stack of tablets on a table. He dragged his oil lamp closer. *Songs from the Founding.* It was a collection of poems Mahalath gave him on the day they were betrothed. The tablet opened with words about date palms:

> *Broad in covering,*
> *Sweet to our lips,*
> *The date palms guarded the founding of the City of Kings,*
> *but the tamarisk, soaring above us, supplied relentless strength.*

Reading those first lines of the poem reignited a memory of date palms and tamarisk trees Shammah couldn't fully reassemble in his mind. Although the Gardens of Destiny were filled with the trees, why did the distinct, but stately trees sometimes prompt sadness? The deadly mistakes he made in Nifla's date forest had introduced a fresh, tragic memory, and sadness poured over him again. Too many mysteries begged to be explored, but Shammah didn't have time to ponder these things. He put the tablet aside and wiped his face with the back of his right hand. Tomorrow he would present himself to his father.

On the third day of waiting, just before evening, the winds swirled, cooling the hot air. Shammah headed to the king's quarters. He walked past Chazon and Gila in the courtyard without a word. Frustration bruised Chazon's heart. Shammah hadn't answered his requests for an audience, and Aleph had revealed nothing. Chazon felt surrounded by a heavy and tumultuous cloud.

As Shammah disappeared into Aikah's rooms, Mahalath came into the courtyard, accompanied by her sister Rina. The sisters' slave hovered in a corner, rubbing his folded arms. Chazon suspected the slave also thought the visit was ill-timed.

"My lady," Mahalath said, addressing Gila while twisting a fold in her sparkling robes the hue of red apples. "I understand Lord Shammah has returned to the City of Kings. I have not been given word of his condition. I thought—as his betrothed—I could do something. You know, my lady, help him in any way."

Chazon folded his hands to keep from speaking. Mahalath worried about her future. The throne was too close to ignore.

"Thank you for your concern for my son, Lady Mahalath," Gila said. "I am certain he will want to spend time with you as soon as he has met with the king. Much happened on his expedition."

"But the Mikana did not injure him?"

"No, my dear. He was not."

Mahalath clasped her short fingers together. "Please do not hesitate to let me know, my queen, if Lord Shammah has need of me."

"Of course," Gila said.

Chazon and Mahalath chatted as they strolled from the palace, with Rina and their slave trailing behind. She surprised Chazon with her knowledge of the political dealings of the nobles and scribes. Her parents had schooled her well.

When they neared the Gardens of Destiny, the winds increased, and a retinue of soldiers approached them. Dahv was among them, handsome and confident in his blue uniform. He nodded his head toward Mahalath for several moments until his horse pawed the ground impatiently. As she watched Dahv leave, Mahalath caught her breath and stumbled.

"Are you well?" Chazon held her right arm for a moment then let her go.

Mahalath lifted her left hand to her mouth, then dropped it. The curls framing her face danced with the winds. "A rock in my sandal. What were we discussing? Yes, yes. I agree with your description of the forums Lord Shammah once led. They brought hope to our people."

Her breathing became shallow. "The scribes miss the debates. I have overheard them complain in the market. Ah. No need to go farther. Thank you, my lord. My father's house is not far from here."

Mahalath scurried away with the slave and Rina, who hissed at her sister in reproof.

Chazon, studying them as they left, crunched his eyebrows into a dark line. Aleph had answered Chazon where the priest hadn't even posed a question.

After sunset, the sky churned into dark gray. Lightning and thunder showered the palace and the Gardens of Destiny. Unperturbed by the storm, Aikah studied Shammah, who stood like a date palm, majestic in its quiet. Aikah had longed to see his heir, so grateful that he was alive, but he also wanted to thrash him in every corner of the palace. Shammah—the one he chose over Dahv, the one who captured his heart, had disobeyed him. Because of his recklessness, soldiers died and a Mikana warrior had lived to chortle with his kin.

The gathering winds fanned through the open balcony window, stirring the heavy curtains. Three slaves scurried to light oil lamps, which, when lit, cast faint shadows over large reliefs showing Aikah, sword in hand, charging toward a crowd of Mikana warriors.

One slave gaped at Shammah and nearly tripped and fell. Shammah leaped to grip the youth by the elbow.

"My lord, I'm clumsy. I deserve a beating." Though he was shaking, the slave clung to the oil lamp.

"Say nothing else," said Shammah. "Have I not slipped many times before the savior-king of Seth? My limbs felt like water. Dread captured my soul. Do you feel steady now?"

The slave offered a timid nod and rushed from the chambers.

Scowling, and untouched by Shammah's gesture toward the slave, Aikah slid from a narrow couch in his bare feet. With a practiced swiftness, he slapped Shammah.

"My heir. My right arm. My chosen hope," Aikah said. "I chose you above the sons of my loins. I brought you from the marshes and reared you as my heir. To wield the sword as I would. To slay my enemies as I would. To display the power of my throne."

Another slap.

"Does weakness entrap your lips? Why do you cower with no debate? Where are your philosophies? Where are your epic tales, scholar-son?"

"You despise my epic tales, Father. They are folly compared with your battles. 'The only real blood is the blood staining my hands.' Have you not muttered those words to me moons upon moons when your goddess gazes upon us?"

"You will not woo me into an argument when I will not be persuaded. You extend kindness to a slave but how do you explain disobedience that cost me men? What do you say to their fathers and mothers? To their wives? To their sons and daughters?"

Aikah slapped Shammah a third time. Blood flowed along the line of Shammah's lips, but he remained immobile.

"My words you cannot understand."

"Why not? Do you speak the tongue of some unknown enemy or people?"

"Anger cannot fathom the sorrow within me."

"I shall not pretend to divine the obstinance within you. Leave my presence. May the deserts embrace you as your father. Enthrone yourself among the nomads. Lift your scepter with the worms."

Shammah took a long look at the gardens. He had planned to reconstruct the irrigation channels and plant more flowers and vegetables when he returned from Nifla. He plucked a droopy rose from its bush not far from where Chazon watched him. Shammah brushed his fingers together as the rose petals fell on the ground.

"Those soldiers should not have died," Shammah said. "Only the limbs of that Mikana warrior should be scattered across the earth."

"A softened and humbled heart betters the man," Chazon said.

"I grieve my men, but not my father. No softening has occurred."

"It must. The throne will be yours."

"A dung heap of blood? I do not desire Aikah's droppings."

Shammah climbed up on his horse and caught sight of Aikah staring down at him from his balcony above. "And Aikah, my constant lamentation, does not want me to have it."

"His heart lies," Chazon said.

"You search for pure water in a sewer, tutor-priest."

"May our lessons in these gardens guide you."

Shammah resisted voicing the foul words that sprouted in his mind. "Tell the queen... tell my mother... I wish her peace."

Slaves who had been waiting nearby with several camels bearing supplies were ready to leave the garden with him. With a wave, Shammah led them forward. He didn't turn when he heard Gila call to him as she ran from the palace.

"Son of another woman, adopted son of my heart, may the winds of your wanderings bring you back to me!"

No, mother, Shammah thought. *May my wanderings imprison me.*

Gila paced before Aikah. Her stormy face confronted his tangled expression. Without acknowledging her, Aikah snatched a date and chewed it. Gila stirred his restlessness and uncovered his sense of failure and loss. He didn't want to see or answer her.

"Does the rose bush overcome the date palm? It does not," Aikah said. "If I cannot control the steps of my heir, how can I lead an army? Do you want the Mikana to rain fire on us?"

"Why not shave his head in shame instead of choosing this spectacle? Transgressions do not rot in Shammah's bosom alone."

Aikah arched a brow. The hurt and humiliation he'd inflicted on her was a sadness for him. He reflected on how he had kidnapped Gila and her sister from the Cove of Revealing. Gila's sister had died during the journey, but Gila lived to be his queen. He often wondered if Gila wished she had died.

Before he could utter words of regret to Gila, She'iya saun-tered in from an adjacent chamber, glowing with an air of defiance. She approached the king and stroked his neck. The concubine's touch dizzied him.

"What do you know about the heart of the king, barren queen of Seth?" She'iya asked.

Gila straightened her shoulders, ready to release a verbal arrow. "You sup on the king's lusts, but dare not speak to me, leech. I may feed my imagination and pierce your heart."

"Then I will address the Proud Lord of the Seven Gates," She'iya said. "My love? For the queen's severity, what gentle kindness may I offer you instead?"

"Mind your life," Aikah murmured. "Gila is my queen."

"Yes, my lord," She'iya said. "But may I tend to your heart?"

Gila left the chamber abruptly, her robes fluttering in a lament.

CHAPTER THREE

STORMY SOULS

Gila sat alone in the gardens, trapped in a prison of sadness. For three years, she had mourned the beloved son who had never returned. Keeping busy with her duties around the palace and her charities in the City of Kings never replaced his presence, but the rhythm of helping others guarded her from despair. For every act of cruelty Aikah imposed or permitted the priests of Livnath to place on the poor, she attempted to balance with food and shelter and affection. Sometimes her efforts felt futile, especially on this day, when unexpected shadows of sorrow surrounded her.

The queen had longed for the day when Aikah's brutal ways with her would end, too. Year after year, he bounced between showing affection and spouting humiliations. She knew that he loved her, as a youth with little understanding, but the gnarled roots within him shackled and lured him toward selfish chases. He pursued She'iya, he toyed with Dahv, and he punished Shammah with exile. Dark secrets polluted Aikah's body and soul. The night Aikah brought Shammah to the palace after his raid in Nifla against the Zuzim, the child had clung to her. At the boy's touch, years of childlessness fell from her. Then, one night, long after the boy had curled in his bed, Aikah slipped into her chambers. He kneeled beside Gila and fidgeted.

"The boy is pleased with you," Aikah said.

"He is a thoughtful child," she said. "He misses his mother."

"I want to keep him," Aikah said.

An inner fire lit Gila's face. "Banish the concubine from my presence forever, and I will mother the child. I am moved by him."

The rustle of a breeze flowing through her chamber could be heard. Aikah reached for Gila's hands. As he bowed his head, she remembered how he had first caressed her in longing when she became queen. She curved her lips in a bittersweet smile and placed her hands on his glossy curls.

"I have caused you tremendous suffering, and yet you continue to show me respect and kindness," he said. "I am unworthy of you."

Apprehension dusted Gila's whispered reply. "Bring your soul to rest. Perhaps we will find love again."

"I am a king with political enemies on every side," Aikah said. He took Gila's hands in his own. "I cannot run away and sing to you in the hills."

"No one is asking you to abandon the kingdom," the queen said. "The people made you king after Kish died with no heir. Your military success and your father's reputation made you Seth's choice. You are the savior-king. But accolades cannot compensate for what a man needs to love, to grow old with dignity, and to die with honor."

Aikah dropped her hands. "Your words flow like the imaginary waters that consecrate Chazon's tongue. Care for the child and train him. My throne is his."

"My sadness is that we won't bear a son together."

"And whose choice was that? You decided to keep me from your chambers. Not me. I did not overrule your decision—something I never would allow another breathing woman in Seth to do. You brought childlessness upon us. I have remedied that problem by making Shammah the one to carry my name."

Gila sighed. "You know the truth of why we cannot bear a child together. Because of it, I will one day lose you."

She saw the clouded look in Aikah's golden-brown eyes, but she turned to the boy sleeping in her chambers. "What happened to his mother and father?"

"Livnath chose the boy. There is no more to know."

Gila didn't believe him. Aikah thrived in complexities, and his devotion to Livnath surpassed her priests, who cut themselves and wailed in the temple tower.

"Neither you nor I can explain the mysteries surrounding Livnath," Gila said. "She creates a luminous night sky and promptly ushers in bedlam into your kingdom and into your soul. My king, is she truly a fountain of mercy and love?"

His fingers curled around Gila's right wrist. "Never question her."

Chilled by the memory, Gila lowered her head and pressed her feet into the dirt near the seat.

"Is the queen in prayer?" She'iya traipsed over from a nearby path.

"The queen is not, but that doesn't give you permission to speak to her," Gila said, standing to her full height, an ache in her back raging.

She'iya bowed before the queen. Gila noticed the small swell at the concubine's stomach.

"May I speak?" She'iya asked.

"You want to tell me that you will bear another child for Aikah."

"Not only will Shammah not make it to the throne, but the children I bring into the palace will outnumber him."

The pain in Gila's back throbbed. She'd asked Aikah to banish the concubine, but he never did.

She'iya continued. "You bring him nothing. You are a farmer's cart without vegetables, a field without barley crops, and a storm cloud without rain. Your adopted seed will bow to mine."

"Stop, and I will spare your life," Gila said.

She'iya rubbed her belly and giggled. "You sound pompous. 'Stop,' says the queen. No one heeds you except for a few doves cooing in the bushes."

Gila stood up. She pressed her jeweled dagger into She'iya's stomach until the concubine writhed.

"Stop," Gila said.

She'iya's mirth ceased. She bowed and returned to the path only to pause by a patch of poppies. She plucked several flowers.

"Do not, She'iya," Gila said. "If the child within you brings you pain, let one of the royal physicians treat you with medicinal plants. While I despise your presence, I will slay you by my blade, not a poppy plant."

She'iya giggled again. "I crave its juice."

Gila warned her again. "It is not good to sleep on draughts of wine and poppies. You are with child."

"An admonishment from the barren one."

She'iya skipped up the path toward the concubines' chambers. It was the last time Gila would ever see her.

CHAPTER FOUR

PLACES OF REFUGE

Flames danced in an elaborate fire pit. Storytellers clustered in corners, murmuring their tales. Harpists stroked their instruments, accompanied by a single drummer.

At the center of the crowded hall was Queen Erela. Lovely, young, and already accustomed to power, she greeted guests while stealing glances at Shammah, her latest target for conquest. Shammah sipped his wine. He wanted to be conquered.

He and Peleg had traveled for three years throughout the territories near Seth. None of the kingdoms brought them rest like these months in Midvar. The country was a place of liberation, where people shared prosperity, where progress appeared in well-planned cities and their gentler monarchy. Erela, like her late husband, the king, sought counsel from elders such as Havilah, Shammah's personal host.

Havilah offered Shammah more wine. Both men watched Peleg as he whooped during his wins at a board game with savvy players who wanted to relieve him of a bag of gold. They didn't know Peleg as Shammah did. The sailor's discernment was keen; he missed nothing, even when a fellow player sought to cheat him.

Only a roaming monkey, one of Erela's palace pets, distracted Peleg. The monkey climbed terracotta pots and squealed every time Peleg grunted or threatened the creature with a tickle.

"Peleg's gambling acumen rivals yours," Havilah said.

"He grew up a thief," Shammah said.

"Then how did you come to befriend him? You were in line to be king."

Shammah sighed. "Distant and lonely journeys. Besides, Peleg has not proven himself false."

"A commendable choice. You do not fear risk."

"Respect is a better word."

Since that night near Nifla, Shammah had tried to understand the choices he made. The morning after the confrontation with the Mikana, his commander, a man with a lifetime of battles streaked across his face, had waited for orders, while Shammah had stared out at the clearing, the bodies of his dead soldiers strewn about on the ground.

"How many?" Shammah asked.

"Thirteen."

The survivors gathered the fallen. Scattered on the ground were the torn ropes that had once held the Mikana warrior. Shammah had slipped to his knees and flung his helmet, hoping to throw away his regret.

Erela's monkey squealed again. Shammah kneaded his jaw, trying to wipe away the memory that never faded, and trying to conceal his preoccupation. He knew Havilah was observing him, seeing more than Shammah wanted to share.

"Great men respect fear as an enemy, but they never forsake their place," Havilah said.

"For if they abandon their place, evil men rule," Shammah replied.

Havilah lifted his wine cup. "Your tutor taught you well. You recited one of my favorite proverbs."

"Like any priest, Chazon demanded to be heard. He kept me at my lessons when I wanted to chase birds or build mud houses, then rewarded me with studies of the stars. He even built a crystal lens so I could see them more clearly."

"A priest taught you the ways of scholars? But you don't claim allegiance to the gods," Havilah said. "You do not practice rituals. You give nothing for the moon, the sun, or the sea. Unlike your companion, Peleg. He invokes his goddess with every gurgle."

"To my shame, I am certain, and to the everlasting displeasure of the gods. I see no strength in them to alter the things that matter to me."

The monkey lunged at Peleg, but the sailor outwitted him and earned a playful smile from the queen.

"The queen delights in Peleg's amusements," Havilah said.

The drumming lowered into a sultry tempo. Queen Erela placed her fingertips on her throat before addressing the bemused architect beside her. Flattered, the architect gestured to describe arches and pillars. Shammah grunted. Poor man. Erela would never desire him.

Shammah straightened as he spoke to Havilah. "She misses her dead husband and exploits those who fawn over her. No one challenges her mind."

Havilah answered with a dark purr. "It was an arranged marriage with a wealthy, doting king who adored an ambitious child."

"She should reconsider being queen and being in love. Thrones addle the mind and curdle the hopes. She should be as I—without kingdom and without affection."

"Wounds do not heal rapidly, do they?"

"They do," Shammah said, his voice harsh in a room filled with laughter and music. "They are the flowers sprouting from a neglected tomb."

With a languid hand, the architect signaled a scribe who brought a tablet. Intrigued, the queen traced the tablet's etchings.

Shammah swallowed the rest of his drink. After a moment, the queen locked Shammah's gaze as the drumbeats became ominous.

Havilah called for more wine.

The wide space of the Midvar library featured large windows facing orange groves. To the slaves watching them, Shammah and Erela appeared to be in love, but Shammah knew they were only flirting with the idea.

Erela halted and bowed before an alcove inside the library that held the clothed statue of a goddess. Shammah strolled past. Before rejoining Shammah, Erela murmured a prayer.

"She notices your silence, you know," Erela said.

"They all do," Shammah said, his voice trailing off as he entered the room. Tablets lined long tables, and scribes dotted the room, either etching or organizing tablets.

Erela strutted with pride, a coy blush tinting her cheeks. "The king left this for me. His dream fulfilled."

Shammah picked up tablet after tablet. The unexpected feast of knowledge that lay on the tables stunned him.

"The histories of your country are here. The epics. The poems. Several works are from my kingdom. Your husband was a scholar-king. What if my travels had brought me here before he joined his fathers? What conversations he and I could have enjoyed."

Her fingers lingered on a tablet as she glided around the table in her saffron-colored robes. He could smell the fragrances of spices flowing around her.

"He would have envied you," she said. "You long for a dream of your own, don't you?"

Shammah returned the tablet to its stack with reverence. "Where is the rest for scholars in a nest of warriors? Seth is too small."

Erela came up alongside him and stroked his cheek with a light finger. "A bear behaves as predator and protector. Is it forbidden to war with a heart of wisdom?"

She sauntered past him like a whisper. As his sober expression faded into yearning, he long to shed the burden of not knowing where he belonged if he wasn't Aikah's heir. With every day in Midvar, with every embrace from Erela, the vision of building a library for his people waned like a melancholy moon after shedding its burst of fullness. Seeking refuge from pain meant abandoning many of his dreams.

"War is not my calling, lovely one," Shammah said.

Erela danced away, and, without a pause, he followed.

CHAPTER FIVE

REBELLION

A voice emerged in the quiet.
"Dead man!"

Aikah jerked upright on the reed mat and wiped damp coils from his face. He heaved like a spent runner. His attention shot over to the balcony. No one was there.

He grabbed for the short dagger his father had given him long ago. As he did, above him, a sword of amber flame plunged from the ceiling and landed near his face.

"You chose punishment," the voice said.

"Name my transgression."

"Your blood oath seeded iniquity."

"What is that to you? Return to your tent in the sky, whatever god you claim to be. I serve Livnath."

"You are a lion of slaughter, but you protected the prophet's son," the voice said. "Choose the impostor at your own peril."

"Who are you to dictate to me? I am the savior-king, the Proud Lord of the Seven Gates. May Livnath smite you. Come to me, Shamgar! Enter!"

Aikah scanned the door, eager for his bodyguards to enter. The smoking sword above him singed tendrils of his hair, and Aikah worried that a multitude of flame-breathing beasts snarled around him.

The voice dropped to a whisper. "Rebellion finds fertile soil within your heart. Will you not abandon it?"

Then, with a burst of flame, the sword disappeared.

Aikah willed himself not to cry out again. He rushed to the chamber doors with sweat-soaked hair and a wild expression.

Guriel, the leader of the three bodyguards, stepped forward. He frowned. "My lord?"

"Did you hear anything,? Aikah demanded.

"No, my lord," Guriel said. "None of us did. Forgive us."

"Do you smell smoke?"

"No, my lord. Shall I enter your chamber?" Guriel began to barrel toward the king.

Following him was Na'iym, unsmiling and unintimidated. Behind her was Amar, burly, watchful, and mute.

In reply, Aikah waved his hand dismissively toward the Shamgar, reentered his chambers alone, and slammed the doors. He stroked his hair. No burned coils. He lifted his gaze toward the gray-white moon and its drifting clouds.

"Livnath, protect the savior-king from my enemies on Earth and in the heavens," Aikah said. "Do you hear me?"

With a gasp, he paused at the stone relief. A large, scorched crack pierced the relief from top to bottom.

Commanders of Seth, ablaze in bronze armor, stood out among their companies. They stationed themselves on the walls and throughout the City of Kings. Some companies hid behind the low hills, tinged with the hues of the dawn, that ringed the city.

Aikah refused to give the Mikana any advantage. His blood oath with Livnath strengthened his sword against them. For decades, he obeyed every instruction she gave him to destroy, and in return, she kept him and Seth safe. She trained him to discern the weaknesses and powers of the Mikana, and he passed this information to Shammah and Dahv. Yet only Dahv seemed to have heeded his lessons.

"Sleep flees from me," Aikah said to Chazon, who stood to his right.

"Settle your life. Secure the throne," Chazon said.

"I thought my contract with Livnath was enough."

"Your agreements conspired for the day forever reek of the night."

Aikah dragged his lips into a frown. "Are you unable to draw words from a more cheerful realm?"

"While I witness you threaten the kingdom's future? You defy the will of Aleph," Chazon said.

"When these beetles from the north tunnel back into their burrows, we will discuss whether the will of your gloomy Aleph satisfies the king."

"Ever certain of your military might over the Mikana? It will not always be so in the City of Kings."

"Under Livnath's banner, we have victory over them."

Chazon grunted but said nothing else.

Aikah signaled Dahv to step closer. His firstborn son, the off-spring of She'iya, stood to his far left, preening as if he already mastered the world. Dahv's pretensions reflected Aikah's habits as a flippant and impatient young man driven by ambition and enslaved by Livnath. To forgive his son was to forgive himself.

Dahv's close friend, Commander Lehabim, was a snobbish older soldier who prided himself on noble ancestry from Arba in the North Country. Lehabim served the army well, but his counsel sometimes betrayed Dahv. The commander encouraged Dahv to distance himself from the men and to choose savagery for effect. Lehabim fed Dahv's rage. Unfortunately, Dahv didn't discern how his anger blocked the things he needed from others, such as discipline and loyalty.

Snatching the throne from Shammah was where Dahv's direction was clear. And against Aikah's better judgment, he indulged Dahv's hopes. Encouraging Dahv to think the throne was his satiated Aikah's anger with Shammah and needled Chazon.

"Your reinforcements at the other six gates were farsighted," Aikah said. "It relieves my worry."

"Do not the histories tell how you caged these dogs for twenty years? I follow in your steps, my lord," Dahv said.

"You inherited your mother's crooked nature. Now practice my wisdom. You must apply the night arts to rule one day in my place. You will not withstand the Mikana with weapons and wit alone."

"Of course, Father."

Aikah frowned, suddenly reflective. He remembered the phantom voice and the flaming sword: *Choose the impostor at your own peril.*

Faint images of a Mikana contingent emerged on the northern horizon. They sauntered toward the city on hairy, double-horned beasts draped with crimson tassels and purple ribbons.

Smoke trailed them. When they reached the wall, the Mikana arranged themselves in military formation. Most of them sat twelve- to sixteen-feet tall astride their beasts. Cicerya stepped forward, embellished in gold from head to toe.

He wasn't the top commander, Aikah knew, but Ciycera's pompousness overlooked that fact. Ciycera's half-man, half-dog face flexed as he focused on Aikah.

Dathan, the scribe, caught his breath as if swallowing a camel. Aikah clenched his teeth in frustration; weakness flooded the scribe's heart.

"I will hammer your filthy bones to this gate!" Ciycera shouted.

"You approach my kingdom without cause," the king replied. "Misunderstandings never existed between us."

Vermin. The Mikana always had seen themselves as the sly ones. But Aikah knew he could be just as cunning.

"I don't understand the need for threats," he said.

Ciycera offered a foamy grin. "Commander Anash sends you this message: Prepare for surrender. One Mikana escaped your military trap in Nifla. On his way back home, he humiliated your pathetic heir. Now it's time to destroy your entire kingdom."

A warrior played a long-necked lute. The Mikana and their beasts marched in disjointed rhythm as the odors of burning flesh rose to the top of the wall.

The foul scent transformed the cooler winter breezes into putrid, broiling air. Soldiers puckered their lips. Some rocked, hypnotized by the stench surrounding them.

Two archers toppled over the wall. A Mikana warrior caught the pair before they hit the ground. He slapped the men over his beast like fish.

Dathan's face drooped as the heat—smelling of rotting meat—intensified. Chazon caught the scribe's slipping tablet. Like Aikah and the soldiers on the wall, the priest perspired in the steamy air. None of them uttered a word.

Ciycera called out to the people huddled beneath the wall and in their nearby homes. "Citizens of Seth! Your savior-king betrays you. He strangles your babes before they take a breath. Drink milk from the bosoms of your rightful lords!"

He twisted his odd-shaped head toward Mattan, one of Aikah's trusted commanders who hailed from the desert tribes of the Rabbah.

"Descendant of Rabbah, and my distant relative! Why live with mere men?"

Mattan, arms folded as he stood on the wall near Aikah, didn't reply.

"By my star-born fathers," Ciycera said with a toothy snarl. "I will feast on your carcass."

The flesh-burning heat and stench of the Mikana faded, the notes on the lute halted, and Ciycera and his contingent turned northward.

Aikah's ears ached from the noise of his enemies and sweat curled the hair at his nape. Dathan coughed deeply until he trembled.

The king turned to face him. "Your bones clatter like cups."

Dathan thinned his full lips. "The stench made me think my line would die with me, the childless only son of my father."

"And yet you live," Aikah said.

The king raised his hand skyward and brought orange flames down to lick at the hooves of the Mikana's beasts. Several members of Ciycera's entourage, unable to control the creatures they rode, fell into the flames.

Ciycera dragged his beast from the fire and glared back at Aikah.

"Livnath's night arts won't save you, Aikah!" Ciycera shouted. "Not this time!"

Flames soared about him as Aikah swung his hand. Horrified, Ciycera and his surviving contingent galloped away.

The city drifted from stillness to activity once again. Aikah, Chazon, and Dathan, guarded by the Shamgar, descended the steps safely behind the city gates. People emerged from their houses under the direction of the soldiers.

The king nodded to citizens as he returned to the palace. Their fears tugged at him. He refused to tell them that if he were to die before the Mikana attacked, he couldn't guarantee their security. The night arts granted to him by Livnath ended with his death.

"Are we safe, King Aikah?" shouted one farmer standing near his ox.

Aikah addressed the man and the growing crowd. "Your king will do everything in his power to protect you. Do not listen to our enemies. They will fill you with fear."

"We have grown tender as grapes after decades of peace," said a metalsmith covered with soot. "We can't attack the Mikana. They're stronger than we are. Their beasts would crush us."

Numerous citizens grumbled in agreement. The Shamgar moved closer to Aikah.

"The king tells the truth," said a narrow-faced merchant.

A scribe waved a tablet, seeking Aikah's attention. "What if the Mikana breach our walls?"

"Their beasts are huge," said an older woman.

Aikah stopped walking. He held his soldiers back with a gesture of his hand. The crowds never troubled the king. Never. Throughout his life, Aikah ignored or mocked what people thought about him. He only worried about Livnath. Always, Livnath.

"War is brutal. In victory or defeat," Aikah said. "But expect humiliation when you believe you can't possess the gates of your enemy before a single arrow is sent."

"Livnath gave you weapons," the metalsmith said.

"I judge when to reveal the kingdom's full strength." Aikah held the metalsmith's gaze until the laborer moved away from the crowds.

"Well said." Chazon spoke in Aikah's ear as they left the crowd and neared the main temple tower. "But can you comfort Haran?"

"Ask your Aleph for patience," Aikah said. "I do not perceive Livnath has any left for Haran."

Haran, the high priest, and several younger clerics, stood at the base of the massive tower built in honor of the goddess.

Aikah knew Chazon suspected he could never pass the temple tower without recalling the night the priests dedicated him to Livnath at the uppermost level of the building. Aikah remembered Chazon's boyish confusion when the priests carried Aikah to the temple platform.

All those years ago, Livnath had arranged Aikah's ascent from obscure farm boy to savior-king.

Haran slipped in front of him and bowed with respect. "My lord."

"Haran," Aikah said.

"The Mikana spoke of a blood oath, my lord. Is this true?" Haran clasped his hands in front of his substantial belly.

"Are you asking whether I betrayed Seth?"

"My lord, if the country sways toward destruction, shouldn't you prepare your people?"

"Trust me, Haran. For once," Aikah said.

The king moved from the cluster of priests toward the palace. He glimpsed Chazon nod at Haran as he departed with the king, Dathan, and the Shamgar.

"The favored lackey…" Haran spat at Chazon.

"A friend," Chazon replied over his shoulder.

"Curse you, Aikah!" Haran said.

"Remember your place, Haran," Chazon said. "We are no longer boys in Yaphah."

Aikah faced Haran with an opaque expression. "You cannot burn where Livnath already has poured pitch and ignited a blaze. May she show you mercy, high priest. You will need it."

Once Aikah reached the palace, he charged into Gila's chambers, restless and livid. He hadn't bothered to remove the dust that flecked his garments and hair. After the encounter with the Mikana, and then Haran, he sought refuge with Gila, hoping her presence would soothe his spirits.

"I need more time." Aikah paced before her, seeking attention and not getting it.

Gila searched for a tablet on a shelf and then settled on her jeweled couch. "Forgive me, my lord, but you knew they would return."

"You remain angry with me."

"You test my love with cruelty."

"You need not worry about the throne."

"Why should I not?" Gila asked. Her voice rose as she put the tablet aside. "Your volatile moods and rages suspend us in involuntary mystery. Maybe you will calm down enough to give us clarity. All I see is She'iya's backbiting son seizing Shammah's inheritance like a raisin from the king's table, while the Mikana dogs howl outside the gate. Tell me, what do you see?"

He sat beside her. "I have dodged the Mikana and endured the exasperating presence of Haran. Where can I find peace?"

"Your rest from trouble does not preclude acknowledging the truth."

"I am dying, Gila," Aikah replied with heat. "Livnath has told me this. You and Chazon know it."

Aikah could feel Gila's body relax, and the anxiety within him eased.

"My love," she said. "You cannot stop death, but you can die with honor. Secure the throne for Shammah. Protect us from chaos."

CHAPTER SIX

BLOODY PROMISES

M erchants offered Mahalath agate, beads, and dyed linen. She picked through their wares, wishing she hadn't agreed to accompany her sister to the market.

The scent of turmeric and garlic from a nearby stall over-powered her.

"Will you not look?" Rina asked. "Father wants you to keep your garments updated in case the king summons you."

Frustrated, Rina continued with a pout. "Do you hear me, Mahalath? Lord Shammah will return. Everyone knows Dahv cannot be king. He's the son of a concubine. One day you will be a king's wife. Not a hen to fishermen and farmers. Choose something."

"Indeed. Then where is my soon-to-be husband? Am I not beautiful enough?" Mahalath stopped to chew a nail. "Why does he not beg the king to let him return so he can marry me?"

"You know you are beautiful," Rina said. She flung her braids, a gesture of teenage self-confidence. "Once you are married, the studious and wandering Shammah will be all you ever wanted. Now will you please choose something? That ruby stone flatters your pale brown skin and your black hair, and that little mole…"

"You are certain of his loyalty."

"You will be Shammah's queen; but heed my warning. Flee every threshold Dahv crosses. Anywhere you see him. You war like lovers among the rose bushes."

"What? I sparred with him since childhood. I am his dragonfly," Mahalath said. "He's my annoying locust. It is nothing more. He could never be called my husband."

"The king and our parents have agreed on this plan. Dahv may not be convinced," said Rina, enraptured by linen offered by an insistent merchant. "Sister. The famed Midvar linen. I must have it."

Mahalath followed Rina into their cart, rubbing her thumb across the cloth the merchant sold to her. Instead of feeling assured, she felt naked. Her sister had identified a secret she didn't consciously possess.

She looked forward to debates with Dahv because he challenged her and allowed her to do the same—unlike most men in the noble classes. He was a playmate, a family friend, and a man who by birthright had direct access to the palace and the upper classes, but she never perceived him as the man who would pay a bride price for her.

The sisters spent another hour touring the market, but when they neared one of Livnath's shrines, Mahalath motioned for their slave to stop their covered cart and jumped out.

Rina poked her head from behind the cart's sheer curtains. "I knew your musings about Dahv and your future marriage to Lord Shammah would make you run to the patroness of the city," she said. "While you prostrate in her shrine, ask her for henna. I did not see any at the market."

Mahalath bit her upper lip. "Why do you mock a request to the goddess?"

"If she will not provide henna, what can she do?" Rina giggled and smiled at a sailor before concealing herself behind the curtains.

A priestess greeted Mahalath at the shrine's entrance, which stood beneath crimson and silver banners lined with serpents.

While male priests dominated the temple tower in the center of the city, the legendary hill of heaven that opened to the skies, women oversaw neighborhood shrines like this in the City of Kings. Mahalath thought Seth demeaned priestesses and insulted all females because women received second-class status, although the patron deity of the City of Kings was Livnath.

The priestess outstretched her tattooed hands. The farmers who trickled into the shrine brought food and animals. The priestess couldn't miss that chance to boost the shrine's treasury. The priests hoarded the wealth and left the priestesses near destitution. Mahalath would send a food basket when she returned home. But she wasn't in the mood to give money.

"A petition for Livnath to help the poor? Many suffer," the priestess said.

"No." Mahalath shook her head.

"Prayer for protection from the Mikana? From an abusive husband?"

"No."

Her head bowed, the priestess led Mahalath into an alcove where a silver oil lamp etched with serpents illuminated the room. Mahalath prostrated on a blood-stained mat. Above her was a ten-foot-tall clay statue draped in linens.

"The absence of my betrothed keeps me from fulfilling the ways of women," Mahalath said.

In a flicker, the lined eyes of Livnath opened. The smudged red on the statue's lips darkened. The statue became flesh.

"Commit to me. In blood," Livnath said.

Mahalath hesitated. The priestess never required her to cut herself, although she knew others had pledged themselves to the goddess in that way. Fresh blood on the mat indicated that someone had done so that morning.

Livnath pursed her lips at Mahalath and leaned down. "A higher vow for a higher petition."

Mahalath reached for a nearby bowl and knife already caked with blood.

Wincing, Mahalath cut her right arm. Blood oozed down and speckled her ruby-colored robes.

"What will you require of me?"

"What is known and not known."

Mahalath gasped as the wound healed before her. Even the blood disappeared from her hands and clothing. She knew Livnath possessed power, but now she'd witnessed it. Her heart pounded. Moisture gathered at her nape and forehead.

"Will I bear the king's sons?" Mahalath placed her fingertips to her lips.

"Why are the daughters of Earth content to unite with mere men?" Livnath's laughter rocked the shrine with a force that drove Mahalath away.

As she raced outside, the priestess, lounging at the threshold, spat with glee.

Dahv watched a slave ignite a fire in a small grate in the Gardens of Destiny. He came up alongside the slave and stood until the man noticed him.

"My lord," the slave said. "Perhaps you are unaware, but you cannot be here. By orders."

"Whose orders?"

"King Aikah. The gardens belong to the king's heir."

"Soon I will be your king." Dahv jerked the slave's arm until he nearly broke it. The slave hobbled away, moaning.

Dahv stretched. It was time for him to claim what was his. The gardens were also the last place anyone saw his mother three years ago before dying in her sleep and taking her unborn child with her.

He pulled herbs from his robes and tossed them into the flames.

"Livnath, secure my birthright as the king's firstborn," Dahv said.

His confidant, Commander Lehabim, and Qayin, the assistant to the high priest, joined him near the fire.

"Even Aikah cannot overrule the line of succession, the line of blood," Qayin said.

"Are you certain? Have the scholars confirmed this from the histories? I was told that the children of concubines couldn't inherit," Lehabim said.

"The priests rule Seth, my lord," Qayin said.

Dahv's fingers slithered over the dagger at his waist. Qayin's smug religiousness didn't reassure him. "Do not deny my claim once I seek it."

From a darkened path, Chazon rushed toward them, stirring a nest of mourning doves.

"You trespass."

"You guard these gardens needlessly," Dahv said. Just the presence of the scowling priest angered him. "My father cast out your charge long ago."

The three men encircled Chazon. The priest looked unperturbed. "The ravens still seek to roost with the doves."

"Where are your armies to overturn my claim?" Dahv growled.

Lehabim struck Chazon's right arm with his whip. The priest stumbled. Before Chazon recovered, Lehabim hit him a second time. Dahv grabbed Lehabim's arm.

The flames in the grate crackled, and a vine of smoke coiled upward. Jubilance poured through Dahv, and so did a halfhearted kindness. Livnath had answered him; there was no need to beat the priest.

"This is a sign from the heavens," he said. "Livnath confirms my claim."

For a final insult, Lehabim shoved Chazon before the trio left.

Chazon leaned against one of the Ten Pillars. With his left arm, he waved over the fire. It withered to darkness.

Aikah watched the scene in the garden from the balcony above. He flexed his large shoulders, then pounded his thick fist into his hand.

"She'iya, your presumptuous soul lives in the heart of our ambitious son."

He took a deep breath. In the lamplight coming from his chambers, he saw that the healthy skin of his right hand was fading into gray.

CHAPTER SEVEN

MOURNING A GHOST

The curse, once it started, took rapid hold of Aikah's body. He lifted his torso with his muscled arms and breathed in spurts. He reached for a jeweled cylinder seal etched with bearded bulls and yanked a tablet away from Dathan.

Aikah knew that his striking looks had dulled into gray pallor and thinning hair. But he was still king. He studied the words he'd asked Dathan to prepare. His sight was leaving him. The cuneiform wedges on the tablet rose and dipped like ships carrying him on choppy waters to the place of the dead. In his mind, he could hear his own voice, stronger and unintimidated, reading the tablet:

> "I, Aikah, the savior-king of Seth, the Proud Lord
> of the Seven Gates, declare that Lord Shammah,
> my adopted heir, shall ascend the throne and lead
> the army of Seth at the time of my death. He alone
> receives my throne as his birthright. By the will of
> the king, this decision no one can revoke, overturn,
> circumvent, or deny."

Aikah rolled the cylinder seal on the tablet. He slumped back on his reed mat. Dathan grabbed the tablet before it fell. The scribe wrapped the tablet in a leather pouch and retreated to a corner.

"Your fears will hound me into the underworld. I'm the one being eaten alive, not you," the king said. "Chazon's Aleph protects you from this. Rejoice in my punishment."

"How can I? I've served you since I was a boy."

"Yes, and you will tend to this tonight. Did you handle my earlier orders?"

Dathan bowed. Aikah searched the scribe's face; for a moment, the old, angry fire burned from Aikah's eyes.

The king fell back into the pillows. "When was the last full moon, Dathan?"

"Twenty-two days ago."

"How many stables in the palace?"

"One hundred in the City of Kings," Dathan said. "Thirty-five at each gate of Seth."

"And the number of workers?"

"Five-hundred-and-ninety during harvest periods. Two-hundred-and-two at all other times, except during war."

"I will miss even you," Aikah said.

The king turned to Gila and Chazon. "Shammah will not return. There's... I wish... But there's not enough time."

"I sent for him," Chazon said.

"I am repentant too late."

"You have fulfilled the will of Aleph."

"No, the generosity of Livnath has done this. For that I do not repent," the king said.

He twisted his body, furious that life was seeping out of him. "Believe as you wish, Chazon. You always have."

"We share the trait of obstinacy."

"Surely there was more that made us friends. We both love him…but you are a better father."

"You could still deny Livnath, Aikah. Aleph is a breath away."

"She wooed me to her forever."

Aikah saw the priest's jaw sag but addressed Gila. "I was your husband of humiliation. I should have explained who I am. What I am."

"You were a boy seduced by a goddess, Aikah," Gila said.

"Give me no excuses. Though I betrayed you, you are my love, and you deserve truth. Aikah said. My mother made promises to save my father's life. Her oath to Livnath will take my life. I also made bloody promises to become the savior-king, the Proud Lord of the Seven Gates. I killed and killed."

At the moment of Aikah's confession, Dahv raced through the doorway, a firestorm searching for something to consume. The Shamgar blocked him.

"Father!" Dahv said.

Chazon motioned for the Shamgar to let Dahv pass. He nodded toward a spot where Dahv could stand. "But do not touch him," the priest said. "His sickness can endanger you. Only Aleph protects us."

"Where are the royal healers? No matter. Father. Your blessing."

"You have it."

"Declare me king before you join our fathers," Dahv demanded.

"Our fathers do not summon yet. The throne is not yours."

"Sickness thrusts your mind down meandering paths. I am your blood son and firstborn."

Aikah could hear She'iya's tawdry ambition in Dahv's voice. The king bristled at the sound. "And you are not whom I choose, after all."

"You promised my mother," Dahv said.

"Drunken hymns to indulge a petulant concubine. I have forgotten my pledges."

"You exalted me. And he is not here. For three years, we have mourned a ghost. Can we not bury him in our minds, if not in the tombs of the outcasts?"

"Perhaps your lust for the throne devoured my favor," the king said.

Aikah waved away Dahv's comment and sank down into the bed. "Where is Shammah?"

"By the gods of the underworld that will soon hold you captive, you insult me. Your blood son." Dahv pushed toward the king, ready to strike him.

Gila, flanked by the Shamgar, walked between them, and pressed her dagger into Dahv's belly. "Your mother learned eternal quiet after crossing me. Shall you become my pupil?"

"Witch." Dahv grunted as she pressed the dagger into him.

Aikah managed a smile despite his torment. Gila, as always, was queen.

CHAPTER EIGHT

RESTLESSNESS

R ain drenched the mud-brick building surrounded by desert palms. Sagi hammered copper and pounded pain. Utensils, toys, and jewelry surrounded him. His graying hair was slick with the sweat that dripped along his unshaven jaw. His mutterings echoed in the makeshift workspace.

"Rest," said his wife, Abelia. He hadn't heard her come in, but she leaned against the doorway, her head and shoulders wrapped with a rough shawl.

He loved Abelia, but she didn't understand how precarious their lives had become. The priests demanded taxes. They stole land from friends of his who were farmers, like they were. The priests overlooked the aristocrats' delinquent payments and financial manipulations and dogged the poor.

Sagi's artisan skills gave his family an advantage. Sales of his copper products supplemented the barley crops and sheep they grew. But crops from last year's harvest emerged leaner than expected. The rains would help the future harvest, but not the obstacles of today.

Their predicament pummeled Sagi's hopes, spinning him into sleepless nights where he envisioned his children begging on the street. But Abelia behaved as if no worries existed from sundown to sunup.

"The nobles and merchants in the City of Kings don't rest," he said. "They buy."

"The barley crops and livestock will satisfy us."

"Do you want us to suffer, wife? The priests will come, knocking on our doors with sticks, their bellies bound by red robes and chains of gold, demanding payment for their temples and rituals. And what will we give them? Barley soup with bits of lamb? Skimpy vegetables? They will want more. They always do. If they don't get it, they'll snatch our land. They'll sleep in our beds. Think about our friends to the north. They lost everything."

"They will not come for us." Abelia's tone was soothing.

He remembered hearing the rhythms of her voice for the first time. A caravan traveling through the Desert of Akron had camped outside of Chaniya at the Third Gate with their wares. Abelia chatted with a merchant. From a short distance, Sagi saw her dark hair framing her ivory-colored skin, rose-tinted lips, and brown eyes the hue of bear fur. As he listened, he felt her summon him. And he replied. Months later, he asked her father if Abelia could be his wife.

Sagi felt the melody of her words caressing his heart again. This annoyed him because he felt she ignored his inner sufferings. He slammed his hammer, cracking an unfinished pitcher. After taking a deep, angry breath, he stretched out his arm in apology. Nothing.

Abelia was gone. Gloom dropped over his shoulders like the droplets pelting the roof. Once again, his anger had edged out tenderness.

Moments later, Tamiym entered the workroom. She shed her hooded robe and shook out the rain. She examined the utensils, her fingers a feminine imitation of Sagi's hands. *My firstborn, a woman, and the wise son I longed for,* Sagi thought. He trained Tamiym to protect herself with dagger and wit, and her mother taught her to dream and study. Chaniyan tradition looked to sons as rightful heirs, but in his daughter Tamiym, Sagi felt she deserved favor because she represented the best of him and Abelia. Peace settled on him because of Tamiym's presence. Affection deepened the bear-brown of Tamiym's eyes, which were so like Abelia's. The difference was that warm flames sprung in Tamiym's eyes, ignited by love or anger. Sagi put down the pitcher and picked up a pair of earrings etched with lilies.

"Your mother. She loves these. It took me days to carve the stems with the perfect curve."

Tamiym didn't seem to care about lilies and stems. She stood with her arms folded, her smile drawing tension from him.

Sagi put down the earrings, quieted by the rain and his daughter.

"Have you noticed, Father? Sometimes the rains sound more terrible than they really are," Tamiym said. "They threaten, but they promise, too—because the rains bless us with plenty."

Shammah tossed in his sleep. He was dreaming. It wasn't a new nightmare, but the same one that dogged him. The affliction greeted him daily, a guardian from the underworld that posed a threat and induced fright by its mere appearance. In the dream, the sun rose with a harsh, orange glow. A growl interrupted the stillness. Shammah and his men encircled the warrior as he stirred. Shammah inserted an arrow into his bow.

One of his soldiers, a farmer's son who served all the gods in Seth because he trusted none of them, thrust arrows into a steaming black brew.

"By the sea gods, by Livnath, by anything not mortal, may these be enough," the young man cried out.

At the commander's signal, the soldiers positioned their bows. The Mikana warrior awkwardly rose to a height of fifteen feet. As he straightened, he gained his full strength. His gold and amethyst necklace gleamed like its own daylight.

In the dream, Shammah muttered, "What nightmares have you brought to me?"

The warrior's inner embers sparkled and distracted some of the soldiers with their unearthly glitter. The Mikana swung its half-man, half-dog face toward the soldiers.

"Slay him!" The command passed through Shammah's lips when the warrior charged toward the men.

The howls of dying soldiers lifted skyward as the sun became a full day.

The sounds of cooing from the palace balcony in Midvar awakened Shammah. He swung open the carved shutters. A sapphire sky turning to day boasted star after star. On the balcony railing, a dove fluttered. Shammah stood still to take in the view, and the bird perched on the fingers of his right hand.

White and brown hues stroked the bird's wings. He recognized it as a bird from Seth.

"You fly far from my gardens," Shammah said.

Chazon sent it. The bird carried a message on a sapphire-and-silver chord hanging from its neck. Shammah broke the tiny seal and read: *His body fades, but his heart no longer lies.*

Shammah's smile disappeared. "I will not come home, priest," he said as the bird blinked at him. "May my father greet his fathers without seeing my face."

The dove lifted from Shammah's fingers.

It had been days since Shammah had seen Erela. She kept his mind distracted from his father and Seth, but he guessed she was conducting rituals for her goddess. When he asked Havilah about Erela, the counselor murmured something unintelligible and focused on the tour of city projects. Shammah didn't press him, but Havilah's silence mystified him.

The two men ambled along several streets until they reached the corner where workers were repairing the scorched bricks of the citadel. The laborers complained that the dimensions of a series of bricks were off.

A foreman yelled at the craftsmen as he reconfigured his specifications. Shammah looked to Havilah to intervene. He didn't.

The foreman demanded that the craftsman adjust the bricks. The craftsman bobbed his head and pointed to a sinking section of the wall. The foreman lifted his hand to strike, and the craftsman relented and attempted to fit the bricks together.

The bricks hit the weak point of the structure. The wall collapsed, killing the craftsman.

"Let us leave," Havilah said.

"Why did you not intervene? The foreman was unreasonable," Shammah said.

"The foreman's brutality profits the queen. He oversees successful projects throughout Midvar. The craftsman, alas, can be replaced."

Disgust rippled through Shammah. The superiority in Havilah's voice was the type of elitism he decried in Seth. But this wasn't his country or his throne. He reined in his distaste.

"I envy your endless supply of craftsmen," Shammah said.

"Does my perspective offend you?"

"I cannot comprehend it."

"This is our way of life," Havilah said.

"And your silence about the queen? How long will she be with her goddess? Is that your way of life?"

"You tread where you don't understand, my lord."

They moved on, examining the well-planned streets. When they reached a public bath, Havilah boasted about the drainage system's features.

Small rocks fell from a nearby wall, distracting Shammah. He saw the dove again from the Gardens of Destiny. Unsteady, the bird sought a resting place on the wall. The bird couldn't find one. Loneliness and guilt swirling inside his heart helped Shammah understand the struggling dove.

Shammah felt his life was fixed like the boundaries of Seth. They left Midvar several weeks ago; once their boat passed the Dragon Islands, they would be home. He maneuvered his sky disk, trying to read the constellations.

Peleg whistled and came up alongside Shammah near the curved tip of the vessel.

"It will be good to be in the City of Kings," mused Peleg, inhaling the sea air.

"Will life have changed when we return?" Shammah asked.

"We will reach your father in time."

"I wanted to stay away."

"He's your father."

"He's king."

"The Seven Gates will be yours to rule," Peleg said.

Lightning surged within the clouds, causing the sailors with them to gaze upward with anxiety. The vessel dipped.

"Or forfeit," Shammah said with a grim tone that wasn't because of the agitated waters.

"You can return for the queen."

"I prefer to return for her library. Her rituals for the goddess number in the multitudes."

Peleg groaned in mock frustration as a mist settled on the vessel. The waters they traveled began to toss them in a frenzy. Shammah and his seven companions gripped the sides of the small craft, relying on the sails that barely kept them upright.

"Spiteful gods guard the Time Sea!" Zephi shouted to Shammah.

"Pray if you wish," Shammah said.

The faithful could be the most vexing at the most stressful times, Shammah thought. Zephi was a devotee of the sea king who allegedly reigned near the First Gate in southern Seth, near the Cove of Revealing. Let Zephi call on his god. Shammah would observe the movement of the stars. From his earlier calculations, the shores of the Dragon Islands should appear soon, unless they were off course.

"Help us, god of the waters," Zephi said. "Overlook our trespasses. Whisper to the sea."

"My lord, pray to Livnath!" Peleg cried.

"Make your own entreaties," Shammah said.

The vessel dipped again under the curl of a large wave.

"Maybe now is the time to change your mind," Peleg retorted, rubbing water from his eyes.

"The mist is worsening," Zephi screamed as the men muttered, cursed, and vowed fidelity to their wives and concubines. One man pledged a noon sacrifice of grain and sheep if he was allowed to live.

"Maybe the skies have confused your great sea god as they have confused me," Shammah grunted. He searched for an opening amid the mist. The air seemed clogged with moistened dust.

"We must sacrifice," Zephi said. "We must fill their watery gateways with human blood."

"No lives will be sacrificed on this vessel," Shammah shouted as the waters became more frenzied.

"Seawater poisons your patience," Peleg said to Zephi.

"We'll sacrifice *you* first," Zephi replied.

"Be quiet!" Shammah yelled.

Zephi reached for a dagger tied to his waist. Shammah, moving toward them, struggled to overcome the brutal rocking of the vessel as Zephi lunged for Peleg, who jerked away.

Peleg's hands clawed at Zephi until the older sailor nipped Peleg's neck with his dagger.

Rage overtook Peleg. He grabbed Zephi and knocked them both over the side of the vessel. Another great wave, and Shammah and the rest of his men tumbled into the sea.

CHAPTER NINE

THE WATER PEOPLE

Chazon clutched his head to tamp down the vision coming to him. Visions dominated his life. They had begun
decades ago when he met a shepherd in a field. The man had
offered Chazon water, barley bread, and salted seeds. Before
Chazon knew it, their conversation had carried from morning
into evening.

When Chazon asked where the man was from, the shepherd explained that he lived in the shadow of Aleph, the mountain where many people of Seth refused to travel because of its
rugged terrain and severe storms. Those who ventured near its
foothills when tracking a lost lamb or a wandering ox swore by
Livnath that fire erupted from the rocks.

The shepherd spoke with lilting words untied to Earth. When
he promised that Chazon would one day protect kings, his words
became swords exposing Chazon's heart: the lie he told his mother
about the cracked mud bricks. The argument he instigated with
Aikah and Haran. The shepherd laid Chazon's thoughts bare.

How old was Chazon when he had met the shepherd?
Twelve? Fourteen? After the man left him on the mountainside,

whistling to his sheep, Chazon received the shepherd's words as anchors of truth he would cling to for life.

In this vision, Chazon, could see images of seawater and Mikana soaring over the palace walls consumed him. He saw a Mikana warrior flying toward the priest and shouting at him. The gold and amethyst necklace around the warrior's neck blazed before curling off and slithering into a sparkling serpent.

The vision ended. Chazon gasped for breath and writhed on the palace floor. Still unfocused because of the vision, he didn't fully comprehend that Dahv, Lehabim, and Qayin approached. All he could do was utter the word pounding in his mind.

"Unsafe," Chazon said.

"Who is unsafe, blundering priest?" Dahv asked. "Shammah?"

Dahv stepped over Chazon. "If so, may Livnath dispatch a sea dragon to swallow the interloper whole."

When they left him, Chazon continued to groan, his knees tucked to his waist.

"Live, Shammah," Chazon said. "Live."

Shammah dreamed of darkness. Salty water streamed through his throat. Perhaps the enraged sea god had punished him for his insolence. Would Aikah rejoice at the death of his adopted heir, an ill-begotten monarch?

As Shammah's mind swam, he awakened. There was a moldy green light. Shammah groped in the sand, willing his body to stand. How long had it been since his vessel capsized?

He searched the shore, strewn with wood scraps and cloth. Padding across the sand, he saw the bodies of his companions. He checked each body and counted six. One sailor still breathed. It was Peleg. His wound wasn't as severe as Shammah had assumed. Zephi had grazed his neck.

Shammah kneeled and tore cloth from his robes. He bound the injury.

Peleg's eyelids fluttered. "Is this the resting place of my forefathers?"

"Not yet. The waters overcame our vessel. You and I survived."

"Zephi?"

"Lost to us," Shammah said.

Peleg gasped and lifted his trembling hand toward a cave in the distance where light emerged. A dark green banner was visible, along with the silhouettes of chanting foot soldiers.

"We are below the sea—the home of the Water People," Peleg whispered.

"Can you run?" Shammah murmured in Peleg's ear, his eyes fixed on the cave's opening a mile away. "They see the remains of the vessel, but not us. There is a cleft of rock behind us. If we crawl, we can hide."

"You can't hide from the Water People," Peleg said. "They are spirits."

"And we are thoughtful men. Move with me."

The two men crawled across the sand. The chanting grew nearer. Sand and debris caught on Shammah and Peleg's hair, fingernails, and skin, but they reached the rock, which led to another cave. They crawled to the deepest end of the opening.

The torches of the Water People glowed as they picked through the shipwreck with thin, pale green hands and kicked at the corpses of the dead sailors. Slung around their necks were long nets, and in their hands, they carried small hooks. They chanted as they searched the shore.

Inside the cave, Shammah picked up a piece of driftwood and scrambled the tracks they left outside. "When they get here, we'll overtake the leader and hold him as a shield," Shammah said.

"But there are ten or more warriors. And they are taller than the sails of our vessel," Peleg said.

"Aim for the leader. Pretend he is a merchant, and you are helping yourself to his wages."

"And how will we escape? We cannot live below the water, not like them."

Shammah's head throbbed. He had no plan. Stories about the Water People poured forth from the mouths of men who dreaded the open waters. Shammah had dismissed the yarns because the sailors described the Water People like they were sons of the gods. Fears of ruling deities polluted Seth, a free-flowing sewage of thought that kept men weak and incapable of forging their destiny.

"We will return the way we came," Shammah told Peleg.

When the Water People entered the cave, the two warriors in front held torches and scanned the walls of the cave's opening. The light didn't hit the far corners where Shammah and Peleg huddled.

The leader emerged from the middle of the group. He growled in a tongue that Shammah and Peleg often heard from gray-haired sailors. Chazon had offered him lessons about the language of the Water People, but he had refused to study, and Aikah didn't demand he learn.

The leader tipped his chin upward and sniffed. "You are here, and we will wait."

Shammah nodded at Peleg and they both reached for the leader, stabbing his arms and shoulders. Shammah's dagger that bore the king's seal slid into the leader's shoulder. He couldn't retrieve it.

Shammah grunted at the loss of his dagger and noted how easily he and Peleg wounded the leader. As the creature fell, they used his slumping body as a shield.

The leader moaned at his companions, who tried to capture Shammah and Peleg with their nets and hooks. Shammah and Peleg blocked their strikes, sustaining light wounds while the leader's head lolled on his neck, framed by twists of pale hair.

Shammah and Peleg worked their way to the entrance and switched places with the Water People, who tried to attack them without further injuring their leader. Then Shammah and Peleg backed out of the cave.

"Don't let them escape..." The leader moaned as Shammah and Peleg dodged the other warriors.

Shammah thought about his lessons. How he wished he'd been a more diligent student.

"Would you dishonor your leader's body with your weapons? Will not the dragon gods slay you for adding to the dignity of his death?" Shammah asked.

One soldier cocked his head in laughter. "He fumbles our words like a babe."

Another soldier twirled his hook. "Kill the dogs."

"We can't hurt our own," the first soldier said.

Shammah and Peleg ran. Once on the shore, they dropped the leader's body and dove into the waters. The soldiers screeched in anger when they reached their leader, who had already died from his wounds.

The Water People flung their hooks into the water as Shammah and Peleg swam away. One clipped Shammah's left arm. He yanked it out and wrapped a good arm around Peleg.

As Shammah searched for light, Chazon's face appeared. The priest mouthed the word: "Live."

Shammah scanned the miles around the beach where they settled to rest. Where had he and Peleg landed? By the sun, he knew it was midafternoon. He would have to wait until night, when the stars appeared, to determine a more precise location.

For right now, he and Peleg would have to eat before their bellies burned with salt water. Shammah cleared the sand where Peleg lay and checked the sailor's wound; already skin had begun to fold over it. He checked his own arm and bound the gash with cloth from his robe.

"Maybe I should be a physician instead of a king's heir," Shammah murmured.

Peleg stirred. "I dreamed of a face."

"It was Chazon," Shammah said. "Priest of Aleph and my childhood tutor."

How Chazon appeared to him was another riddle to unravel, but Shammah was certain that the waters parted for them when the vision appeared. Shammah began to say more, but then he heard a soft snore. Exhausted, Peleg had fallen asleep.

Shammah rose on weak legs, waiting for the dizziness to ease. Which way should he go? Figs, a wild goat or boar would be a bounty for a man after being thrashed by the sea.

CHAPTER TEN

SECRETS BELONG TO THE PRIESTS

A sahel led Shammah past the small mud houses of the bustling city of Yaphah—a coastal port populated by merchants, artisans, sailors, scribes, and priests. As they walked, they observed men carrying grain and vegetables to market. Goats and chickens wandered around, chased by children learning to manage their animals. A group of grizzled men sat not far from the city gate, judging civil disputes. The Sixth Gate wasn't ornate like the entrance to the City of Kings, the Seventh Gate, but it intimidated with its high, thick walls.

When the two reached a wide house with doors of beaten copper and silver, Shammah estimated that the home boasted about a dozen rooms. Asahel opened the door without knocking and was met by four slaves. One of them, a middle-aged man about Asahel's age, moved forward and spoke. The three others waited for their orders.

"Where is the commander?" Asahel asked.

"He has recently returned from a patrol in the south near the Second Gate at the Forest of Elihu," said the older slave.

"There were reports of stolen livestock. Would you like us to alert him to your presence—and that of your guest?"

Dirtied, bloodied, and reeking of the sea, Shammah didn't impress the slave. Shammah had seen this so many times before. The slave's condescension mirrored the pretension of the priests, nobles, and merchants in the City of Kings, who reveled in their wealth at the expense of the poor.

"Nabal, guard your expression," Asahel said.

The slave bent his head. "Yes, my lord."

"You must go further than the name of foolishness your mother gave you," Asahel said. "Please tell the commander that I need to see him when he is willing. We'll wait for him in the central courtyard. Prepare a goat for us and bring fresh water while we wait. Also, prepare a room with fresh garments and water for my guest to wash."

Nabal bowed. "Your wish."

All four disappeared into one of the rooms.

Asahel chuckled at the bedraggled Shammah. "Let's feast after you are refreshed. Your smell would confuse the livestock!"

Both men howled with laughter as Asahel led Shammah down the corridor. Once Shammah dressed and slaves tended his wound, he returned to the courtyard.

"Now we can eat," Asahel said. "Would you like water? Or beer? The commander may have rare wine."

"Fresh water and wine," Shammah said. "The sea sours my mouth."

"I sent other slaves to retrieve your friend," Asahel said. "And I've summoned the physician to tend to him."

"I am grateful."

"Ah. Of course, you're grateful. I found you roaming the shore."

"You found me with the handle of your dagger."

"It's the way I greet trespassers."

Shammah grunted. "I was lost. Home is in the City of Kings. It lies days away."

"I like you. Despite being nearly drowned, you fought back. It's why I invited you here. To talk with you more. Fortunately, the commander grants me rooms here and allows me to entertain guests."

When the slaves served their meal, Shammah ate heartily.

He sipped the Yaphah wine. It rivaled what he tasted at Erela's table.

"Satisfying, Asahel," Shammah said.

The soldier grinned. "No doubt the Existing One makes it so. Aleph touches even the wine."

Shammah forced himself not to reply. *Yet another of the faithful*, he thought. Chazon no doubt would tease him about his encounters with those who believed in the deity of the depressing mountain.

The other slaves beamed as Asahel described the offerings of their city while Nabal stiffened as he sliced more meat and bread for the table with precision.

Asahel shook his head as the slaves left the room. "Nabal clings to old ways that could do my lord more harm than good."

"What do you mean?" Shammah said.

"Some old sailor told me this adage," Asahel said. "'A dark thought hides the illumination of fresh understanding.' Nabal clings to the class warfare my commander's family upheld. But the commander is different. Strong seedlings don't emerge from the soil of anger and repression."

"I look forward to meeting the commander. 'I sit at the feet of princes who reward wisdom wooing them at the city gates.'"

"What an interesting expression," Asahel said. "Where have I heard it before? Was it a sailor? No, maybe it was one of the sea merchants. But the saying is from Yaphah. Where did you learn it?"

"My childhood tutor. A priest," Shammah said.

Asahel slid to the floor and bowed low. "My lord. I didn't know. I didn't know…"

A man, fresh from bathing, oiled, and wearing fine robes, entered the courtyard at that moment, with Nabal trailing behind. Commander Eitan, Shammah guessed.

"Asahel, what are you doing? Introduce your guest."

"I don't have permission to rise. Only one priest from Yaphah tutored a child in the City of Kings. It is our friend Chazon. Commander, before me is King Aikah's heir."

Eitan bowed immediately. Aghast, Nabal managed a bow as well.

"My lord, I entreat your forgiveness," the commander said. "I am Eitan. I have visited your father's palace when you were absent. There are no images."

Shammah stood "I have been an outcast for too long for images to be made. Please. Rise. I should have shown my seal. I only told Asahel my name—a common one among our people."

He pulled out the seal Gila had given him. Despite the shipwreck, the seal—bearing the face of a man with the body of a four-winged hawk—hadn't been lost, having been bound to him.

"I also should have remembered. Yaphah is the ancestral home of my father. And Chazon."

The skies unfolded above with batches of stars. Here, on the roof of Eitan's home, Shammah sensed that the seasoned soldier was world weary, and that it was in Yaphah where he came to rest.

For a moment, the two men stood in silence as night fell. Lamps were being lit. Shammah could hear children begging to stay outside longer. He breathed in the fresh scent of the sea from the nearby shore.

"I returned to Seth because Aikah is dying. I received a sign."

"From Chazon?"

"Of course. He trails my steps."

"You will see your father," Eitan said. "I would accompany you, but king and heir must meet without unnecessary fanfare."

"Do you divine the entrails of lambs to determine life or death?"

Eitan smiled, unoffended. "I first saw your father during the war. Wails from men and women soared from the villages. Some village buildings burned. Our dead lie unburied. We fled and huddled in the hills as the Mikana shrieked and howled around us."

"Ah. The battle in the Aijalon Valley."

"The Mikana crushed most of our forces like river pebbles. We waited for Aikah to give the next command. We gathered around fires while he stayed all night in his tent. At dawn, he emerged. He instructed us to get women from the village and encircle them with jugs of drugged wine and beer."

"The temptation succeeded."

"Beyond human hopes. That night, the Mikana welcomed the distraction. They drank and flirted with the women. One by one, they fell into a stupor. We rescued the women, then bound the drunken warriors' hind legs with ropes. Soldiers cut off their heads with sickle swords and drenched them with water. Perhaps this helps you understand your father's rage about what happened during your failed mission."

"It does not," Shammah said. "When I was a boy, my father's military amazed me. Now that I am a man, his rage and arrogance astound me."

"War delivers burdens we are ashamed to carry." The commander paused. "May I show you something before you leave my home?"

Eitan pointed to a mountain to the southwest.

"Chazon took me around its base when I was younger. Do you fear it?" Shammah asked.

"Aleph is a place of secrets."

"Secrets belong to the priests," Shammah said.

"When you understand who you are, you will turn away from the roads that don't reach the gate of Aleph."

"Chazon loved that saying. I despise it. Its thorn scrapes my mind. I hear no poetry or wisdom in it."

"Your doubts do not fade, my lord," Eitan said.

"I did not imagine them. Like the claims of the other gods, like the promises of the night arts, Aleph hides beneath earthly mists, supposition, and the inhumane ambitions of men like my father. Commander, my doubts spring from deep foundations."

Eitan smiled again; his face carried the piercing expression that accompanied foresight. Older sailors Shammah had met on his travels wore the same look after battling decades of storms. They advised and counseled the younger men who insisted on taking a vessel into unpredictable weather or too close to an enemy's port and stepped back when they refused to listen. Like the seasoned sailors, the commander didn't appear smug. Only certain.

Shammah felt Eitan wanted to warn him; prepare him. Instead, Eitan inhaled and spoke to Shammah with a commander's dispassionate tone.

"I will send four slaves to accompany you. I also understand you lost your dagger during your skirmish with the Water People," Eitan said. "When you depart for the City of Kings, I will give you another."

Sunset dusted the evening sky. The priests of Livnath operated with more transparency in Chaniya than in the other cities. Nevertheless, they collected money for the Temple of the Moon and their personal upkeep more than they paid homage to the goddess, Javan believed.

As the local magistrate, he witnessed their self-indulgent lives daily. The clergy paraded through the markets, examined their farms, kept an excessive number of slaves, and arrived late at the nobles' feasts. They ridiculed the scholars at their schools with an abundance of religious fervor, rules, and intimidation. Donations and promises of food or property fueled favorable responses from the priests. The people neither loved nor respected them, but they feared them when they conducted secret rituals at the change of the moon.

The City of Kings rarely interfered, except for tax collection through Livnath's ever-greedy priests. Consequently, the royal tablet that arrived from King Aikah astounded Javan. The message revealed that the king who led at the behest of Seth's clergy had broken from the priesthood.

"Javan. A cup of beer before you go home," called out his friend Uz from an outdoor table on the winding street.

Uz was one of the city's scholars, an expert on the Desert of Akron and its secrets. After a few cups of beer, Uz could become a pitiless storyteller who imprisoned his listeners until far into the morning.

Javan needed to alert him to the king's message, but he wanted to ponder the implications first. Chaniya never had endured a war, though soldiers attended their schools and sought the counsel of their scholars. The king's orders could birth an uprising that neither Javan nor anyone else could stop.

"Tomorrow I will stop by. We will talk then," Javan said as he kept going in his horse cart.

Javan knew Uz wouldn't be alone for long. Men and a few women who chose to ignore Uz's indelicate remarks about his former wives and concubines would question him about the existence of the gods or the lasting influence of the epics. It was this familiar feeling of community that Javan didn't want to lose by executing the king's orders without careful planning. Self-governance levied enormous costs.

When his cart pulled up to his two-story house, five Chaniyan leaders waited in his courtyard. He speculated that his wife, Adara, served these unexpected guests his favorite meal: warm bread and barley soup. He also guessed that she had found fragments of goat to intensify the broth. Javan sighed. The guests would leave little for him.

"My friends," Javan said, entering the courtyard. "I'm always glad to have you visit, but why this meeting? I would have returned home sooner had I known."

"Adara has been kind to us," Reu said.

The man's thin frame and frail voice evoked the reeds he sold for living—which he did better than anyone else. People always demanded reeds, even in a desert city like Chaniya. Everyone looked forward to Reu's small caravan when he returned from the Great River. He was efficient and fast, and a merchant with few words. But he could be as picky as a babe about what he ate and drank.

Javan wondered whether Reu had irritated his wife. Adara preferred uncomplicated meals and no unexpected guests.

Javan's eyes met his wife's as Reu spoke. Although she blushed, he knew she was one poorly spoken word away from striking her husband with a bowl. The sudden flurry of guests forced his family to neglect essential household chores to entertain Chaniya's esteemed leaders.

"Adara and my daughters are my heart and my greatest riches," Javan said.

At his words, Adara offered a genuine smile before returning to the interior of the house. *Perhaps she would not crack a bowl tonight,* Javan thought.

"We didn't find you in the magistrate's quarters, so we decided to visit you here," Reu continued. "We heard rumors that King Aikah sent out special orders. But no one knows what they are."

Javan sat on a stool near the fire pit in the courtyard. He stayed silent until Adara returned and served him food. His was a large enough portion, with ample meat and bread.

He smiled with gratitude, then waited until Adara and his daughters left them.

"This discussion will remain with us. If you have loyalty to the priests, leave now," Javan said. "If you speak one word of this, I will call you into account as magistrate."

No one left the courtyard. Javan pushed on. "I've meditated on the king's instruction. The cities of Seth now possess self-governing powers. This is an emergency step King Aikah has imposed. The throne still rules Seth, but in case the throne falls, the king wants to protect the cities from the priests and nobles. I believe he also expects a major attack from the Mikana.

"We have to make immediate decisions to establish a form of government," Javan continued. "The king will send a small company to Chaniya to back up our leaders against the priests and their security."

Reu let out a gasp and almost slipped from his stool. The four other men were equally shocked.

"We're free!" exclaimed Adina, a popular farmer who organized security patrols for Chaniya's farms against warring nomads from the nearby Desert of Akron.

"Don't forget how freedom brings new cares," Javan said. "If the priests lose authority, will Chaniya still prosper? Temple commerce is a large reason why Chaniya isn't a rich city. But it's also the reason we're a satisfied one."

"Chaniya will prosper," Reu said. "We're a town of thinkers. A new form of government allows us to enact what we only debate about in our forums."

"But will Aikah's heir heed the instructions set up by the king?" Adina asked.

"I have no reason to think otherwise," Javan said. "Lord Shammah is King Aikah's choice, and King Aikah reinforced Lord Shammah's future ascension by another tablet, issued after this one. The king's seal validates it. We are to say nothing. Our role is to obey."

"If the orders are so secret, I wonder if those in the palace know," Adina said. "Maybe even the heir doesn't know how his father seeks to protect his inheritance."

The terrain shed date palms, vegetation, and animal life. Bits of rock lay scattered. Straight ahead loomed Aleph, shadowed, unwelcoming, and stern. Daylight didn't dim its gloominess, and Shammah wished he felt better while he and Peleg rode southeast. Four hooded slaves, sent by Eitan, accompanied them, and Shammah felt uneasy. They were taciturn figures who concealed their faces. Nothing was servile about them.

"Perhaps Commander Eitan cut out their tongues?" Peleg quipped.

"But they must follow my orders," Shammah said. "I intend to pass Aleph on our way to the City of Kings. Not ascend it. They misunderstood my instructions."

The four started singing in unison, jarring Shammah and Peleg with surprise:

For destiny we serve,

For life we die,

For thee, we seek.

They repeated the song and took turns singing. The melody changed each time. Sometimes it was a sudden roar; sometimes a wistful murmur. Their voices never broke the rhythm, as if music imbued the words themselves. Shammah heard the notes from stringed instruments and the thump of drums.

Eitan's men drew his attention. They sang a simple chorus to an unseen audience with a singularity of focus that bothered Shammah. *The gods must be at work. Their manipulations would soon manifest.*

Shammah pulled the reins on his horse. "This journey does not please me."

Peleg hung his shoulders. "I feel something sapping my breath…but the singing isn't that bad. At least we know they speak."

"Time to rest the horses," Shammah said.

The four slaves dismounted. Shammah rubbed his throat. Like Peleg, he struggled for air. He slid from his horse to breathe. Once his feet touched the ground, the earth expanded and jutted upward into a sheet of soil, vegetation, and rock.

The hill was becoming a mountain.

Hours later, an amber hue lit the evening sky. Eitan's four slaves walked with a pronounced awkwardness. Their strange gait puzzled Shammah, and he strained to detect expressions on their faces beneath their hoods.

"We're the victims of Commander Eitan's night arts," Peleg suggested, looking assured of his skills of observation. "It was the pomegranates. They brought sickness upon me, and this must be a vision, a daydream, though it is night. I had two of those pomegranates. My mental capabilities are…disrupted."

"Five pomegranates," Shammah said.

"All right, six. Another is in my robe."

"What are the odds of us reaching the City of Kings?"

Peleg tossed a tiny stone dice in his hands. "Twenty to one."

Before Shammah could answer, the moon crept from behind the dense clouds.

Peleg cried with elation. "Livnath! I can give better odds now that she's here, my lord."

His voice knifed through the singing and the four slaves stopped mid-verse. He exchanged glances with Shammah, who noticed that the slaves' wheel-like movements had accelerated. Peleg's words apparently agitated them. The slaves increased in size to about twenty-five feet.

Stunned, Shammah and Peleg tripped over rocks to escape from them. Shammah longed for the horses they left at the mountain's base.

But the four slaves followed briskly, their hoods falling from their heads. Instead of one human countenance, each slave possessed the bronze face of a lion, an eagle, an ox, and a man. Each had four wings that slipped from their cloaks.

Peleg collapsed. "What creatures are these? They're unnatural beasts."

"Your silence, Peleg." Shammah reached to help him.

The four slaves waved their wings and walled Shammah from Peleg.

"He cannot follow the king's heir," the slaves roared.

A donkey appeared a few feet away. Peleg gathered his strength and sprinted toward the animal that was tethered to a skeletal tree. Astonishment chained Shammah to the soil where he stood.

"Lord Shammah! Run!" Peleg jumped on the donkey. "I'll send help."

The lifeless tree crumbled to ash.

ABOVE THE SAPPHIRE STONE

U nbridled anger flowed through Shammah. Gusts of wind and clouds wound around the four slaves while Shammah clung to a large boulder and scowled upward at them.

"Who are you?"

The four slaves shrank to their original size. The hoods concealed their faces and wings once more. Shammah steadied himself.

"The Four Faces," they replied. "We're among the host that guard the throne of the Existing One."

Shammah masked his fear with imperiousness. "Why bring me here? I do not believe in any god. Existing or dead."

They didn't answer, but the ground trembled. Wide-eyed, Shammah gripped the boulder. His thoughts flew from tablet to tablet that he had read since his boyhood: about the Earth's dimensions, the skies, the roaming of kings. He even scrambled to remember what Chazon said about Aleph. No thought could he capture for long. The mountain Shammah deplored as irrelevant and lifeless was cogent and living.

He wiped the sweat from his jaw. "I never wanted my father's world. The gods sanctify chaos. Each one of them."

He looked ahead and gasped. The moon, a moment ago cloaked by drifting clouds, appeared to tumble toward him. Shammah fled like a child running from a desert tiger. He wondered how the moon could fall from the sky, and why it seemed to be rushing toward him.

Shammah rolled. Trapped between the barren terrain of Aleph and the face of the moon, mounds of jagged stone cut into his knees.

"The skies deceive us. The moon is not a goddess," Shammah said, waiting to be crushed. "It is a rock."

He clenched his eyes shut. Too much Yaphah wine had birthed this nightmare. His mind would clear soon, and the visions would evaporate. Peleg waited for him somewhere. Soon they would head home to the City of Kings, and the odd, singing slaves would be a memory.

Shammah opened his eyes. The moon seemed to lie at his feet. A screeching cry accompanied it. Shammah stood openmouthed, reaching for each breath. Then, the orb faded.

Thousands of tablets appeared. They floated into clumps of smoke. The remains transformed into projectiles that crashed into circling planets. Stars whirled into a cylinder of light. The *kimah*, along with the *kesîl*, rolled out before him.

The Four Faces started singing their hymn again, and overhead, multitudes of voices joined them. Beyond Shammah's sight, he could hear the flap of heavy wings. Grinding wheels rotated, and a platform of sapphire stone lowered above the mountain.

Shammah stretched to see above the platform but could not. He was near giving up and slumped on the ground. He hugged his knees to his chest and prepared for the platform to bury him. Death in the bowels of Aleph would end his suffering and regret. Shammah watched the platform descend, and he slid into darkness.

The visions came in rapid sequence. Light beamed where Shammah stood. Crowds surrounded him. Gila smiled at him with pride. The crowds yelled his name. "King of Seth!"

Then, a heavy mist swallowed the image like a closing fist. Shammah heard Gila scream his name in grief.

Holding on to the rocks of Aleph, Shammah then saw himself as a boy. He slept near a wall of tablets. Stirred awake by loud cries, he realized no one was with him. He started to run from the house, then returned for a tablet. Once outdoors, he sprinted toward a burning field.

Sprawling before a tamarisk tree was his mother, Emunah. A body hung from the tree.

The boy Shammah cried out: "Mother!"

"Keep running, Shammah," Emunah said. "Your father is dead."

Soldiers cheered around the tamarisk and restrained his mother, who rose to wave at Shammah.

The boy stepped toward her. Aikah, covered with soot, blocked his way. The boy threw his tablet at him, and it fell on Aikah's sandal. Aikah smiled, a crooked expression dusted with a threat.

"Your mother wants me to care for you," Aikah said. He thrust the sobbing boy onto his horse.

Shammah retched on the rocks and knuckled his drenched face dry.

A few hours later, the Four Faces squatted before him, roasting plump fish. Shammah shuddered. He understood nothing. If he couldn't calculate how the four transformed themselves from tall slaves to giant beasts, he couldn't explain fish on a mountaintop.

"I will not ask about the presence of fish without a water source. The moon. The stars. The suspended sapphire stone. The visions. My mind cannot hold the answers."

Nonetheless, when they offered him fish, he devoured it, consoled by its tender sweetness. No sea he had ever traveled had produced such flavorful meat.

When his stomach was full, he crushed fish bones with a rock to quash what happened to him. The Four Faces watched and waited until he couldn't take the weight of their gaze anymore.

"What do I say to a dying king who murdered my father and exiled me like a rodent? What do I say to the boy within me who screams at me from my forgotten past about that dreaded tamarisk tree? Who asks why I have forgotten my true father? A man Aikah hung?"

"Speak with love," said the Four Faces.

"It's impossible to pour fragrance into a filthy pot."

"A curse that took Aikah's mother's life will consume his. He also made a blood oath of his own. It is now required of him."

"You describe a non-existent diabolical convergence. I was summoned because Aikah faces death. It is the natural way of men. But you are not men. You are traveling spirits commissioned to hound me. Does the platform accompany you? What lies above it? Perhaps your calculations offer less insight than mine because you are nightmares—phantoms from my mind. You sow fear, but do you produce understanding?"

"Dare you doubt what we say?"

The Four Faces rose, their bodies elongating skyward. Shammah felt his limbs shake as a whirlwind closed in on him.

CHAPTER TWELVE

A GARDEN IN THE WEST

Light rain dampened Sagi's tunic. Tamiym, her wrists shimmering with silver bracelets, offered him a handful of dates. He frowned as their horse cart rumbled over the muddy, uneven road they traveled.

"You should have more."

Tamiym bit into a date. Her father worried as much as he hoped. As she always did, she tried to ease his stress. "What I have is abundance. You do much for us."

"My labors envelop me. Your mother tells me this. She tells me many things."

The sun overtook the rain, but Tamiym felt a lingering gloominess. Nothing seemed fair. She hoped that the goods she and her father sold in the City of Kings would be enough to keep their farm in Chaniya. Financial inequities divided families and friends throughout the city. They had even dislocated her parents' marriage, turning them into lovers out of joint with the beginnings of their love.

"Life will get better." Tamiym focused on a date.

"And my crops wait at home for my tending—while I sell in the City of Kings."

Shammah landed upright in a pile of mud. The walls of the City of Kings rose from the horizon. The Four Faces took off their hoods. Amber light glowed about them. Their wings throbbed with power.

"Why are you not going with me?" Shammah asked.

"We may not accompany you. The Mikana will soon attack the City of Kings. It will fall. If we set foot in the City of Kings now, the Great Wars will begin before the appointed time."

Shammah steadied himself in the mud. "What Great Wars? The Mikana have not attacked us since Aikah ascended the throne. Sometimes they raid a small border city, but the king's soldiers stop them quickly. What happened with me—with my men—was an aberration. It speaks more of my mistake than the Mikana's intention to invade us."

"Extinguish the nightmares of the Mikana from your mind, Shammah," the Four Faces said. "You need strength for the wars to come."

Shammah wondered whether the Four Faces could see his heart beating before them. Then he felt anger that they'd witnessed his fragility, like an old man who resists the help of his younger and stronger son.

Before Shammah could retort, the Four Faces shot up into the air as wind and fire.

The sun emerged at full strength, drying the droplets on Sagi and Tamiym's cloaks. To the west, four hooded men in a field of emmer wheat captured her attention.

Tamiym nudged her father. "Who are they?"

"Soul-stealing priests taking a poor man's crops, probably. We grow old waiting for King Aikah to shut their greedy mouths."

"Indeed," she replied. "Aikah is a savior-king for wars, not for the needy, the sick or the lame."

Tamiym's inquisitive expression intensified. "What are they doing?"

"Who?"

"They don't look like overfed priests," Tamiym continued. "These men are lean. And tall. Very tall."

As she spoke, life-sized blooms sprang up around the four men. Date palms shot skyward and kept growing. The lush garden transfixed Tamiym and her father. The horse pulling their cart—and the one tied behind it—remained on the path, even though Sagi neglected the reins.

A song floated toward them:

Sing now,

Sing again,

A garden opens its gates in the West.

"Father, what did you say?" Tamiym asked.

"I didn't say a word, daughter."

"I heard a strange song."

Sagi focused on the reins, but Tamiym, with her back to her father, studied the men as the horse cart rocked along the road.

Shammah was staring upward when a donkey nudged him. He jumped. Hand to his dagger. Behind him was Peleg.

"Them?" he asked.

A reluctant nod from Shammah.

"By the kindness of Livnath… At least you didn't ride two days by donkey, my lord. I don't think I'll ever ride again. This contrarian donkey wouldn't take me back to Yaphah to get help. She pushed me toward the City of Kings. And now I meet you."

"Two days," Shammah said. Had he lost that much time on Aleph? He wouldn't let his mind try to calculate how many hours had passed. Unable to understand what had happened, he stated what he knew, what he could grasp. "I need a horse."

Shammah glared at the donkey. She nudged him with affection. The gesture stoked Shammah's irritation. "Do the gods relish vexing the lives of mortals?"

"Isn't that why we declare everlasting devotion to them?" Peleg asked.

"No," Shammah said. "It is why I refuse."

He wanted to slip to the ground and cry out about what he saw on Aleph, but he knew Peleg wouldn't understand. Livnath was all he chose to know.

Shammah sighed. He needed to reach the City of Kings, to prepare Seth for war, and to face the man he called father for nearly two decades.

At that moment, ambling from the southeast, was a horse cart, driven by a man who looked like a farmer. Riding with him was a young woman. Shammah rubbed his eyes. "The gods are temperamental indeed," he said. "But which deity aids me?"

"Livnath of course." Peleg held out a hand to the pair on the approaching cart.

"Friends," Peleg said.

"Friends," Sagi replied, slowing down the cart. He placed his fingers on a dagger at his waist. Shammah suspected that another weapon lay at the man's feet. Farmers always worried about robbers snatching their produce as they traveled to market.

"My lord needs to borrow your horse. May he borrow it?"

"I cannot oblige you." Sagi clucked to his horse.

Shammah stepped in front of the cart. "We need to borrow it," Shammah said. "I am Lord Shammah, son of King Aikah. I've been summoned home after a long exile. The king is dying."

Shammah reached for his seal while gazing at Tamiym. She appeared more regal on her horse cart than he did standing on the road.

"Perhaps this will help you trust me."

"The king's seal…" Sagi said. "Please forgive me."

He elbowed Tamiym, who elbowed him back. The man left the cart and bowed.

"I am Sagi. This is my daughter, Tamiym. We're from Chaniya."

Shammah studied her. She lowered her head and went to the rear of the cart, appearing to Shammah as elegant, reticent, and astounded. He turned to Sagi.

"What is your trade?"

"I am a farmer and an artisan," Sagi said. "My daughter is my right hand."

"Your work must find favor. Horses are rare. Expensive."

Sagi beamed. "They're the blessing of trading with caravans from the Desert of Akron."

Shammah followed Tamiym to the rear, where she caressed the mare. She placed a saddle cloth on the horse. He reached out to help her attach the yoke. Her hands fumbled as they worked together.

Their hands touched as he stroked the mare's jaw. Tamiym moved away. The horse whinnied at Shammah's caress.

"How beautiful and dignified she is," Shammah said. "A gentle touch is all she requires: from farmers, from kings."

Shammah sensed Tamiym studying him. He knew his appearance mystified her. He smelled of sweat and dust and maybe even fish and vomit. Bracelets, earrings, and rings didn't grace his body. Nothing on him signaled his rank; all he had was the seal Gila gave him three years ago.

He took in the shadows that dusted the skin beneath her eyes. Her lustrous braids, bound at her nape, revealed high cheekbones the color of dark honey. Every movement on her face bore secrets Shammah yearned to learn.

When he returned to Sagi, and Tamiym had settled in her seat, Shammah felt composed again.

"The palace will return this horse to you. Where will you lodge?"

"The merchants' quarters." Sagi paused. "Lord Shammah, may you greet the king before he joins his fathers."

Shammah hesitated and waited for Tamiym to speak—or to be able to catch her gaze. Neither happened. He climbed onto the horse. "A reward awaits you for the mare and for seeing my friend to the City of Kings. Please take this good man with you, as I must reach the king."

Smug, Peleg grinned at Sagi.

CHAPTER THIRTEEN

THE CURSE

Mud-splattered from his ride into the City of Kings, Shammah kneeled at Aikah's side. A suffocating rottenness permeated the room, despite the balcony's open windows. Guilt clutched at Shammah. He slowed his breathing. This man, complex and horrible, had been his father for most of his life.

Shammah kneeled before the dark-gray form of Aikah. Gila, with a cloth held up to her nose, stood behind Shammah. "You've returned in time, my son."

Aikah's frail hand hovered over Shammah's bowed head. Shammah reached for him, but Chazon snatched Shammah's hand, then gently let it go.

"Even in love you cannot," the priest said. "The curse has advanced to its most dangerous stages in the last few days. It can infect you with death. Aleph protects us if we do not touch him. I will explain later."

Aikah dropped his hand into his lap. "I've squandered much."

"Please forgive my stubbornness, Father," Shammah said.

Aikah leaned forward again. Tears flowed along his shriveling cheekbones. Locks of his hair fell with every movement.

"Remedy what I have done," Aikah said. "In the Desert of Akron, you will find a hidden cave."

"Father, the histories are in the libraries of Chaniya."

"Not every truth arises from the knowledge of men. Before I brought you here, I followed your father to the cave."

Shammah trembled. Aikah blinked with understanding.

"He was a man of philosophies without swords. I don't atone for your father's death. I killed him at the demand of Livnath, and he died in the name of Aleph. I chose you because of the desires swirling in my own heart. I know that now."

Shammah bowed his head. He hid fury mingled with sorrow. Aikah hung on to his arrogance even when facing death.

"Go to the caves and save Seth from the Mikana and save the throne from…"

The ceiling opened.

"Shamgar!" Chazon shouted. The bodyguards rushed into the room.

"Go, Shammah! Take the queen!" Chazon said.

Shammah leaped and shoved Gila to a far corner of the room. A Zuzim warrior, about seventeen feet high, peered down into the chamber. He shrank his form to about nine feet and stepped into the room; his appearance was stunning: a red mane, a tunic of jewels, scalding green eyes.

The Shamgar crouched low before the warrior. They drove their swords at its legs. He swept them away. The Zuzim, amused by the torment he caused, lifted Aikah's body and twisted it between his fingertips.

"Your dying is as putrid as your mother's. She cried out like a babe when I clenched her bones."

The king moaned. His body glowed with an inner flame. Aikah shook as the Zuzim grinned. Shammah felt rage bubbling within him.

"You trespass," Chazon yelled.

"You instruct me about my prey? I've longed for the day of his rottenness. He slew our children. I still hear their cries."

"Aleph!" Chazon snapped his arms skyward. Water and wind ripped into the room. The priest, backed by an unseen force, manipulated a curling wave around the Zuzim.

Another wave dragged the unconscious Aikah from the warrior's grasp and placed him on the floor. The waters engulfed the Zuzim, although the rest of the room remained dry.

"Where is the heir?"

The Zuzim turned his head to face Shammah and Gila.

Shammah rushed toward him, dagger exposed.

"You have no rights here!" Chazon said.

"You have no power, priest." The Zuzim stretched out a reddish hand that slipped through the flooding water. He looked at Shammah. "Heed me. I am power. Doubt no more."

Shammah hesitated. Pounding questions ignited within him again. The Zuzim extended his hand. Shammah felt his grip on his dagger loosening.

"Curious from birth. I must have you." The Zuzim wagged a dripping, jeweled finger at Shammah. "What you see is truth, adopted son of Aikah. He was no father to you. Call me father. Make me first."

Shammah felt like a man awakened from sleep. "Pestilence, bow to your future king," he said.

He dug Eitan's dagger into the Zuzim's thigh. To Shammah's surprise, fire burst forth from the weapon. Simultaneously, water poured over the warrior at Chazon's direction. The Zuzim vanished with a flicker. The ceiling closed shut.

Shammah was heaving, trying to end the incessant questions prodding him. Chazon collapsed. Sweat and water soaked his body. The priest crawled to where Aikah lay. Gila was already there, weeping.

Chazon stood and spun toward Shammah. "Hesitation in the face of evil is the work of foolish men. The Zuzim drew strength from you. Deliberations mean nothing if you do not know when to fight or when to act. Too many people sacrificed for you to entertain carelessness. Did Aikah's punishment teach you nothing?"

Shammah shoved his dagger into his belt. How fire erupted from the weapon Eitan gave him would be a meditation for another time.

"Is the king dead?" Shammah sounded mellow.

"He lies with his fathers," Gila said.

Shammah's jaw flexed. The burden he dreaded was now his. He was the new savior-king of Seth, the Proud Lord of the Seven Gates.

"I never expected the unholy thunder of Aikah from you," Shammah said to Chazon. "Leave me."

"Now that you are king, you will not hear me?"

"I do not require your tutelage."

Peleg vowed never to ride a cart again. The tedious journey, during which he attempted to engage Sagi and Tamiym about things he knew nothing of—crops and livestock—made him eager to smell the dirty, narrow streets of the City of Kings. He yearned for the beer of the lower classes, that mind-numbing brew that would make him forget being jostled in a cart, carried by a donkey, and hunted by four creatures with shifting faces.

"Did you grow up in the City of Kings?" Tamiym asked.

"I never knew my mother," Peleg said. "My father left me with a family when I was three or four. I couldn't identify him if he sold me linen in the market."

"Horrible," Sagi said.

"My best teachers were the thieves who taught me how to slide fish from the sailors' tents and bread from the baker's ovens before they noticed. They taught me how to feed myself, barter, and get work."

"Did you ever learn to read tablets?" Tamiym asked.

"Lord Shammah urged me to read with him; however, epics and the philosophers weren't as exciting as the mayhem I was accustomed to hearing from the thieves and the temple priests. There was one epic that intrigued me—one that told of the great flood that terrified our gods."

"I have read that one," Tamiym said. "But the way the priests retell the story, the gods fear nothing."

"Lord Shammah noticed that as well."

Peleg knew Tamiym's interrogation was just beginning. Suspicion dripped from her voice. "How did you meet him? I mean, you and Aikah's heir are unlikely companions," Tamiym said.

"Sailors always are. I was assigned to one of his vessels," Peleg said. "We sailed the Time Sea together and drank beer on forlorn nights. We sent back jewels from the East for the king's treasuries. We traded with caravans and arranged for imported wood and stone to be brought to Seth."

"Such bounty could have clothed and housed several cities," Tamiym said.

Peleg saw Sagi chastise her with an elbow. "Lord Shammah is quite extravagant with the poor. I hate to say it, but some sailors doubt whether he should be the heir. He's kinder than King Aikah. His generosity makes him appear weak. The rich of the City of Kings—and many of those who wish they could be as wealthy and haughty—display cruelty and little compassion. The poor, the slaves, the scholars, and the merchants who understand that our economy can't flourish in constant oppression, well—and I don't blame them—they admire him.

"All kings are tyrants, dictators, and despots," Peleg continued. "They have to be. But don't repeat my words. I beg you. They could get me killed."

Sagi's cart rocked toward the enormous gate of the City of Kings. Six human-headed bulls in headdresses with flowing beards and coils of hair stood sentry at the Seventh Gate. The bulls were forty feet tall and dated back to the time before King Kish, and before the Mikana had invaded the north.

Peleg sighed. "Home."

A guard stopped them and scanned the cart bed and their belongings. He dismissed them with a wave. He and his men were preparing to close the copper-plated, two-leaved gate as night fell. They had reached the city in time.

"Is all well in the City of Kings? How is the health of King Aikah?" Sagi asked.

"The king died before sunset," the guard said. "Lord Shammah is king. The city mourns and rejoices."

The three didn't say a word as Sagi guided the cart through the crowded streets. When they reached a corner, Peleg mumbled, "I hope they parted as father and son."

He rubbed his knees with his hands, then jumped from the cart and twirled on the ground, solemnity gone. Merchants and farmers getting to their quarters for the night walked past him with their baskets and sheep, but Peleg continued his survey with an expression of open wonder.

A long breath. Then an unabashed snort. "Can you believe it? I sailed with him, ate with him, and fought with him. He was my friend, and now he is the king. Do you think he can find a palace room for me to sleep?"

"Maybe not," Tamiym said. "He cannot trust you with the king's treasury nearby. You do not seem the type to resist temptation."

"You're right," he said and took to dancing again.

CHAPTER FOURTEEN

RITUALS AND RESTRAINT

The queen's private rooms were as elegant as Gila: fragrant blooms on a table, jeweled coverings for her bed. Shammah joined her on the balcony and wrapped an arm around her shoulders.

"The balcony was Aikah's favorite places to think," Gila said. "He implored Livnath more here than at her palace shrine or at the temple. From here, he could remember the responsibility he had, and from the balconies, the people could see the king. I know that Aikah didn't require it, but I almost wish I had the courage to throw myself from the balcony so that they could bury me with him. He hurt me, but being without him, flawed as he was, without the goodness he also gave me, nearly hurts as much."

"He escaped to the balconies. I escaped to your rooms, Mother," Shammah said. "Or, the Gardens of Destiny."

"You do not approve of me arranging my death?" Gila asked.

He kissed her hair. "The king was wise and loving not to require it. The practice is barbaric."

He paused. "Your rooms comforted me when father spun into one of his moods, and when Dahv taunted me about my studies. Peace winds alongside you like a river."

"Dahv is a cunning bear who hungers for the throne. Aikah's tablet reinforces your claim."

"Where is it?"

"In Dathan's safekeeping."

She pulled away from him. "Have you reconciled with Chazon?"

Shammah didn't want to be harsh, but he needed to be direct. "You question my judgment?"

"Will arrogance carry you to destruction?"

"When Chazon atones for his insolence, I will listen."

"Don't tarry for atonement. Chazon bruised you, but you will need him."

They watched the first strokes of sunset slip below the horizon.

"Later, describe your journeys from us," Gila said. "Aikah sent you off in a rage, but his heart longed for your return. He would want to know what met you along your path."

He thought of what he learned from the Four Faces. He wouldn't add to her sorrow to hear him retell how he saw his birth mother and dying father in a vision. That telling would come at another time.

"My journey is not over, Mother," he said. "I still travel it."

Through a slave, Shammah instructed Chazon to schedule Aikah's burial within a day. This meant that many of the people who knew Aikah in Yaphah wouldn't know of his death in time to reach the City of Kings.

Chazon agreed with the decision. The decay in Aikah's body was contagious. Chazon refused to allow the royal morticians to help him prepare the body for burial by saying that Aikah wished the priest to care for him alone. As Chazon prepared the body for burial, he remembered Aikah's sad description of how his father had sent him away so that he could prepare his mother's body for cremation after she succumbed to the Zuzim curse. Chazon wondered how Aikah's father knew to burn the body and remain safe.

The priest bound his hands with rough linens and moved Aikah's decomposing form to a cot, covered it with reeds, and tied it to the cot with heavy cloth. He minimized the odors wafting from the body with myrrh before summoning the Shamgar. The bodyguards, their bodies covered with linens, carried the cot through a passageway the royal slaves used to bring food from the kitchen. Slaves weren't present because Chazon told the palace they could attend the noonday and evening sacrifices.

Chazon and the Shamgar heard the wails from above as they descended into the passageway. They went into a walled-off storage room that featured a small oven that King Kish installed for special dishes he wanted late at night. Slaves baked bread in the furnace. Chazon planned to let Aikah's body burn in a separate rack deeper in the oven. After this, while offering some excuse, he would tell the slaves to seal the oven.

When the wailing reached its loudest at the temple, Chazon waited for the animal sacrifices to douse the city with smoke and fumes. At the same time, the priest and the Shamgar cremated Aikah's body.

"Aleph, help us," Chazon sighed as the flames consumed the corpse.

Chazon wouldn't let the Shamgar collect the ashes until after he had placed them in a closed container. Only then would he allow them to fulfill the rest of the plan—their last act as the bodyguards of Aikah.

They rested until the evening rituals took place. When Chazon heard the first wail and saw the rings of smoke, he instructed the Shamgar to take the ashes and place them in the sarcophagus already in the tomb carved for Aikah. Chazon added one of Aikah's robes.

When they left the mound-like structure, only footsteps away from the palace, they sealed the heavy doors of the burial tomb with bitumen.

"Existing One," Chazon said, "please protect us from any remnants of the Zuzim curse. Even in the ashes. Keep us free."

He pulled out a small bottle filled with myrrh and other ingredients and sprinkled its contents on the men.

"This will take the foul scent of the curse away," Chazon said. "At least from us."

The Shamgar stepped into a small grove to get the horses, leaving Chazon alone. In that same moment, Qayin and several of his slaves rode up in a horse-led cart.

The priest of Livnath cocked his head with a grin. "Did you have to help King Aikah reach the place of his forefathers?" Qayin asked. "It's one thing to refuse the help of the royal morticians to bury the king, but does the priestly duty include burying the king in solitude?"

Qayin's presence surprised Chazon, and it meant that the priests had noticed Chazon's ruse.

"A loyal friend's duties reach far," Qayin said. "And are we not all loyal to our dead king? Is that not why all the slaves are attending the night's ritual in his honor before Livnath while you do not? Do I have to summon Commander Lehabim to beat you again to get the truth?"

Chazon bowed, flexing his full lips. His wounded arm ached, and he longed to sling dirt clods across Qayin's smirking face, but it wasn't the day of reckoning.

"I'm sure Livnath overlooks your choice to leave the sacrifice early."

Qayin jumped from the cart, intending to menace. Chazon was unimpressed.

"We must go," Chazon said, walking away. "Shamgar!"

Guriel, grim-faced and ready to pin down any of Qayin's men, emerged from the darkness with a horse.

CHAPTER FIFTEEN

TRUE RIVALS

Mourners passed by the sealed tomb, dabbing their tear-stained faces: enemies of Aikah, friends, and paid mourners who wailed like wolves. Nobles and priests argued about succession, and sailors congratulated themselves about the scholar prince who had journeyed with them on many voyages.

Shammah knew many of them were lackeys and foes who wanted access to the throne, though they critiqued it. His heart filled with pity, however, when Aikah's five concubines bowed before him. Though privileged, they were shunned women who lived for decades amid finery and lovelessness. Aikah treated them like indulgences and brought them to the palace against their will.

"You are free to stay under the protection of the palace or return to your families," Shammah said. "You have no obligations to me."

"My name is Cheberith, my lord." She was a low-voiced woman with stooped shoulders. "Will you guarantee protection for our sons?"

"I am king." Shammah's tone was gruff. "It is so."

Cheberith smiled in gratitude and led the group away.

Moments later, Dahv sauntered up to the king and bowed. "A fruitful kingdom feeds on loyalty," Dahv said. "Our father demanded its sweetness."

"As will I," Shammah said.

"When we dwell on failures from long ago, we blind our sight."

"Or sharpen it."

"My brothers and I pledge fidelity to your throne, my lord," Dahv said. "Our loyalty flows from Aikah to you."

Shammah inhaled. Dahv had been a liar since they were children. Flattery coated his love of prevarication. Ever-present was his thirst for the throne. By all mortal rights, Dahv, not Shammah, should be the Proud Lord of the Seven Gates. A volatile Aikah had forced them to become competitors, and Shammah was weary of the game.

"Fidelity proves itself," Shammah said. "May I be your first witness."

Dahv bowed and moved to a crowd of merchants just as Mahalath slipped away from her sister and a cluster of noble-women. She planted herself near Shammah as he studied Gila, who stood before the tomb.

"You are generous," Mahalath said.

"No, my father the king was," Shammah replied. "He spared the queen's life."

"Will you assume your father's quarters?"

"My small home in the Gardens of Destiny is sufficient."

Suddenly, Chazon barreled toward them, eyebrows tucked together. When Shammah glimpsed the priest, he raised his hand, and the Shamgar barred Chazon.

Shammah listened to Mahalath, not distracted by the irritation he suspected brewed in Chazon.

"In time, we must become what we are destined to be," she said.

Shammah patted her hand and noticed dull, chewed nails. She slipped her hand away from his in embarrassment.

"I feared your estrangement from the king would separate us forever. Anxiety overwhelmed me. Now the king is gone. Do we remain in covenant?"

"Free yourself from uncertainties, my lady," Shammah said. "I will not abandon King Aikah's pledge."

Shammah lit a lamp at the Ten Pillars. He rubbed his fingers over the carved markings of Aikah's name. He heard feet crunch tree leaves and pebbles. Shammah turned. From behind him, Peleg found a bench and tossed tiny stone dice in his lean hands.

"You do that too well." Shammah removed his right hand from his dagger.

"Learning to hide from rogues who beat me gave me the gift of stealth," Peleg said.

"Perhaps you should write a hymn about the murky life you endured. Your former companions will drink to your success."

"And my enemies may return. Your life is more curious— less common than mine. And as I can neither read nor write, and prefer not to, you write the hymn."

Peleg paused. "You never told me what happened on Aleph—with the four terrible ones. Do they breathe fire? Or cut open the earth when they sit?"

Shammah peered into the crystal lens. The constellation of Aryeh shone before him. He jerked away from the lens. "Their wonders defy understanding. I rule with what I comprehend."

The memory hounded him, but he refused to explore what it meant. He refused to allow the gods to rule his mind, no matter the power of their night arts.

He changed the subject and ignored Peleg's open-mouthed expression. "Sagi and his daughter. You left them well?"

"They tolerated me. Tamiym wants to send me to one of the priest-run schools. She sees me living as a scribe. My affection for blissful illiteracy unhinges her. I'd better not tell the whole story about my past as a child. It may break her heart."

"Tenderness? I wondered what lay behind that stern exterior," Shammah said.

Another question simmered on Peleg's face. The sailor missed nothing, but Shammah chose not to give Peleg the satisfaction and discuss Tamiym.

"The procession. The coronation," Shammah continued. "After their conclusion tomorrow, we will prepare our people for war. My father hid too many of our troubles. He made agreements in the dark. It is time to tell the truth."

Peleg's voice rose. "The rumors are true, then?"

Qayin had never stood so close to a Mikana warrior. He held his breath, hoping the warrior wouldn't kill him with a blow of heat. Though they were enemies, under Aikah they had forged a truce because of the king's victories. Sometimes the Mikana tested Seth's good will, like in Nifla when Shammah encountered them, but they knew Aikah's sword was nearby. Now that the king was dead, it was an opportunity to pledge a new covenant.

Ciycera towered over Qayin. The priest felt heat on his face and sucked in his breath. He couldn't change the plan. Qayin, remembering the Mikana's powers to make people feel as if trapped in a furnace, wondered if Ciycera would torch the date palms where they stood.

"The high priest of Livnath wants to offer me Aikah's heir so that he and his conspirators can live?" Ciycera mused.

"We thought we could barter the king's heir to buy us continued peace," Qayin said.

Ciycera guffawed as if hearing a joke in a tavern. The loud cackle stirred Qayin's horse and petrified his slave, who scurried to a palm trunk, clutching a small figurine of Livnath.

"This gives me deep amusement," Ciycera said. He studied Qayin as if the priest were a flea escaping its brood by the riverbed.

"Aikah was felled by the Zuzim curse, but he was a worthy opponent," Ciycera continued. "Why would I want his adopted son and heir? What value is he to my people? Why shouldn't I snatch his inheritance and drag his body through the fields?"

"The priests want to forge a bloodless agreement with the Mikana and the Zuzim," Qayin said. "You would be in covenant with the heir of our choosing, but that heir would submit to you. Commerce could grow more between Seth and your people. We all would profit."

"A bloodless, profitable agreement? You are ambitious."

Ciycera pulled out his sword and stroked its blade without drawing blood. Saliva dripped from his jaw. Drops fell on the weapon.

"You confirm to us that Aikah perished because of the Zuzim curse," Qayin said. "You take Lord Shammah's life on the day of the coronation. The priests will declare it an act of Livnath. You proceed with your attack as planned."

"Ah. You have no problem sacrificing your own people? This covenant is not bloodless after all."

"Unintended casualties. It's necessary to conceal our, er, relationship," Qayin explained. "In return for murdering Aikah's heir, and crowning a king who will pay you tribute, you will give the high priest and myself immunity from the Zuzim curse. We also agree to increase your commerce within Seth's borders. The financial year for our merchants will arrive in two moons after the barley cutting, and they want it to be lucrative."

"You are certain? The 'unintended casualties' may be numerous."

"Yes."

"Then it's done," Ciycera said.

He shouted into the shadowed date palms behind him: "Dathan!"

Aikah's skinny slave-scribe slipped from the night darkness and bowed before Qayin, who exclaimed, "This is proof?"

"Speak," Ciycera said.

"I have the tablet," Dathan said. "The original tablet sealed by the king that confirms Lord Shammah as his heir. Without it, Lord Shammah's claim is invalid. I can… alter it."

Dathan tried to control his features. "King Aikah trusted me to keep it safe. You see; I hid behind a cracked door. Saw him perish from the curse. The Zuzim squeezed the last of life from him. I served six-hundred-and-seventy-six weeks beneath Aikah's foot. No more."

The slave rubbed his arms as if they helped him to remember his triumph over Aikah. "My lord might also want to know something else now that King Dahv will be on the throne. Once King Aikah decided to announce Lord Shammah as king, he instructed me to do something I couldn't sabotage—"

"Enough," Ciycera said.

Dathan slipped back into the shadows.

"What else did Dathan have to say?" Qayin asked. "Other than Chazon, he was the one who knew everything Aikah was doing."

"That's beyond the reaches of our agreement," Ciycera said. His green eyes shone with heat.

Qayin felt intoxicated by the sticky warmth, a desire so invasive and foreign that he almost collapsed. Perspiration soaked his throat and chest.

The heat subsided, and Qayin shuddered. His wits returned.

"Do we still have the original agreement, priest of Livnath?" Ciycera asked.

"We do." Qayin caught his breath.

"Good," Ciycera said. "Pray you are a worthy partner."

Haran stacked salted meats and bread on his plate. Qayin barely veiled his nausea. The high priest's incessant consumption of rich foods perplexed the younger and leaner priest. It seemed as if Haran satisfied the hunger of his sorrow with delights from the oven when he could end his grief by wielding power on behalf of Livnath.

"Your news excites me," Haran said. "I rejoice at the mention of Aikah's pain. But how does that further our hopes? The throne belongs to Shammah."

Haran piled meat into his mouth. Qayin tried not to watch.

"I discovered a luscious morsel about Aikah's death." Qayin smirked as he said it.

"Does Dahv know?"

"In part," Qayin said. "His ignorance will benefit us later."

Haran gobbled a chunk of bread. Delighted.

CHAPTER SIXTEEN

THE FESTIVE CUP

B linding streaks of noonday sun glimmered on the embroi-dered robes of nobles, whose faces and jewelry reflected the sun. They stood closest to the procession and squirmed to catch the gaze of their new savior-king.

Shammah felt suffocated by the rowdy crowds and the pull of greed and power. He heard jostling to his right but kept moving his horse. The sooner the coronation and the feast were over, the sooner he could meet with Seth's commanders and prepare for war. Shammah searched for someone who would reassure him that this madness wouldn't last. Queen Gila stood at the temple's summit. He looked to the right as Chazon charged his way to the front of Shammah's entourage.

"My lord, please hear me. I must speak to you…For your safety…For your understanding. Your father would have wanted you to heed me."

"Do you forsake your words at the king's deathbed?" Shammah used the same dry, hard tone he'd heard Aikah use to belittle others. He ignored the tinge of sadness when Chazon appeared older and frailer to him for several moments.

Chazon said nothing.

"Then you are denied," Shammah continued. "Denied, you hear me? Now, get out of my way."

The royal entourage of slaves pushed the priest aside.

Peleg carried no rank, but he pushed through the clusters of people so that Shammah could see him. He ignored the nobles, frowning and shooing him away from the procession.

At last, Shammah had seen him. The king lifted his hand, his gold and lapis lazuli diadem sparkling, and grinned. He dismounted his horse and climbed the temple steps.

"May we not forget the days at sea!" Peleg shouted to Shammah.

Peleg glared at a noble who shoved him aside. Then he shouldered him in return.

"You don't want me to speak? My dagger has slashed one hundred throats," Peleg said. "Should yours be next?"

The noble pouted before retreating from the growling Peleg, who sauntered closer to the entourage. The sailor was behaving at his braggart best. His impudence would remind Shammah that he wasn't alone.

When Shammah reached the summit, the pleasure he had felt in seeing Peleg vanished at Haran's greeting. Ablaze in scarlet with gold crescents, the high priest's face was as stern as his garments were brilliant.

"King Aikah's choice," Haran said. "It is also nearly the new year because the barley and wheat harvests are beginning. May this be the Year of the King."

Shammah kept his face as stoic as Haran's. The self-indulgence in the demeanor of the corpulent priest revolted him. People starved while the high priest ate. The new king forced himself to remember.

"High priest," Shammah said.

Haran frowned and motioned to the coterie of scarlet-robed priests. Two priests carrying torches moved toward the altar of wood where a strangled lamb lay.

Queen Gila stood nearby in golden robes. Like a warming ray of sunlight, she smiled at Shammah, and for moments he rested in its glow. While warmth flowed from Gila, feeble hope trailed from Mahalath, a cool mystery he had never deciphered. The soon-to-be queen, the daughter of a noble house, simpered before Shammah like a gnat to fruit. He favored her with a clipped nod. Amid a den of conspirators, he hoped he could rely on Mahalath as an ally.

"Though your moon is not with us, Livnath," Haran said, "link your strength with the sun. Bless our new savior-king—chosen by your slave Aikah."

Though noonday sacrifices were common, an altar bearing a lamb signaled a significant spiritual transaction. Shammah remembered Aikah performing the rite once, after he defeated the Mikana. He was a youth, but he remembered being awed and repelled by Aikah's devotion to the goddess.

The two priests lit the sacrifice. Flames swarmed into the air. Cheers erupted at the base of the temple tower. Haran raised his arms and searched the sky.

"Livnath!"

Clouds hid the sunlight. Grayish, silver light wound itself around the structure in a throbbing funnel. Shammah's heart dropped. Sudden winds arrived and gained speed until the crowds quieted. A howl roared from the clouds. Shammah's body tightened. The Shamgar hugged the jeweled handles of their swords. The howling escalated as a priest handed Haran a golden cup. He took it in both hands. It was the festive cup, formed of gold and silver, etched with fig leaves and date palms. Every king of Seth had drunk from it.

Shammah felt uneasy when Qayin moved into Haran's place, raised his arms upward, and resumed chanting to Livnath.

The cloud cover settled into a greenish mist over the temple summit. Hawks emerged, first flying upward as if freed in celebration. Then they flew toward Shammah, who held the festive cup to his lips. He dropped to the platform. The Shamgar raised their swords and struck. The hawks dodged them.

While Shammah saw his soldiers trying to break through the cloud to rescue them, the Shamgar huddled around him. They cried out as they sustained wounds on their back and legs from the wild, malevolent birds. Light struck through the dark cloud of hawks, twirling like torrents of water.

Meanwhile, soldiers rushed up the temple steps, but it was too late. A burst of wind swept Shammah and the Shamgar away. Drops of their blood splattered the platform. Moments later, another set of soldiers, led by Commander Lehabim, overtook those who had attempted to protect Shammah.

Gila screamed and the crowd wailed. Not far from her, Mahalath stood frozen. Gila guessed she was unaware of the conspiracy. As the queen slumped down, she felt hands taking hold of her. Chazon. He had rushed to the platform to reach her. The queen wiped away her tears. An image of a younger and stronger Aikah appeared in her mind. With Aikah only days in the underworld, the temple priests had destroyed the line of succession by murdering his adopted heir.

What night arts had carried away Shammah and the Shamgar were unknown to Gila, but she held Haran and Dahv responsible. She jerked away from Chazon and snatched a dagger from her robes, ready to pounce.

"Livnath has rid us of this curse of an heir," Haran said, picking up the bloodied cup that had fallen from Shammah's hands.

The high priest motioned to Qayin to retrieve the royal diadem. After searching with several slaves, Qayin shrugged. The diadem wasn't on the platform.

"Livnath has slain him," Haran continued. "She rejected Shammah as the heir. Don't be saddened; rejoice. Livnath has disrupted the line of succession and revealed her choice. We understand from King Aikah's own scribe that he preferred his blood son, his firstborn."

"Falsehood!" Gila screamed. Each of her limbs throbbed. "You dishonor a dead king with a liar's testimony."

The queen felt violated by the high priest's voice and mocked by the moaning wind that mimicked the throaty voice of the concubine She'iya, smirking at her from the underworld. Gila tasted the salt of her weeping. She was a broken loom in an unraveling world.

Haran, with a backbone he never had displayed when Aikah was alive, calmed the crowd. "The queen is saddened by the death of her adopted son and heir. But the goddess has revealed her will."

Another cry rumbled through Gila as Chazon gripped the queen's hand that held her dagger. She resisted for several moments, her fingers clawing at the weapon. Slowly, she relaxed and the gasps and trembling limbs stilled.

"Aleph will avenge," Chazon said.

Dathan ambled toward Haran, eager for public attention, but fearful of it too. "It's true," Dathan said in a loud voice while holding up a tablet. "Dahv is Aikah's choice, and Livnath's choice."

Nobles gathered below the summit and yelled, "Livnath's choice! Livnath's choice!"

Haran shooed away Dathan and motioned to Dahv, who stood on the steps below the summit with Aikah's five concubine-born sons. Conspicuous submission. Dahv appeared compliant, even though the hunger for conquest hung over him.

Dahv ascended to Shammah's place on the platform. Haran held out the cup that an attendant refilled. The new king drank slowly, staring at Mahalath over the cup's rim. Gila turned her head again to the younger woman who ogled the platform, remaining motionless as a pond.

"Livnath, please bless your choice for the savior-king," Haran pleaded.

As the high priest made his plea, the sky turned clear and bright again. Dahv seized the moment and addressed the people, straightening his shoulders as if dropping an unseen burden.

"We will run toward a fresh future, and I swear to protect and bring prosperity to Seth," he said. "I swear to obey our patroness, the goddess Livnath."

The crowd roared in reply.

Dahv bowed like a loving son before Queen Gila.

"Livnath has chosen me, my queen, but I regret that Livnath chose to remove Lord Shammah from his inheritance," Dahv said. "I mourn the loss of your son, my dear brother. Please come to me. I will fulfill your needs as he would have done."

"You are kind in the face of this decision by the goddess," Gila said. She was grateful her words didn't come out in a shriek. "I ask that I be able to leave the court and eventually return to my childhood home. I also want my slaves freed without reprisal."

"It is fulfilled," Dahv said, bowing again. "I will see to assigning your escorts."

"I thank you, King Dahv," Gila said. "But Chazon will care for all I may need."

Dahv turned to Chazon, who stood by with his head lowered. "Serve the queen," Dahv said. "Do not return."

Chazon escorted the queen from the platform. Gila sighed with anxiety as they sidestepped people who called her name or tried to seize her. Resentment rode beneath their shouts and a brooding hung over the city as word of Shammah's death and Dahv's ascension spread.

"Gila, why live in the palace since Aikah lies with his fathers? Live with me." The man yelled while waving a half-filled cup of beer that dripped onto his tunic.

"My son died in Nifla under Shammah's care. The gods are just," shouted a woman who spat at Gila as she elbowed away from her.

A man and woman snatched a section of Gila's robes, and Chazon punched their hands to release it. It was unmistakable.

Dahv's coronation had released reckless anger among some people in the City of Kings.

When they reached the street, Gila spotted a man with his right arm bound in clean, but frayed bandages, while carrying a stick with his left. The man rushed toward them, pushing away those in his path. Gila reached for her dagger. Chazon glowered at the man as he unsheathed his sword to guard Gila from a trio of belligerent merchants who muttered curses.

The man bowed quickly, then expertly separated them from the trio by thrusting his stick. "My queen. Priest Chazon. My name is Raah. King Shammah would want me to help you."

"Why do you help us, friend?" Chazon's question emerged in a growl. He was wary, but Chazon and Gila followed with caution because the only safe path was the one Raah created for them.

"I won't injure you," Raah said.

When they reached the palace, palace guards surrounded Gila. She extended a hand to Raah. "I am grateful. But why did you attend to us?"

"King Shammah came to my home and expressed his grief and sought forgiveness for my son's death in Nifla. I was heartbroken. I was angry," Raah said. "But seeing the king's heir on my doorstep brought me hope. We embraced. We wept. I vowed never to forget."

Gila's normal breathing returned. "Your arm, Raah. Please let me bandage it."

When Raah left the palace, a slave trailed him, carrying supplies. In silence, Gila and Chazon watched them walk away until they reached Shammah's chambers. Gila touched stacks of Shammah's tablets and the star-gazing instrument Chazon made for him. Then she sat on a bench and broke the quiet.

"Dathan altered Aikah's tablet," Gila said. "I am sure of it."

"Yes," said Chazon. "I have also identified Dahv's unexpected ally."

"Who? Has Dahv dragged his conniving mother from her tomb?"

"Mahalath. At first, she chewed her nails nervously, stunned by what happened to Shammah. Later, horror shifted to reluctant, but loving admiration for Dahv."

"Her father would welcome a change of affection toward the new king," Gila said. "E-ven's gaze never has wandered far from the throne."

"Livnath killed Shammah," Peleg said. A bearish noble, annoyed with Peleg's cries as the cloud of hawks dispersed, pushed him to the ground and placed his foot on the sailor's neck.

"Dahv is Livnath's choice, sailor. Rejoice. Shammah was an impostor. Drink up."

Other nobles danced and sang around the pair, oblivious to them as they cheered the new king. Merchants, who never missed a chance for commerce, sold smoked meats, barley bread, and beer in kiosks draped with banners of gold and scarlet. Steps beyond the kiosks, artisans, farmers, and slaves celebrated as the sun beat down on the City of Kings.

But from his place in the dirt, with the noble's smelly, leather-clad foot on his neck, Peleg could see others, as stunned as he, pushed about by the crazed mobs.

Poor fathers wrapped their arms around their weeping wives and children. People scurried from the temple base. Slaves attended noble families with glum faces. Dejected scholars clustered together, and those merchants who chose not to sell wares at every opportunity closed their tents and carts, tears streaking their cheeks.

Laughing, the noble released Peleg with a jerk. The sailor crouched on the ground for several minutes until the noble sauntered away. Despondency replaced the bold joy Peleg expressed as Shammah had ascended the temple steps.

Two pairs of hands grabbed Peleg by his arms and helped him up. He looked up to see Sagi and Tamiym.

"You're bleeding," Tamiym said.

"An old wound," explained the sailor as he rose, his words slurred with sorrow. He tore a piece of cloth from his garment and wrapped it around his neck. "A noble stepped on the place where I was healing. May a sea plague invade his house."

"Come with us," Sagi murmured.

The three made their way to where Sagi had rented rooms. The city was a mixture of festivity, shock, and sobriety. Soldiers left their guard posts to celebrate, and opportunistic thieves stole from the merchants, who sold beer and wine to the lusty crowds. Peleg had never seen the City of Kings this unbridled.

Outside their quarters, a palace slave stood with Sagi's mare. Freshly cleaned, the mare bore a jeweled saddle cloth and a new yoke. The finery on the horse would feed a family for a year.

On his coronation day, Shammah hadn't forgotten Sagi and his horse. Peleg wanted to shout to the slave that the new king was dead, but he couldn't utter the words.

Sagi took the reins from the slave who seemed to have waited for them, despite the coronation festivities. Tamiym attempted to give a bag of grain to him in gratitude. He refused.

"Lord Shammah already has provided for my family beyond my expectations," the slave said.

The mare secured, the three spoke to each other in their quarters. Peleg paced and pulled at his hair. "Shammah didn't want to be king."

Sagi started a fire in the hearth. "Lord Shammah's death was a manifestation of the goddess I've never seen or heard of before," Sagi said. "We witnessed a human sacrifice. That hasn't happened publicly since the early days of the city.

"I don't remember an appointed heir ever being taken by the goddess like that. Given power, yes. Rejected with a sign in the sky or struck by plague, yes. But this? There isn't even a body to bury."

"More reason for us to sell your work and return home," Tamiym said.

"It's not our family alone who is at stake here, beloved one," Sagi said.

"The aristocracy is deaf to our struggles. I will not listen to theirs."

"Is this what we taught you?"

"You taught me to respect every class in Seth, Father. But this is a problem for the City of Kings, not for Chaniya."

She moved toward a shelf that held grain stored in bins and other food items. She reached for salted meat, a few apples and cucumbers, potatoes, and onions from beneath a worn cloth.

"I should have our meal ready shortly," Tamiym said.

Sagi left the dwelling and stood outside. Peleg rubbed his stomach, but not from hunger. Churning within him were memories of the king's heir and their travels.

"Lord Shammah saved my life," Peleg said. "Why couldn't I have saved his?"

CHAPTER SEVENTEEN

DESIRE

Dahv savored the touch of his royal robes as Joktan, one of his slaves, examined the royal tailor's work. Joktan purred with pleasure about the fabric and the fit until Dahv waved away the slave. Dahv walked to a large table stacked with tablets.

His fingers traced tablet etchings that tied his name to Livnath. Aikah would have been proud that his firstborn son seized his rightful place by the power of Livnath. His father often stressed how a king must rule from the skies. Well, today Dahv won the throne because Livnath killed Shammah for his sake.

Dahv wished he could savor his solitude longer, but he overheard Qayin speaking with soldiers in the courtyard. At another time Dahv would get his bearings in his father's quarters. The spare chambers confused him. Why had his father lived this way when he had access to every luxury? Never had he slept on a worn reed mat or appreciated Aikah's murals depicting his victories over the Mikana. A more soothing room of gardens and water pleased Dahv, and he would one day redo the king's private quarters.

Qayin sauntered into the chambers, only to admire the king's robes. "Being king suits you," Qayin said.

Dahv placed a hand on Qayin's shoulder when the priest entered. "Livnath has paid me a great honor today. I am humbled."

"As we all should be," Qayin said. "We implored her, and she answered with her fist."

The priest's tone bewildered Dahv because it bore none of Qayin's usual snobbery. In fact, Qayin appeared bemused as he turned from Dahv and paced the length of the room.

"We don't know when the Mikana will attack, but we must be ready," he said. "We need the support of the noble families if we are to minimize the historic liberties of Seth."

"Do you pledge your alliance with me, as Chazon served my father?"

Dahv felt an inner reproof for his impetuous request to Qayin, but he reassured himself that the decision was justified. All kings required counselor-priests to make them wise on the Earth and with the gods—even priests they didn't trust. He was no different.

Qayin bowed. "As you wish, my lord."

The priest led the king outside of the room. A new Shamgar that Lehabim recruited now served King Dahv. They placed their right hands over their chests and bowed. A longing for his father crept over the new king. Aikah's bodyguards served as elegant assassins recognized for their precision while the guards Lehabim chose for him appeared surly, like crusty criminals emancipated from prison.

The Shamgar followed as Qayin continued through the corridor to the large courtyard where Aikah had spent time with the noble families, along with Dahv's mother and his other concubines—reciting poetry and listening to epic tales.

Dahv's half brothers—the five sons from the other concubines—entered the courtyard along with the best families of Seth, including Mahalath's. They waited for Dahv to be seated at the oblong table festooned with banners and loaded with goat meat, vegetables, barley bread, dates, jars of beer, and cups of wine.

"My young brothers and friends. We mourn the heir, but we are thankful. Are we not grateful for life and prosperity? Livnath spared us all. Let us feast in honor of the goddess."

The nobles sat down hungrily, and the area gradually filled with laughter. Dahv leaned toward Mahalath. He placed plump figs from his full plate onto hers. "Eat from my platter. Drink what my cupbearer brings. Dine with your king."

Dahv refused to conceal his pining after years of wishing he was the king's heir. Shammah was dead. Nothing stopped him from making Mahalath his. "Will you grieve long?"

"Lord Shammah will not be forgotten so soon," Mahalath said.

"You hardly knew him."

"The king betrothed us."

"Because of your father's status," Dahv said. "Yet your heart beats for me."

He thought he saw relief in her eyes.

Mahalath clutched her right arm.

"Are you unwell?" Dahv asked.

"Perhaps I have eaten too much," she said.

"You have eaten very little. Walk with me for a moment. Perhaps the illness will pass."

Dahv rose from his seat and offered his hand.

Pride curdled within Dahv. He saw Lord E-ven smile as his daughter rose with the king. Mahalath's father continued a loud debate with a noble who owned vast parcels of property.

"We need laws to cover those expenses for the nobles," E-ven said. "We don't have to pay for every irrigation project in the fields surrounding the City of Kings."

"But we own most of the land, and we bear the responsibility," the other noble replied, his swarthy face flushed with irritation.

"My family goes back to the sacred founding of the city and its dedication to Livnath. One of our ancestors was king," E-ven said. "What you say never has been done."

Dahv felt smug as he guided Mahalath to the perimeter of the courtyard. A union with Mahalath would delight E-ven. Now that he was king, Dahv knew he was more appealing to her family.

He selected a rose on the fringes of the courtyard. He rolled the stem between his fingers, broke off the bloom without the thorns, and placed it in her thick coils of hair.

"This does not smell as aromatic as the scent of almond oil in your hair," Dahv whispered. "I ask you again. Will you grieve long? I ache to bring you joy."

"As propriety demands," Mahalath said. "You are the savior-king, the Proud Lord of the Seven Gates. My response will match that."

Dahv laughed, snagging the attention of the nobles, before they returned to their debates.

"Ah. That has changed. Will you now surrender your swords? Your barbs?"

Mahalath smiled. "It is true. We do debate with intensity."

"Should I start an argument about the role of women in the kingdom?"

She blushed. "My lord, you know I believe women should share freedoms with men that our code does not allow. They should receive the same treatment as men when it comes to marriage, adultery, property, and education.

"The code should be reviewed by the king, whose authority comes from Livnath," Mahalath said. "Half of the elders in the noble class do not know the boorish requirements of the code, and they should initiate the changes. The priests are horrible to the priestesses. Women suffer more economically than their male counterparts. Men should not have such power that they dominate women. Women should have every right—"

She caught herself. "My lord, please forgive me. We are celebrating your coronation."

Dahv folded his bullish, date-colored face into kindness as much as he could. "Don't subdue the luster of your wit and words. They're as beautiful to me as the curls of your hair, the curve of your cheek."

"I am glad the king is pleased."

"Very."

Mahalath almost lost her step. Could she hear the coarse desire pouring from his voice? Did his passion offend her?

His breathing grew heavier as they stood together. He was grateful when Qayin approached and whispered in his ear.

"I must go now. Please excuse me, my lady," Dahv said as Mahalath offered him an uncertain smile.

For the first time in Dahv's life, his beloved protagonist, the woman who had sparred with him since childhood, appeared bemused by his presence. The sensation of potency boiled within him.

Many of the people gathered on the steps of the temple tower appeared sluggish from the previous day's coronation.

Good. Warring for what is mine has been useful, Dahv thought. So were the sleeping draughts he ordered placed in the beer and wine during the celebratory feasting. The bait of platters of food and endless pitchers of drink lured the people into submission. How many times had he suspected his mother She'iya enticed Aikah to her chamber with juice from the poppy plant? She had tutored him unknowingly in the night arts of deceiving through drink without giving him a direct lesson.

"Citizens of Seth, our days of feasting will stop sooner than we planned. My scouts informed the throne late last night that they estimate the Mikana will attack within three days," Dahv said. "We will have to evacuate the city for safety. I know this imperils our harvest and our property, but until we defeat the Mikana, I declare martial law to protect you. Evacuation begins at dawn."

He ignored the screams and slurred murmurs of people gathered on the steps. "My friends, martial law is a temporary state. We need to protect you by keeping the streets clear. We must protect our food supply. We must keep order. Once we drive back these foul beasts, everything will return to as it was."

"What guarantee do we have? You could steal everything we own," yelled one man.

"In our history, no one has implemented martial law. Even during war. Why now?" cried a tailor, a length of linen looped around his neck.

Dahv nodded at Lehabim, who signaled to his soldiers to infiltrate the crowds, their swords and spears held high.

The complaints ceased.

The five younger sons of Aikah never returned to their quarters. *The cruel nature of Aikah reappears in the bosom of his firstborn son, Dahv,* Chazon thought.

Six assassins stormed the tavern where the five younger sons were drinking, along with their friends, and killed them. When he was told, Chazon knew that Dahv orchestrated the murders.

Restless, the priest shifted on his narrow bed. He felt lost. In his mind, he could still see the concubines as they made their way through the city, weeping as soldiers carried the bodies of their dead sons. They reached out to Queen Gila, but an armed patrol surrounded the queen, who sought seclusion in the Gardens of Destiny. They reached out to Dahv, but he declared his dead brothers rebel supporters of Shammah and cast their mothers from the palace.

Shammah had been the only person gifted for this moment in the kingdom's history until assassins violently plucked that revelation from Seth. All the petitions, the tutoring, and the longing to see Aleph work through Shammah toppled for Chazon during those rib-crushing minutes on Livnath's platform earlier in the day. The priest couldn't find comfort. He couldn't.

Chazon passed his left hand over his damp forehead. Decades ago, he forsook the ways of Livnath, but as grief tasted like bits of moldy bread, the old practices called out for Chazon's return.

"Please speak, Existing One," he whispered.

He reached for a tablet and flung it at a wall. Abandonment clenched Chazon's chest and throat, and he couldn't suppress the complaint on his lips.

"What have I done wrong? Why did you not rescue Shammah from death? Have you abandoned Seth? Have you abandoned me?"

Like a whirlwind, the priest took another tablet, and then another, and then another, and swung them around the room before collapsing on the floor.

Eitan stopped south of the City of Kings in barley fields owned by the palace. Slaves harvested what they could. The slaves must have been trying to save crops before the Mikana marched on the City of Kings. Having missed Aikah's burial, the commander longed to have seen the coronation, but was delayed by storms. As he was traveling to the City of Kings, thinking he would reach the city in time for the days of celebration, he was intercepted by a messenger sent by Chazon.

Word about Shammah's death had confounded him, and because of the priest's terse message, he suspected Chazon was numb. As for himself, Eitan had been rigid before his men. Only now, as he and Asahel slowed their horses to a trot on the dirt road, did the commander relax.

"I had such hopes," Asahel said.

Eitan smiled. "Didn't we all? We can sit before the mystery of the Existing One and wait. But I admit that the hurt is beyond the horrors of war."

The commander peered down the road at an approaching retinue led by Chazon. Who sat in the covered cart of the nobles? Chazon spoke of confronting the Mikana and overthrowing King Dahv. Had he won support from someone in the upper classes? Eitan's face brightened as Chazon's horse drew nearer.

"It is good to see you, Chazon," he said, jumping off his horse. Eitan, Asahel, and Chazon embraced in the middle of the road.

"By Aleph!" they yelled in unison, grasping a moment of happiness.

They were like young men again, untried, eager to test the boundaries of their destinies. They stepped back to examine each other, noting how time had passed and troubles had come.

"It has been too long." Eitan slapped the priest's back.

"Yes," Chazon said. His dark brows weren't ominous for once. "Asahel, I have missed your stories. Promise me a tale of Yaphah at the fire tonight."

"You will have your wish," Asahel said. "I have one about a lazy king who drank himself to death, and his wife took the throne."

Asahel paused. Eitan understood. They were no longer care-free men, and the throne of Seth was in jeopardy.

"War is upon us," Chazon said. "And within us. King Dahv has declared martial law."

Eitan groaned. "How near are the Mikana?"

"Scouts say they will strike in days," Chazon said.

The commander winced and rubbed his beard. "This will be a bloody war, and one led without the rightful king," Eitan said. "King Aikah had not counted on this."

"How can we produce a rightful heir to stop Dahv? Lord Shammah is dead," Asahel said. "The whole situation seems hopeless. What country survives that violates its own code by seating an impostor king?"

"And they may outnumber us," Eitan said.

"We can count on it. That's why we must travel to Chaniya and consult with the scholars about the caves in the Desert of Akron," Chazon said. "It's the only way to save Seth from the tyranny of the Mikana. Aleph, in mercy, has shown me this."

"Chazon, but the caves are described in a tale told to children, are they not? And what about the City of Kings? Should we not return there and fight?" Asahel asked. "What good are we out here when Seth implodes at its foundations?"

"No doubt the Mikana will make a spectacle of the royal court before they overtake all of Seth. We have very little time to defeat them. The answer lies in Chaniya. Aikah's instructions were for Shammah to go there. We must go in his place."

Eitan placed a hand on Chazon's shoulder. The priest's jerky movements and slow, slightly slurred speech replaced his usual fluid, but pacing gait. The commander could only imagine the burdens the priest bore. With Aikah succumbing to the Zuzim curse, and Shammah murdered only yesterday, Chazon appeared as an injured soldier unable to conceal his ghastly wound.

The priest moved toward the cart and pulled the decorative curtain aside and said, "This should cheer you, my friends. Please welcome Gila, the Queen of Seth."

Gila stepped from the cart and accepted Chazon's hand with the practiced grace of a veteran monarch. Eitan and Asahel bowed before her.

"Friends of Chazon, let me see the faces of dear ones he loves."

The kindness rippling through Queen Gila's voice and filling her gaze caught Eitan off guard. She was almost ethereal, a mournful cloud that refused to block the sun. During all the years of Aikah's reign, he'd never visited the palace when she was present, and the commander regretted not meeting her during sweeter seasons.

Eitan remembered protocol and kissed her outstretched hand. "My queen."

The commander couldn't help it. He wanted his lips to touch Gila's fingertips again and again.

CHAPTER EIGHTEEN

THE WORK OF THE GODS

The fire, the songs, and poetry sung by the men in the camp were consoling, but Eitan discovered comfort in the pools of Queen Gila's eyes.

"You thought these days of impending war would not come because of Shammah," Gila said as they sat before one of the fires.

Chazon didn't look up from the flames, and Asahel hung his head, so Eitan assumed the question was for him.

"I had hoped he would reign like none other; that I would see a peace sanctioned by Aleph," Eitan said.

Gila smiled at Eitan's words but addressed his lieutenant, who appeared forlorn. "Asahel, I understand. Turbulence existed between my adopted son and my husband but hope also flourished between them. For all his many flaws, my husband knew that Shammah would make an extraordinary king. In the end, the king's sins did not overcome his love."

"Perhaps if Aikah had openly declared Shammah his heir—as we had begged him—Shammah might be alive today," Chazon said. "He remained unforgiving until the opportunity to endorse him publicly was lost."

"Stubbornness was one failing my husband didn't conquer completely—like many of us," Gila said. "He did make amends with Shammah privately before death."

Asahel reacted with a horn blast of a sniffle.

Eitan ignored him. "But in your grief, you seem peaceful, my queen. May I ask if you follow Aleph?"

"I am curious about the dark mountain because of Chazon," she said. "Livnath demands and destroys. Aleph may make requirements from its followers, but I sense benevolence that my husband never experienced. Livnath is volatile and willful. Our sea gods in the Cove of Revealing aren't as cruel."

She paused with a winsome smile that made Eitan flush. "But those sea gods are unreliable," Gila said. "Tell me, what god is true? We serve at their pleasure and die at their choosing."

Eitan didn't know whether he should defend Aleph to the queen. He waited for Chazon to say something; he was the priest. Eitan didn't want to offend the woman whose voice soothed his mind like fragrant oils.

"Aikah never overcame his mother's death, so he replaced her with Livnath," Chazon said. "Livnath visited Aikah by the riverbank, and he said she foretold his future. I have heard reports from other men about Livnath visiting them as a beautiful, cooing woman who prepares meals for them.

"By the time Livnath visited Aikah, his father couldn't guide him on a different path; he was sick and mourned his wife. As a boy would, Aikah created a new mother. Livnath didn't curb his selfishness, and she didn't stop his savagery. She incited it. Demanded it. Aikah claimed it was freedom, but it was bondage."

The crisp burning of the fire crackled before them for long moments. "My queen," Asahel said. "I follow the Existing One of Aleph because he's there."

"Then you would call Aleph constant?" Gila pressed as Asahel's face wrinkled with emotion.

"If you mean, is the Existing One a mystery that makes sense, then yes," Asahel said.

Then he released another loud sniffle.

Javan, the magistrate of Chaniya, didn't know what to think. None of his meditations, which occurred when he paced his chambers and murmured his father's proverbs, brought any clarity except the nagging thought that a storm surrounded him. Another messenger from the City of Kings had arrived the day before, announcing the death of Lord Shammah and the ascension of Lord Dahv. After the messenger left, Javan began his mutterings.

Chaniya already had established self-governance and appointed elders to oversee civil disputes, including those involving the priests, as King Aikah's orders—sent weeks ago—prescribed. The orders had surprised the Chaniyan priests, but they didn't envision an immediate threat to their status. But King Aikah had also sent another order—classifying it as secret for the magistrates—confirming Lord Shammah's claim to the throne. But which of the orders should Javan follow now that Lord Shammah was dead?

Frustrated, Javan summoned his closest friend, Uz, away from the young astronomy students in the city's library.

When the scholar arrived, he stepped over tablets Javan had stacked around the magistrate's quarters. The cluttered room was evidence of Javan's impatience. Javan suspected that Uz thought he was awkward at unexpected times, pushing forward when he should wait and hesitating when he should attack.

"Did you find an answer?" Uz asked.

"I must prevent civil war in our streets," Javan said. "Once the priests know about this, they will side with King Dahv. Those who prefer self-governance will fight to keep the privilege we gained under King Aikah."

"And as magistrate," Uz said, "you want to do what's legal."

"I'm trying to prevent a massacre."

"Then what do we have before us? Three orders. The voices of two kings. Does one cancel the other? Or do all of them matter?"

"I need more than that, Uz. That's why I called for you."

"The answer is simple."

Javan tossed a tablet regarding temple taxes at Uz's graying head.

"I offer my repentance," Uz said as he dodged the lethal tablet. "Your legalistic blustering keeps you from seeing truth."

The tablet cracked on the floor. Javan groaned. Now he would have to pay a scribe to replace that copy.

"Get to the point," the magistrate said.

"King Aikah was the clear line of succession from King Kish. Lord Dahv was never intended to be the heir, but the priests selected him at Lord Shammah's unexpected death. What should have happened is that the priests should have consulted Seth's history before they assumed Dahv would be king because he was the blood son of King Aikah."

"What you're saying is that they should have come to us."

"That is correct," Uz said. "Chaniya holds the tablets of Seth's history in our library. There is no precedent for this. None. In fact, the queen could have ruled. I mean, it is extraordinary to think of a woman at the helm of Seth because it has never been done, and should not be, in my opinion."

"Must everything come back to your opinion about women?" Javan asked with verbal frost. "The kingdom is at stake."

Uz shrugged, then cupped his head with its cropped coils. "You asked for my perspective, did you not? As I said, the queen alone could have chosen the new king. I do not know whether King Aikah knew that was in the law because it dates to the sacred founding. Educated nobles whose ancestors founded Seth probably knew, but they apparently preferred Dahv to be heir."

"You're saying that King Dahv is guilty of presumption?" Javan asked.

"His guilt is greater than that. He staged a coup. King Aikah anticipated that," Uz said. "He suspected Lord Shammah would be challenged for the throne because he issued the secret order about self-governance, and the second order reinforcing Lord Shammah's claim."

"But King Aikah could've never anticipated Lord Shammah's assassination," Javan said.

"You are correct. I do not think he did, although he was aware of the manipulations of the priestly class," Uz said. "The whole matter is disheartening. Shammah would have been Seth's first scholar-king. But it was not to be."

Uz sighed. "Beer. Do you have any?"

"None. That wouldn't be appropriate for the magistrate's quarters," Javan said.

Uz frowned at the untidy room. "But it would make it more entertaining to be here."

"Perhaps the death of Lord Shammah was indeed the work of Livnath and the gods," Javan said.

"You know better than that, my friend. The 'work' of the gods occurs because of the 'fingers' of the priests. They want to control the throne, and they can achieve that through Dahv's ambitions."

"So, what do we do?"

"Are you still so blind? We fight with the king's company assigned by Aikah's orders," Uz said, rubbing his lips. "I want beer. Are you coming, or will you wallow here?"

Javan rehearsed every word Uz had said. The circumstances vexed him, and the counsel of the scholar deepened the fantastical nature of the circumstances. Decades of peace and power had spoiled Chaniya's magistrate.

He was deep in thought as he made his way to the barracks. Although he hated to admit it, he felt compelled to follow the advice Uz gave him and work with Commander Mattan. They had yet to meet.

Once he was face-to-face with him, Javan wondered if a fresh problem challenged him. Commander Mattan stood several feet above him. Mattan's height and his colorful dress—he didn't wear the traditional blue of the commanders—confused the magistrate.

"At your service. Let me reassure you," Mattan said. "I am the son of a Chaniyan woman. My father came from Edrei in Rabbah. I am of the fifth generation."

Javan relaxed. "Please forgive me. We don't see your people cross the desert to us, except for trade."

Social deftness was never Javan's skill, and he was one of those who had mocked the turbaned merchants from Edrei known for their fastidiousness and love of exotic dishes. The magistrate felt like a foolish rustic. He was also fearful. As a fifth-generation descendant of the star-born, the commander had sworn peace with the citizens of Seth, but his presence jarred Javan.

Mattan found Javan a stool. "My mother was sold into marriage to the people at Rabbah. She escaped my father, whose great-grandfather was star-born. When I was old enough, she sent me to the military, where she thought I would be able to thrive without question. King Aikah understood my mixed lineage and favored me. For his kindness, I am forever loyal."

Javan remembered graciousness. "And for your presence, I am most grateful. Are your quarters comfortable?"

"The accommodations are like palaces," Mattan said. "My men and I are accustomed to patrolling the desert and sleeping with flies and scorpions."

"And have you met with our local security?"

"I have, along with the priests."

"Was there resistance?"

"None that matters."

"No one expected this," Javan said, shifting the subject as if he had held conversations with Mattan for years.

"All that matters are King Aikah's orders," Mattan said. "Dahv acted presumptively at the death of the king's heir. Every commander in the military contingents assigned by King Aikah knows this. They suspected a coup planned by Lord Dahv and Commander Lehabim but never imagined they would succeed."

Javan felt his annoyance growing. "If this knowledge is so widespread, why weren't the people of Seth and its magistrates warned earlier?"

"King Aikah knew there would be a challenge to Lord Shammah's ascension and prepared for it," Mattan said. "But he revealed it to commanders like me whom he trusted."

The commander paused and sighed. "Civil war throws the country into turmoil. However, there's something else that disturbs me."

"What?" Javan was curious, but afraid to hear the answer.

"The alliances Lord Dahv has made—those will determine the source of his military strength to sustain his coup," Mattan said.

"What are you saying?" Javan asked.

"I suspect they're working with the Mikana."

Commander Eron ate the last of his bread. He leaned forward on his stool to study Geona, who rocked their son back to sleep. Their daughter had fallen asleep hours before Eron came home from the barracks in the City of Kings.

Sleep tickled Eron's eyelids as Geona sang to the infant. Home felt restful to him after the tense gathering with the commanders. To regain military strength after the discovery that Aikah's order had thwarted King Dahv in the cities of Seth, Commander Lehabim sought to solidify the companies in the City of Kings and eliminate any disloyalty. Kingdom politics divided the commanders, and Eron dreaded facing his fellow soldiers in civil war, but he believed King Dahv was as much a threat to Seth as the Mikana.

Geona rocked the infant and sang until his whimpering ceased. It was for this that Eron lived: a woman who loved him, children who would gather about him, and enough money to keep them fed and housed. Geona put the baby down on the bed and sat by her husband. She caressed Eron's cheek, and he kissed her wrist.

They had loved each other since they were children playing in the oldest section of the City of Kings; since he had been a dirty-faced boy who protected her from the rude merchants and nobles in the market.

"I will not stop you from fighting, husband," she said.

"Dahv outnumbers us. We could die saving Seth from anarchy," Eron said.

"You could. But you won't."

Eron smiled. "My love, you could lead armies."

Geona dabbed the tears that sprang from his eyes with her fingertips. Then she rose and cleared the table.

Beneath an austere moon, Eron and two commanders slipped into the barracks. One of the lieutenants who expressed support for their cause met them. Together, the men rounded the corner to Lehabim's chambers. The soldiers in this barrack were conducting patrols under the new terms of military rule. Only Lehabim and his bodyguard should be there.

Before they could reach the chamber door, one commander with Eron howled and arched his back. The commander fell forward. A sword wound sliced him shoulder to waist. The assailant was the lieutenant who pledged his support to Eron and the two commanders.

The lieutenant was reaching for the second commander. Eron and the commander exchanged glances.

"Go," the commander yelled as he dodged the lieutenant's sword.

Eron sprinted to Lehabim's chambers. They were empty. He rushed back to the door and saw that the second commander was now dead. The lieutenant who broke faith with Eron and the two commanders was in a corner bleeding and yelling curses.

Judging by the severity of the wound, Eron kept going. The lieutenant would die soon.

Eron locked the chamber doors. He pulled his cloak over his head and smeared soot on his face from a fire pit. He climbed through a small window and slid down the wall.

He heard soldiers shouting, and the air glowed with torch light. Eron flattened himself against the wall. He prayed Geona had followed his instructions about traveling to her brother's farm. If she had not—he stopped himself from worrying. He was no use to her dead. He must disappear within the crowds in the market.

Eron crawled and slid against walls, determined to reach the older part of the city, the southern quarter where he and Geona grew up. Once he was there, he could disappear.

CHAPTER NINETEEN

SEEKERS

Lotan ascended the steps of the Temple of the Moon for the nighttime sacrifice. The priest loved sleeping like he loved eating and drinking, but rest eluded him. Livnath required entreaties and sacrifices to act on the priests' behalf. King Aikah had upset the balance of power. The priest hadn't confirmed it, but rumors were also spreading that Dahv, not Shammah was king. Aikah's heir, the rumors claimed, had been slain by Livnath.

The priest raised his hands, sleeves of his scarlet robes sliding down and exposing bracelets and tattoos. Six priests joined him at the summit, and two of them set an altar with a slain pig ablaze.

"Livnath!" Lotan cried. "Your order has been changed; your will overturned; your traditions overrun. We implore you: give us strength to keep your ways."

At the ceremony's end, the priests doused the sacrifice and cleaned the platform. Lotan returned to his quarters, shooing away anyone who wanted to follow him. He threw off his bracelets and earrings as he entered, and they thudded on the hard dirt floor. He had pronounced Livnath's help to the younger priests, but he worried the goddess wouldn't fulfill his petition, that the elite status he enjoyed would shift like sand. Lotan had plans— plans he dreamed about when attending the priest-led schools as a boy. Dread of the poverty that dogged his family drove him to master reading, writing, calculations, and astronomy.

Lotan became an expert on trade, and that study enabled him to increase the wealth of the temple during the ten years he had overseen it. Commerce surrounding the temple base had increased, and Chaniya itself had grown as a priest-controlled trade route for those traveling to Edrei.

He reached for a glistening clay bowl near the bed, where he often lounged and read. He vowed death before he would release power.

Mattan walked the grounds surrounding the barracks where the military of Seth slept. He reassembled within his mind stories his mother had told him about his father's people: how they claimed to be the direct descendants of the star-born, how they summoned powers from the courtyards of the sky and the bowels of the Earth, and how they killed with fire and plague.

As he turned a corner, a messenger greeted him. The messenger looked haggard but determined to speak.

"Commander," the messenger said, "one of Commander Lehabim's men killed two of our commanders last night. And a third commander is missing. I rode all day to tell you because before the commanders attempted to assassinate Lehabim, they ordered their lieutenants to inform you should Lehabim discover the plot and kill them."

Mattan growled. "How many men side with us?"

"About two thousand. One of the commanders led a double contingent. Commander Lehabim is publicly announcing that Mikana spies killed the commanders."

"When do the contingents receive their new assignments?"

"In about a day," the messenger said. "If the Mikana don't attack first."

"Send word that we will help," Mattan said. He motioned to his lieutenant to oversee the message but refused the unspoken question on the soldier's face: *How would they rescue two thousand soldiers from the City of Kings?*

When Mattan was alone, he went to the hills outside of the barracks in the darkness. He found a high rock, curled his bulk upon it, and closed his eyes.

"What am I to do?" he whispered. After a while, he fell asleep.

While Mattan slept, shadowy doors opened above his head.

CHAPTER TWENTY

FIRE FROM THE MIKANA

"You must evacuate the city tonight," Dahv said. He munched dates from a bowl, licked traces of fruit from his fingers, and glanced at the tablets strewn on the table in the courtyard before him as if they were a bother.

"Your parents and the rest of your household will join the nobles at dawn. Do not argue with me, Mahalath. It is my will."

"I will not leave without my family," Mahalath said.

She stood up in protest. "Let them come with me."

"I cannot afford to show favoritism to any of the families during martial law," Dahv said. "But I can be forgiven for favoring my future queen. Our best soldiers will escort you. I will join you if the Mikana overtake the City of Kings. Until then, the priests at Arba will provide for you and your slaves."

Mahalath shivered. She didn't feel protected; she felt captive. So did her father. Both bristled at martial law. Even as a tool of war against the Mikana, martial law for the kingdom was a dangerous step, a serpent in the storehouse. They also had openly defended Dahv—certain that he wouldn't drug guests at his coronation feast, as the wildest rumors insisted.

Now she wondered if the whispers were true. He longed to cling to the throne and its excesses as the kingdom faced war when he should display the discipline to save it from harm. She never viewed Dahv as a strategist, and her recent feelings of passion toward him hadn't altered her opinion. He could romance her, but she doubted his ability to rule.

As Dahv studied the curls of her hair and the smooth skin of her shoulders, she yearned to debate him as she had when they were children, but her aristocratic instincts warned her to remain docile. The boastful can't endure criticism for long.

"As you say," Mahalath said.

"Your compliance comforts me," Dahv said with a laugh, his bare feet slapping on the stone walk. He placed his hands on her shoulders. "Do not fall prey to anxiety, my rose. Victory is ours, and we will reign together."

He paused, and Mahalath knew he wanted to kiss her; she felt relieved when he didn't.

Dahv bowed. "My queen forever."

"My king."

While she bowed, Mahalath prayed to Livnath that her desire for Dahv as a man would bloom into a desire for him to serve Seth as king.

"Where are the priests?" Dahv asked.

"In the temple tower," Lehabim said with a grimace. "They refuse to leave."

"They think the temple tower will protect them from the Mikana?"

"According to them, Livnath's sacred temple is impenetrable," Lehabim said.

"Their stubbornness is beyond understanding," Dahv said. "What about the palace property?"

"We packed the king's treasuries in the tunnels below the palace and sealed them," the commander replied. "Portable items the king will need while outside of the city are on the carts."

"I know we told the people dawn, but let's evacuate two hours earlier," Dahv said. He scanned the moonlit city from the balcony. "Tell the troops to evacuate the city now."

"Yes, my lord. The soldiers are already in place. The people will resist us. They will say they are not ready."

"Remind them with swords that they either leave their belongings and live or die at that moment."

Lehabim smiled.

"To Livnath," Dahv said.

To might, Lehabim thought.

Commander Anash lifted a scepter in his right hand, signaling for the second wave of warriors behind him to move. Beneath the pink sky of dawn, the Mikana's double-horned beasts crushed rocks and grasses as they headed for the Seventh Gate. Anash yearned to demolish the structures, for they symbolized Seth's refusal to submit.

By covenant with Livnath, Aikah was the sole person who could restrain the Mikana. With his death, Seth was unprotected. The enormous warriors could cross the Tiras Mountains and ravage Seth.

Ciycera, halting his beast with the ease of a noble on a hunting spree, joined Anash at the front lines.

"My lord," Ciycera said. "We have an agreement with Livnath's priest to accept their king. Qayin promised that King Dahv will submit to us."

"He will, and so will these renegade priests," Anash said. "We will pretend to play along, but have we suffered Aikah's arrogance only to endure the feeble demands of these slaves of the goddess?"

Ciycera saluted him and returned to the rear guard.

Seth's soldiers were in place. Anash laughed as thousands of arrows flew at them, but each Mikana beast marched forward, untouched. This generation of Seth didn't possess knowledge of the night arts.

Aikah, Anash mused, *I miss your cunning*.

Fire soared throughout the city. The Mikana stormed the City of Kings. They jumped to scale the wall.

Dahv released arrow after arrow, but there were too many Mikana.

"We must retreat," Lehabim urged. "We misjudged their arrival. They attacked before the fullness of the third day."

Dahv fired another arrow. It landed in the forehead of a Mikana trying to climb the wall. "This is my kingdom, you polluting beast."

"Seth will stand," Lehabim shouted to Dahv as Mikana swarmed near them at the farthest part of the wall. "But we must keep you safe."

Anash sat erect on his beast that was adorned with gold tassels and ruby beads, and he growled at the fading moon. Without leaving their perches on the beasts, the Mikana crumbled the bulls at the gate like stale bread and torched the City of Kings like kindling. His army consumed the city, corralling priest, noble, merchant, soldier, scribe, and poor citizen alike in silver pens encrusted with precious stones that the Mikana created from empty air.

At the city's central section, several contingents of Seth's soldiers waited. When the beasts—who numbered in the thousands—were in shooting range, about two thousand of Dahv's men vanished in a wind of debris that gathered from the city streets.

The winds startled Anash. He lifted his nose into the air and sniffed. Night arts were at work, and they resisted the Mikana. Anash slowed his beast, and the yelling Mikana behind him stopped.

Beasts roared, and the remaining soldiers of Seth ran in confusion. They threw spears at the Mikana while they screamed at each other about the missing men.

"Whose power is this?" Anash bellowed. "Why are some soldiers taken and some are not?"

A shadowy image of a turbaned man appeared. Anash leaned backward on his elaborate saddle cloth. An offspring of the star-born dared to play with him and snatch his prey?

The image of the turbaned man vanished. Disturbed, but unwilling to stop the Mikana assault, Anash imprisoned the remaining soldiers of Seth and instructed his warriors to march to Livnath's temple.

At the temple tower, several of the Mikana warriors struck the building at its summit with their massive swords, cracking its foundation and causing the four-stepped structure to quake.

Shrieks echoed from within. Young priests ran from the tower, only to be apprehended by the Mikana.

Anash chortled with pleasure.

Ciycera pulled alongside him, a yellowish foam soaking his jagged teeth.

"Livnath can't protect them from us," Anash said. "Her acolytes are weak as piglets."

"My lord, you've angered the goddess," Ciycera said. "You trampled her sacred city and temple. You humiliated her priests. She won't be pleased."

"I look forward to sparring with her at another time," Anash said.

When the Mikana reached the palace, their beasts surrounded the structure, trouncing the few hundred palace guards King Dahv left to care for Seth's seat of power. Anash dismounted and ascended the palace steps, tapping his scepter on his thigh.

Palace slaves stared in disbelief as the warrior who rivaled the height of the palace pillars stomped inside on hind legs. Anash paused before several aides, who huddled in front of a wall panel King Aikah commissioned after he defeated the Mikana.

Anash ignored the aides for a moment and studied the relief depicting a Mikana warrior as a fallen dog with Aikah's foot on its neck and a whip on his back.

Anash snarled. "With your body rotting in the underworld, I will desecrate the ground where you are buried."

The commander raised his scepter encrusted with precious stones and lashed the limestone panel, disfiguring the images on the relief.

"Where is your king?" Anash turned to the palace slaves.

"We don't know," said one slave, clutching a hand-sized statue of Livnath.

Anash's body burned, and the stench of frying flesh nearly left the slave unconscious.

"Don't lie to me," Anash said, grinding his teeth, his body exploding with heat.

"They fled to Arba," he stammered before fainting.

"Ah, they depend on Arba," Anash bellowed as he marched out into the courtyard where the throne of Seth stood.

Anash placed his massive frame on the jeweled seat. His warriors brought in a remnant of aides, nobles, soldiers, and priests rounded up from throughout the palace and the city to create a makeshift court.

"Hail your new gods! Your savior-kings!"

The bulk of the northern troops had escorted the nobles and some lower classes to Arba before dawn. Lehabim kept enough men with him to protect the king on the journey from the City of Kings, but he needed to recalculate the route of escape. It was now day, and they couldn't hide in Seth any longer.

He swung his whip. It sliced in half a rose bush on a path in the Gardens of Destiny where they had fled the Mikana.

"Traveling to Arba may be too dangerous," Lehabim said. "The logical move is to head west to Yaphah."

A sufficient contingent could fight the Mikana from there, Lehabim calculated. While he didn't care for Commander Eitan in Yaphah, Lehabim respected his military ability. He also knew they would have to win him over since he was devoted to Aikah and may have supported Shammah.

Even with those considerations, fleeing to Yaphah was still problematic. They couldn't take the normal route because the Mikana blocked the entrance of the City of Kings and encircled much of its walls.

"I know how we can get there," offered Qayin.

At that moment, fire swallowed the summit of the temple tower.

"How?" Dahv stared at the flames crowning the temple.

"An underground passageway that will take us miles from the city without detection."

"I have not seen this on any tablet of Seth," Dahv said.

"You would not have, my lord," Qayin said. "Only the priests know of it. The passageway lies beneath the temple platform."

"Can you not see we cannot reach the temple?" Lehabim crushed his lip when he snapped at Qayin.

"The Mikana have set everything aflame," Qayin said. "The Mikana probably have captured Haran and the priests. Or they are surely dead."

"After the temple, we can reach the passageway through a second entrance," Qayin continued. "To access it, we will have to desecrate King Aikah's tomb."

CHAPTER TWENTY-ONE

THE SCENT OF DEATH

"The seal is broken," a soldier said. Lehabim motioned to the rest of the soldiers to bring King Dahv and Qayin forward. Flames threatened the Gardens of Destiny and its array of date palms and tamarisk trees. While their thick foliage hid their escape, at the tombs, they risked being seen by the Mikana.

Once they were inside Aikah's resting place, Lehabim instructed several soldiers to reseal the structure and go ahead of them to Yaphah—above ground.

"Move the sarcophagus," Qayin instructed the soldiers.

"We're defiling the tomb, not the body, priest. Is there no other way?" Lehabim asked.

"No," Qayin said. "The passageway lies below the sarcophagus. We built every burial area with a tunnel below it to reach the temple. This is the newest, so there is no need to go through the older ones, which may be too dangerous to enter."

"Your priests tended to the king through this tunnel after he was brought here?" Lehabim asked.

Qayin was quick to respond. "When he died, he was buried by Chazon and the Shamgar. They did not call us to prepare the king's body."

"I did not know of this," Dahv murmured. He winced and covered his nose with a fold of his robe.

"Then wisdom led you rightly—you rid yourself of Chazon, the priest of Aleph," Qayin said. "You removed the betrayer from your midst."

Lehabim selected five soldiers to lift the gilded coffin. Beneath the coffin was a wood slab, which the men shifted to climb down beneath it.

"The kings built the tombs this way," Qayin said. "The passageway is an escape for the king if Death captures him wrongly. At King Aikah's instruction, this route ends near the Sixth Gate in Yaphah, his birthplace. Of course, the tunnel also helps the priests travel to and from the temple during burials, too."

"But Chazon didn't need your services," Lehabim said.

"As I said," Qayin replied.

Dahv rubbed his nose. "It's incredible that the priests can stand to be in here. The smell of decay is beyond what I can ever remember with the dead."

The commander's face settled into a thoughtful frown as the group descended into the passageway. *It didn't matter now, but why hadn't the priests of Livnath tended Aikah at his death?* Lehabim's frown deepened. As a veteran of many battles, Lehabim had observed fields strewn with decomposing, mangled flesh. He knew the fumes of death. But the stench in the tomb suffocated like the clamp of a fist. No one was happier than the commander when they moved deeper into the passageway.

"The Mikana have taken the City of Kings!" yelled the messenger from atop his horse. Soot covered the young man's face and clothes.

Chazon straightened his posture like a man barely able to unload straw from his back. The rest of the party assembled near him in their camp outside Chaniya.

"The Mikana?" Eitan asked.

"They arrived before dawn yesterday on beasts and earlier than estimated," the messenger said. "They massacred many of our soldiers on and within the city walls. Are you a commander in this region? You wear the blue."

"Yes, yes," Eitan replied. "But not of this region. What about the citizens of the city?"

"Some evacuated in time to escape," the messenger said. "The Mikana captured or killed the rest. We treat our beasts better."

"And where is the king?" Eitan said.

"Missing."

Asahel guided his horse closer and handed the messenger water from his own supplies. The young man grasped the waterskin in gratitude.

When he finished drinking, he said, "Hundreds of soldiers vanished before the Mikana in the central section of the City of Kings. No one knows who did it or why. A man in a turban appeared, like mist. Witnesses said the image disappeared, along with the soldiers. The unknown phantom filled the Mikana with fear."

"Mattan," Eitan said. "Loyal as ever."

Asahel grimaced. "Nonetheless, the Mikana didn't stop their tormenting stomping through the City of Kings, did they?"

"No," the messenger said. "It worsened the terror they inflicted."

Two thousand soldiers of Seth, having not awakened for a day, slumbered below Mattan's rocky perch. Mattan had received his petition the day before. Aleph had whisked the soldiers like dust from the central section of the City of Kings to the makeshift barracks in Chaniya. Among them was Commander Eron—one of the three commanders who attempted to resist King Dahv's regime.

Mattan, who had lingered on the rocks for hours in astonishment, raised his arms toward the sky. He had done so many times since the soldiers arrived.

"Aleph," he whispered.

Javan's inquisitive expression moved Chazon. By Javan's face alone—crossed with wrinkles from too much sun—the priest guessed the magistrate was kind.

"Magistrate."

"Yes, may I help you?"

"I am the priest Chazon. I served King Aikah. With me is Commander Eitan, and his lieutenant, Asahel," Chazon said, waving a hand. "We are here to learn."

"King Aikah. How do I know you tell the truth? King Dahv is now the savior-king," Javan said.

Chazon pulled Aikah's seal from inside his robes. "This identifies me as King Aikah's counselor."

Javan examined it and stood back. "By the hot sand of the desert, what will happen next?" he said, dismissing the aide and inviting them to sit. "Have you brought another contingent? Commander Mattan already is here."

"Mattan? Here? Why?" Eitan asked.

"King Aikah sent out secret orders before his death that the cities would act as independent city-states. He sent contingents of soldiers to back them up."

"Why didn't we get such a message?" Asahel asked.

"We may have," Eitan said. "But we've been away from Yaphah."

"May I see these orders?" Chazon asked.

"Of course," said Javan, pulling a tablet from the table and handing it to him. "Did you not know of them?"

"I did not."

"Then maybe you didn't see this one," Javan said, showing him a second message. Chazon read and passed it on to Eitan without a word.

Eitan scanned the tablet. "Sly as ever. Aikah anticipated what Dahv, and the priests were doing and sent out orders, both ensuring the independence of the cities from them and upholding Lord Shammah as king."

"How I doubted him…" Chazon's voice dropped to a mumble. "I thought he died without securing Shammah's place. But he had done it in the best way, knowing that Shammah would face rebellion. He also knew that the cities would support him as king."

"Aleph used Aikah's cunning," Asahel said.

Javan cocked his head. "But Aikah did not count on Shammah being killed. Meanwhile, King Dahv has sent out his orders for military rule. It has caused, er, confusion."

"But to whom is Chaniya loyal?" Sternness flecked Eitan's tone.

Javan straightened on his stool. "The wishes of King Aikah. And, until a scholar friend told me, I didn't know there was another reason to ignore King Dahv's claim to the throne."

"What is that?" Chazon asked.

"A little-known law from Seth's founding says that the queen should lead the nation if the heir dies. Scholars and nobles are the ones who should know," Javan said. "King Aikah may not have, however. He was not born into the noble class."

Asahel whistled. "Queen Gila is our ruling monarch."

Children gathered around Gila's cart as she handed them dates and chuckled with them. She raised an eyebrow when Chazon, Eitan, Asahel, and Javan arrived and bowed before her.

"My lady, you are the rightful ruler of Seth," Eitan said.

She smiled. "Has Aikah visited us from the grave and acknowledged my good counsel at last?"

CHAPTER TWENTY-TWO

ARYEH THE LION

Though her two young brothers adored the company and her mother hungered for conversation, Tamiym felt restless as guests mingled in their courtyard. Peleg had joined her family for a visit in Chaniya after the death of King Shammah six days ago. And when the military leaders, Eitan and Asahel, learned that Peleg was in Chaniya, they came to the house too.

With Eitan and Asahel were the priest Chazon and Queen Gila herself, who put everyone at ease, a touch of honey amid the bitterness. Finding a haven at their home was also Magistrate Javan and his wife, Adara, and the scholar Uz, who Tamiym remembered for his hostile lectures about women. She heard three lectures and decided she didn't want to listen to another.

Javan and the military leaders kept talking about a Commander Mattan and Tamiym half-expected him to stroll into the courtyard. But he didn't.

Tamiym's family never had hosted this many people, and she was grateful for their large home on the grassy edge of the Desert of Akron. The surrounding date palms ushered in an atmosphere of repose, but the setting didn't ease the anxious mood everyone seemed to possess.

Tamiym wondered whether the gods noticed the growing havoc in Seth. Livnath must be lounging in her heavenly chambers. She must be unaware of the turmoil in the land she fiercely claimed. As Tamiym gazed at the sky, she wondered whether Aryeh, the lion, would step down from his starry place and rescue Seth.

Chaniyan scholars often belittled the constellation of Aryeh because rival scholars in Nifla claimed the foot in the cluster of stars was Aleph trampling a serpent. But Chaniyan scholars considered the foot to be that of a man teasing his pet during an era when mortals didn't fear serpents.

The debate was curious to Tamiym because the Chaniyan scholars, who boasted that they didn't worship Livnath, sympathized with the serpent connected with the goddess.

Tamiym found a grassy patch. She pulled apart her braids, her crinkly black hair rippling across her shoulders like a starless night. Usually, she could escape to the rooftop of her family's home and study the constellations, but tonight, she sought solitude away from the crowd.

Tamiym lay down to face the sky. Her hair cushioned her head as she studied Aryeh and imagined a lion tearing at the feet of the Mikana's beasts until they toppled. She peered at Regulus, the star so bright and expansive that it seemed to light up the desert directly before her.

Fearful that Regulus had fallen and left a hole in the Earth, she jumped up. The amber-colored light grew larger. In moments, its outline became a chariot with large, lion-faced horses. In the chariot seat was a tall man, and with him, three other chariots.

She wanted to scream but noted every detail of the scene instead. The chariots crossed the desert, churning sand at high speed.

When the chariots stopped, she recognized Lord Shammah in the first chariot. While she had understood Queen Gila's sadness for her lost son, she now knew why Chazon flexed his hands behind his back, and why Eitan and Asahel, when overcome, strode the perimeter of Tamiym's house. It was about Shammah, but then, it was not. Seth had called his name in mourning, and the stars were returning the true king.

She closed her eyes. When she reopened them, the chariots were gone. Only Lord Shammah stood before her in his coronation robes, his arms across his chest, his diadem framing braids that draped over his shoulders, his skin the color of glistening raisins, and the brown of his eyes sparkling with gold and copper hues.

Behind him stood his Shamgar. They stepped forward with bemusement as the light encircling them remained. One bodyguard hummed with joy.

Tamiym's mind swam with questions, though she could ask none of them.

She struggled to bow, and Shammah grasped her arms with his fingertips.

"My king," she said. The king of Seth… Alive…? How?"

He let Tamiym go. "Ah. This is the first that I have heard the gentle stream of your voice."

She trembled. "Notes of disbelief, my lord."

"The wonder I suspect you feel mirrors my own."

Tamiym's legs trembled. She dug her feet deeper into the grasses. The rightful king was dead, seized by Livnath's malicious clouds and birds. How could he live?

"You stumble over what puzzles my own mind," Shammah said. "Perhaps we could cipher all things over a warm bowl of lamb-and-barley soup. I make a humble request."

"Soup, my lord?" Tamiym clucked like the matrons who strolled the market.

Laughter of a kind she had never heard before was in Shammah's voice, as if he saw the sun, kissed the stars, swam the seas, and now was home.

"Asking for food in the midst of the unknown cuts through your thoughts like an unexpected thorn, does it not?" he asked.

Tamiym attempted to regain her wit and her confidence. Both seemed overrun by Lord Shammah's chariot wheels. "My lord, you did not draw blood, only more queries, more incomplete conclusions."

"Would you do me the honor of feeding my guards and me?" Shammah asked.

"My father and brothers like it, but my mother says my soup needs improvement," Tamiym said. "I also would invite you to bring your horses to our house, but they seem to enjoy other quarters."

"I promise. Your curiosity will not go unsatisfied," Shammah said.

The Shamgar howled with merriment, prompting Tamiym's father and the other men to run from the house, shouting her name and drawing their daggers.

"Daughter! Tamiym! Are you safe?" Sagi screamed as he ran up to them. His wife and their guests followed.

Within a moment, their faces switched to confusion.

Sagi wrapped an arm around Tamiym's shoulders, and Abelia joined them under the stars.

"It's the king," bellowed Asahel, who was the first to prostrate with joy. "To Aleph!"

"How can this be but the work of the Existing One?" whispered Eitan as he craned his neck to the heavens.

Javan swallowed over and over. Uz stroked his beard. Peleg ogled Shammah, transfixed. Gila hugged Shammah. When she released him, she began to weep.

"My son…" she said.

"Why did he appear to a woman first?" Uz asked.

"Why not appear to my daughter?" Sagi slung the retort as he regained his voice and held Tamiym tighter.

"Does it matter now, Uz?" Javan demanded.

"It doesn't," said Peleg, who jumped in excitement. He calmed himself and stepped forward. "Were you attacked by thieves? Did you change vessels?" he asked.

Shammah grinned and gripped Peleg's shoulders. "You sound 'peevish,' my friend, as you once told me."

As Peleg smiled, Tamiym recalled the chariots that carried Shammah and his men from the sky. Peleg was closer to the truth than he knew.

When Chazon stumbled toward Shammah, the priest's sternness vanished. His eyes were bloodshot, his face pale. Shammah bowed. Then the two men embraced for a long time.

"Lamb-and-barley soup is my favorite dish. And this version is better than any I have had in the palace," Shammah said.

Tamiym blushed at the compliment as she gathered the empty bowls and removed them from the table. The king studied her every action—the king who commanded sky chariots to bring him to her home on the edge of the desert.

When she and her father met him on the road en route to the City of Kings, she felt in control. She assessed him in his soiled clothes and his distracted manner as he tried to reach his dying father, a king she loathed.

Tonight, he was in her family's rambling home of mud bricks, a king who had come back from the dead. She felt like the distracted one, mortified by their crude plates, and strong but unadorned wood tables, stools, and benches.

"Thank you, my lord." Tamiym inhaled, trying to regain her normally assured demeanor.

"Please sit," Shammah said, pointing to a stool near him. Her heart sank. Being near him unsettled her.

Tamiym focused on his mother, who dabbed her cheeks as she helped Abelia. Every time Shammah smiled as he ate his meal, Gila seemed poised to sob.

The rest of the room fidgeted and chatted about the soup, the warm bread, and Sagi's spacious home while they waited for Shammah and his men to speak.

Asahel, unable to sit still, stood, rubbed his hands and pursed his lips in a soundless whistle.

Shammah pushed his bowl away. "We died… in a way."

The room hushed. Asahel sat.

"The cloud of hawks carried us to a cave near Edrei, near the remote Fifth Gate in the northeast," Shammah said. "We could see the great forts, but we couldn't reach the Earth. The hawks fled, and the Zuzim bound us and poked our wounds. They tried to taint us with disease, which I believe was the blood curse that killed my father."

Shammah gazed with tenderness at Queen Gila. She nestled in a seat across the table from him.

Guriel picked up the story. "They cursed at us verbally and attempted to strangle us. I have never seen such rage. With all that, we never saw death's darkness. When they resorted to daggers and were about to cut our throats, the Four Faces appeared."

"Not them!" Peleg said.

"Who are the Four Faces?" Queen Gila asked. "Are they gods too?"

"They are the guards of Mount Aleph," Shammah said. "Peleg and I encountered them after our shipwreck near Yaphah. Eitan sent them with us as we returned to the City of Kings."

Tamiym noticed the queen turned toward Eitan, who avoided Gila's glance.

"I petitioned Aleph for them," Eitan said. "My lord, continue."

"Their presence broke the power of the Zuzim," Shammah said. "The Four Faces took us to the summit of Aleph. They generated a wind that brought the sky as close to us as this table. We could touch the stars as if they were this spoon"—he picked up the spoon he used during the meal— "or this cup"—he held out the one he used for his beer.

"Our feet held on to the mountain, but our hearts trailed the stars," Guriel said. "We heard voices."

"One voice emerged above all others," Na'iym said in a tone like the notes of a stringed instrument. "And our wounds disappeared."

At the unbelieving looks from the others around the table, the last of the Shamgar bodyguards, Amar, spoke up. "My voice, stolen from me as a child, returned."

Gila started weeping again. Tamiym surmised that Amar's words touched her because she knew the years of the bodyguard's affliction.

"The sapphire foundation of a throne appeared overhead," Shammah said. "I felt undone before this throne. I was not the king before a man I saw, who beamed with light. I was a boy—a lost man."

Shammah pulled the diadem from his head and glared at it. Tamiym felt he intended to fling it to a wall. She slid the diadem of gold and lapis lazuli from his fingers and handed it to Gila.

"Since Uz says the law allows for your mother to rule in your absence, perhaps she can be entrusted with this?" Tamiym asked.

Shammah twisted his black braids. "I did not know of such a law, but I know with certainty Queen Gila rules with more wisdom. My father knew it too."

"Perhaps. And if so, any insight I possess is only because I walked through many seasons of mistakes and regrets," Gila said. "The throne is yours to rule, my son."

Uz sighed. Tamiym wondered if the show of affection between the queen and her son bored the scholar.

"Who was this man you saw?" Uz asked. "One of the gods?"

"He said his name was hidden," Shammah said, "but I saw a vision in his eyes. The Mikana and the Zuzim crawled before the bulls of Seth. And the bulls of Seth bowed before a sapphire throne. I had encounters on Aleph that filled my mind with wonder... But in the presence of this person, I felt like the interloper with my diadem and soiled coronation robes, for I stood in the presence of utter peace and dominion."

The nameless man didn't intrigue Tamiym. Every epic featured a wise one.

"What about the chariots?" she asked. "Where did they come from? Some priests rattle on about the flying wheels and the gods, but they are often wide-eyed and feverish when they describe them."

"Hardly credible in any scholarly gathering," groused Uz.

"What? Chariots, too?" Asahel asked.

"Oh, those." Shammah emerged from his reverie to offer Tamiym a lopsided grin. "When the vision ended, horses beckoned us from below on the mountain."

"Like the donkey that appeared on Aleph for me," Peleg recalled.

"Exactly," Shammah said. "We stepped into the chariots, and they carried us to the desert, where Lady Tamiym greeted us."

"You heard the king, Uz," Javan said. "Write it on your tablet: flying chariots."

Shammah exhaled. "I've seen ghoulish, unnatural chariots in Midvar that left the rider mute, almost lifeless. Light filled these chariots and surrounded us with joy."

Uz twisted a coil of his beard, deep in thought.

Tamiym understood. A cave suspended in the sky. Flying chariots. The unknown man. Chaniya boasted in its logic, its sensibilities. The entire tale mirrored the rants of Livnath's crazed priests.

The king and his guards had shared their story with sincerity, and their listeners were dumbstruck, but no one dared to challenge the tale. Tamiym suspected Chazon, Eitan, and Asahel understood, but they didn't add to Shammah's words. Neither did the queen.

"My lord, you should know that your father took steps to protect your throne," Chazon said. "He issued secret orders for self-governing cities backed by a military contingent. He anticipated the conspiracy."

Chazon paused. "He hid his plan from me."

"And from me," Gila added. "We both begged him to secure your place on the throne."

"The mystery of my father's love will stay with me forever," Shammah said. "I thought he would give Dahv the throne. I would have delivered it to him."

Tamiym was overhearing the inner workings of the palace at her family's battered dinner table covered with scattered crumbs and drops of soup. Scouring her mind to remember, she wondered whether she had read any story like the one she was living.

"A bit of slumber will help us all," Shammah said.

Tamiym thought the king appeared unperturbed by the doubts surrounding him. Whatever he had witnessed emboldened him to lead with fixed intention.

"At dawn, we search for the caves King Aikah instructed me to find," he said.

"Do you know the location of the desert caves?" Uz said. "As I told Chazon, the elders have determined the caves are a tale told by nomads to their babes."

Tamiym caught her breath. Uz spoke as if he corrected an astronomy pupil. Many a young student had trembled before this tone—she had witnessed it—but the king was unruffled by the scholar's haughtiness.

"Uz, this is your king, not one of your students," Tamiym said.

Before he replied to Uz, Shammah reached for his diadem from Queen Gila. Shammah's hands traced the jewels.

Tamiym wanted to warn Uz to seek forgiveness for his arrogance. Perhaps the scholar didn't understand that in that moment, the savior-king of Seth, the Proud Lord of the Seven Gates, the adopted son of Aikah, expected obedience.

As Shammah paused before replying to Uz, Tamiym suddenly decided: *I want to accompany Shammah to the caves.* She gave her mother a swift look; Abelia seemed to understand and nodded.

Shammah stopped fingering the diadem. "My plans amuse you, Uz? From odd storehouses you find laughter. Babes and nomads will stand in wonder as Aleph fights the Mikana for us and through us."

CHAPTER TWENTY-THREE

CROSSINGS

The fumes from the tomb were suffocating. Commander Lehabim calculated that they had been underground for about a day, gasping as they tried to reach the tunnel's end. The commander wiped grime from his eyes and motioned to a lieutenant to open the door that stood before them.

King Dahv began coughing. Qayin clapped his back, and the heaves stopped. Eyes watering, Dahv blinked his thanks to the priest and turned his attention to the soldiers at the door.

"There's death in this tunnel," muttered a soldier in the rear.

Overhearing him, Lehabim scowled and marched to the soldier, who leaned against the tunnel wall. The commander's elaborate mane, dusted with cobwebs, gave him the appearance of an aged and vengeful deity.

Lehabim's whip descended on the soldier's shoulders several times before he stomped back to the front of the line. The soldier collapsed against the tunnel wall, blood oozing from his forehead and jaw. None of his fellow soldiers dared assist him.

"The passageway is open," shouted the lieutenant tasked with opening the barred tunnel door. The commander and the lieutenant exited first, followed by Dahv and Qayin.

The soldiers took turns hoisting each other out of the tunnel until all stood on the rocky plain near the Sixth Gate.

In the twilight, they brushed off the grime, and Lehabim instructed scouts to survey the area and look for water. He also had ordered them to search for the other contingent of soldiers he sent by foot from the royal tombs. They found damp ground and waited for the scouts' return, but the commander forbade anyone to start a fire.

"When the scouts returned, Dahv asked, "Did you see our men?"

"No, my lord. Nothing," the scouts' leader said.

"Then we must wait longer before we start a fire," Lehabim said.

"Light the fire. The Mikana couldn't have discovered us yet," Dahv said. He wanted warmth. And he needed comfort so he could think.

"My lord, we do not know that for certain," Lehabim said.

"Livnath will protect us," Qayin said.

Dahv cocked his head. He was more than surprised to hear agreement from Qayin.

Lehabim instructed another set of soldiers to start a small fire as the stars bloomed over the eastern sky. As the night deepened, shadows descended and crept around the camp.

A lookout on the outskirts of the camp cried, "The Mikana!"

Lehabim bolted from the ground, elegant despite the dirt and sweat, and grabbed a spear that lay near him. Dahv rose and gripped his sword.

"Protect the king!" Lehabim shouted.

The soldiers circled Dahv, weapons at the ready as the Mikana emerged in the firelight.

Anash loomed over them. "King of Seth, did you think you could escape me? Perhaps you did. Your fires were a welcoming beacon."

Anash lifted a languid hand, and the soldiers and Lehabim all fell back from Dahv and Qayin like drugged men. Then Anash jutted his doglike nose into the air.

"Lord Dahv, as King Aikah's heir, the Zuzim curse flows in your bloodstream. You won't die by an assassin's hand like your younger brothers."

Aikah never confirmed the Zuzim curse to any of his sons who were born of concubines, but they all wondered if they had inherited it. Rage flared inside Dahv. *If Anash speaks the truth, may Aikah lie with worms of torment in the underworld,* he thought. Dahv remembered his half brothers, whom he had ordered slain. His thoughtless murder saved them from the death-curse that may face him now.

"As far as the rest of you, the same curse now lies in your flesh. I detect its stench," Anash said.

He leaned forward on his hind legs, his eyes torches in the darkness. "Your bodies will rot with fire because you exposed yourselves to the Zuzim curse in the king's tomb."

The soldiers gasped.

Dahv swallowed his fear. He wouldn't submit to the Mikana. Maybe Anash was lying.

"Surely there is another choice?" Dahv asked.

Hot salvia dripped from Anash's teeth. "Become one of us."

Mahalath, her slaves, and their military escorts, neared Arba. After days of riding, they finally reached the old city, almost as ancient as the City of Kings. It was known throughout Seth for its fine apparel and lavish homes. In the morning light, Arba looked as impressive as the City of Kings.

Mahalath felt alone. Still holding the reins, she grabbed her right arm because it ached.

The guards on the wall raised spears in greeting, and the captain with Mahalath waved his sword in return. When the captain's arm extended, a spear shot from the clouds and pierced his heart. The captain failed to pull the spear from his chest before he fell from his horse.

A soldier in their caravan drew his weapon and searched for the attacker. "Where did that spear come from? Arba?"

Through an unseen opening in the sky, winged creatures with goat faces and the bodies of men swooped over the captain's men, killing them all. Mahalath and her slaves screamed, slipped from their horses, and raced for the city gate a few feet away, but the creatures plucked the women from the ground.

Mahalath twisted her body between the gnarled hands of the goat-man who held her. She saw Arba's soldiers launch a barrage of arrows at the creatures, but the arrows simply littered the plain.

The creatures holding Mahalath, and the other women, hung in the air as other goat-men swarmed over Arba, attacking men and boys in the streets. Women and older girls howled and fainted when the creatures snatched them by their braids and clothing and carried them away.

Moans drifted over the city, followed by the howling of two goat-men perched at the gate. They sat cross-legged on each towering head of Livnath.

At midday, after hours of waiting in the desert, a burst of fire appeared before Shammah. Startled, Shammah's horse and the other horses leaned backward in fear, their legs spread. The burning image widened into a wall, then parted. Tamiym gasped in wonder, but was dumbstruck again when, without a single command, the king charged into the blaze with the Shamgar following close behind.

"We can't do that," said Peleg, as jittery as his horse. "They can't do that."

Uz hung his head. "Impossible."

"Well, whatever they can't do, I'm going to try it!" Asahel yelled back.

Unheeding the apparent danger, Asahel, Chazon, and Eitan disappeared into the fiery opening, while Peleg, Javan, and Uz hesitated.

"Where did they go?" Peleg cried.

Tamiym never expected to meet death in such a grand manner, but to follow Shammah seemed like the sweeping conclusion of an epic. As a scholar, she couldn't stay back in fear. One day regretting that she didn't follow the king distressed her more than dying.

"Where did they go?" Peleg repeated.

"From here, you will never know," said Tamiym, entering the flames.

CHAPTER TWENTY-FOUR

SANCTUARY IN THE DESERT

Shammah's company crossed by horseback through dark, clammy caves. When they reached the last cave, they dismounted. Chazon nearly swooned. Before them was a bronze sanctuary lit with amber hues. Stillness fell on the priest as Shammah's company sat on the glistening floor that felt plush as pillows.

Three bronze griffins, fierce of face, guarded a golden altar. Two stood at its sides, and the third hovered overhead. The altar didn't touch the floor, but steps glistening with rubies and gold lay below it. Blue and silver curtains enclosed the area and stirred, although no desert breeze passed through the caves. Unimpressed by the golden altar, Uz stretched his legs and fidgeted with his sandals. Chazon suspected artfully aimed complaints weren't far behind.

"The gods possess a fervent wish to make mortals wait," Uz said.

Javan sighed. "Please don't say you're looking for beer. At some point, other things are more worthy of conversation."

"I am thirsty," Uz said.

Tamiym elbowed Uz.

"You reproach me, Tamiym?"

"Possess the waters of your heart and mind," she said. "You teach your pupils this. I heard you."

"I think I remember you attending," said Uz. "A studious one."

"I hid behind a pillar to listen while my father delivered vegetables. You never saw me."

"Of course." Uz cleared his throat. "After so many years of teaching, it is easy to presume you remember the past."

"It is," Tamiym said. "But I remember your words. They were wise, Uz. They protected me when I was a girl with nightmares of desert phantoms."

Chazon smiled. Tamiym was fearless when she confronted the sour Uz, and surprisingly, the scholar didn't mind.

"With that stern voice, you could have taught in the priestly schools," Peleg said to Tamiym.

"I would not accept you as my pupil," she replied.

Chazon understood that humor cloaked their nervousness. They didn't know where they were or what was happening, and the uncertainty made Peleg and those from Chaniya uncomfortable, while Shammah, the Shamgar, Eitan, Asahel, and Chazon sat expectantly.

Suddenly, the griffins shifted their limbs, and a loud rumbling accompanied their movements. Chazon, eyes closed, leaned forward.

"Shammah," a voice said. "The son of my beloved reed among the marshes."

Chazon's heart raced as the voice of Aleph ribboned around them. He bent his head as the voice soothed and thundered at the same time.

"King Aikah sent me here to receive instructions to defeat the Mikana and retrieve the stele," Shammah said.

"Aikah followed your prophet-father here because he presumed that theft or murder brought knowledge. You need not grasp and pine for treasures Aikah coveted."

"I do not understand."

"Would you have believed the unseen?"

"I remain without understanding, but I am grateful for the answer," Shammah said.

"You will need many more answers to rule, Shammah."

"May I have the privilege of possessing the stele to overcome our enemies?"

"You will not conquer your enemies with spears and swords," the voice said, "but you will defeat them."

The caves dissolved.

Immediately, Shammah, his company, and their horses, were back in hot sand. For long moments, silence cocooned them. Chazon couldn't shake off the stillness; he longed to return to the golden sanctuary, but Aleph had closed it to them.

Tamiym's mare nudged her curiously as she stood, biting her bottom lip. Chazon waited for her reactions to the cave, but she didn't engage any of them. On the other hand, Uz was the first to mount his horse and spout an opinion.

"As I thought," he said. "A trick of the night arts. An amber light. I heard nothing."

"None of this is common in the City of Kings." Peleg groaned. "No one is more powerful than the goddess, and, at least, she gives more instruction. The gloomy Aleph is mute."

"Aleph and Livnath are rivals in weak minds," Uz said. "This 'battle' merely amuses mortals who do not conspire with false deities."

Javan hung his shoulders like a heartbroken youth. "I heard music. Faint notes. Only King Shammah heard Aleph's words and sorted the meaning."

"As if the hearing of Aikah's heir only matters in days of war?" Uz demanded.

Eitan drew his horse near the scholar's. "Enough. You ignore the king's kindness and toy with my patience."

While tensions rose among the company, Chazon noticed that Shammah remained seated, cupping a mound of sand.

It unsettled Tamiym that they squandered daylight in caves they could never find again on their own. In a few hours, night would fall. She mused that it was odd that the soothing melody from the amber sanctuary followed her as she rode. She looked to her left, half expecting a person to be singing next to her. Nothing was there.

She clung to her horse and focused on Shammah and Chazon, who rode ahead together with the Shamgar. Peleg rode alongside her, along with Uz. Eitan, Javan, and Asahel rode behind them.

"Real sand. Not a glazed floor," Peleg said.

"The glazed floor felt better than riding," Asahel said. "Didn't you feel the comfort within the sanctuary?"

"What I saw, I cannot believe," Peleg said. "What I heard, I don't comprehend. I heard thunder. Thunder without lightning, without rain."

"Sit in one of my lectures and uncertainty will fall from you like rainwater from a rooftop," Uz said. "All the gods practice the night arts. Do not drown yourself in their concerns. They are not yours."

Tamiym had heard Uz demean the gods and their powers as if they were annoying children in his scribal classes. She
often thought the scholar should be more circumspect with his
words and consider the beliefs of men like Peleg, who built their
lives on the words, wishes, and whims of the gods. When Peleg
pushed back, if only slightly, deciding not to imbibe from the
cup of cynicism Uz offered, Tamiym felt relieved.

"Perhaps," Peleg said.

The sailor jerked his head upward when he heard Chazon
cry out.

"A trap awaits us outside of Chaniya!" the priest said.

"How does he know this?" Uz demanded.

"What do you see, Chazon?" Shammah asked.

"Soldiers wait for us," Chazon said. He clasped the side of
his head.

"Where?" Shammah asked.

"The vision is unclear."

"Have new enemies entered Chaniya?" Shammah asked.

"Commander Mattan's soldiers are on the north side of the
city," Javan offered. "But they're too far away to reach us in time."

Chazon shook his head. "We'll fight them alone."

Asahel secured his weapons. "How many do you see?"

"It doesn't matter," Eitan said.

Peleg grinned when Tamiym pulled out her dagger. "The
lady who rides with us intends to fight. You possess a handsome
weapon. Let me trade my fine dagger for yours. I would like to
see you use it."

Tamiym gave him an icy smile. "You will if you try to take it."

The company reached the outskirts of Chaniya at dusk. They slowed as they approached the border and, as they did, a ring of soldiers assembled. Javan estimated about three hundred gathered before them, some on foot, others on horses, and each in light armor. Adara told him that his eyesight was a gift. At this moment, he was grateful for it. What he could view in the distance helped him to prepare.

Shadows hid the soldiers' faces, but their swords, spears, and bows shimmered. Javan exhaled between his thin lips. The desert was to their backs, and the gate to enter Chaniya was where the soldiers stood, poised to march. Chazon and Lord Shammah's Aleph delivered a warning. But how should the king's company respond?

The company lined up behind Shammah, with Peleg and Eitan riding near Tamiym. As the soldiers advanced, Shammah waited. His company remained behind him. Javan could hear the snorts of the horses emerging from the boundaries of Chaniya and the clatter of the soldiers' weapons.

Javan wanted to call on a god, but he struggled to breathe a prayer. Asahel, who rode beside him, didn't hesitate.

"Aleph, Aleph, Aleph," Asahel muttered.

Shammah lifted his right arm, lowered it, and pressed his knees against his horse.

His company moved with him, the pace of their horses quickening. The soldiers on the wall of the city launched their spears while Shammah's company dodged them.

Shammah shouted, "Don't stop! Don't use your weapons! Ride through them! Ride through them!"

Javan tried not to howl in fear. What Shammah told them to do wasn't traditional military practice, and he had no choice but to follow.

Shammah and the Shamgar, who were in the lead, plunged through the ranks of soldiers. The rest of the company gasped as the spears crumbled and their enemies tottered like sun-dried bricks. Tamiym urged her horse forward.

Uz reached the line of soldiers and halted for a few agonizing moments, transfixed by the soldiers' murderous faces and heavy weapons.

"Can you ever follow someone else?" Javan called out to Uz.

"I can't detect their origin," Uz said.

Javan groaned. His scholar friend of many years sounded foolish, not erudite as he probably intended. As he jerked his horse to the scholar's side, Javan grabbed the reins from Uz. The magistrate pulled the reins of both horses through the line of soldiers. Fragments of bricks exploded in their faces as they passed through.

After Shammah's company rushed through line after line of soldiers, they reached Lotan the priest. Surrounded by heaps of mud, the high priest screamed: "By Livnath, you will not rule Chaniya, and you will not rule Seth."

"Come down and answer to the king!" Shammah yelled.

The priest pulled roots from his robes and rubbed them between his fingers, uttering indiscernible chants.

Javan had seen his work before. "Lotan, let's talk as men. Don't make the night arts a part of this."

Lotan raised his arms and swarms of wasps surrounded Shammah's company: stinging them, agitating their horses, and causing several of them, including Tamiym and Eitan, to be flung to the ground.

"No more!" Chazon shouted.

He blew in Lotan's direction, and a wave of water knocked the high priest facedown. With a whoosh, the wasps halted in midair, then fell.

Chazon's brows formed a dark horizon. "Pay homage to the true king."

"I will not." Water poured from Lotan's mouth.

Chazon said nothing while the swarm of wasps revived. This time, they headed toward Lotan. Before the swarm could attack, an arrow pierced the high priest in his chest and the wasps disappeared.

A narrow-faced man dressed as a farmer emerged from among the mounds of mud. Javan remembered King Aikah's instructions to squelch rebellion. He suspected the man was part of the king's plan.

"Who are you?" Shammah demanded.

The man bowed. "My name is Shur. I waited for an open moment when the priest would show his opposition to King Aikah's wishes. Commander Mattan knew of my whereabouts. And my mission from King Aikah."

CHAPTER TWENTY-FIVE

THE FIFTH GENERATION

Mattan arrived and stood outside the wall of Sagi's family home. He was uncomfortable. Few quarters could hold his towering bulk, and few people felt at ease with him. He nodded and smiled, hoping to be seen as a quiet soldier who wouldn't intentionally injure civilians. Or friends.

When the Shamgar entered the dwelling, trailing Shammah, he noticed Na'iym. Tall and lean, she strolled into the building with a watchful expression. Beneath it, he sensed a well of experience in her confident gait. He bent his head toward her in greeting. Her taut, cream-colored face warmed, then froze again as she took her place near the king.

Chazon raised his hand in welcome. "My king and my friends, this is Commander Mattan."

"Commander," Shammah said. "Now let's plan. Aleph will guide us, but we must prepare for guidance we do not expect. We war against star-born offspring."

Mattan smiled. The young king didn't have the commander's scars and regrets, but he already had detected a difficult truth about the majestic Aleph. Mystery surrounded the paths of the Existing One.

Sagi poured water for his guests. "Do we plan our steps at the whims of the gods and giants?"

Shammah arched a brow and nodded to Mattan to answer.

Mattan didn't hesitate to reply to Sagi. "We fail when we walk without wisdom."

Abelia entered the courtyard, carrying loaves of bread. "They're too afraid or proud to ask to learn more, Commander Mattan. Help us understand."

"Yes, my lady," Mattan said. "The ancients inhabit the clouds and the Earth. They attempt to replicate themselves through the wombs of mortal women. The first generations of their seed are star-born peoples like the Zuzim and the Emim. But later generations look like the Mikana. Or like me, a man from Rabbah."

"Your countenance displays great kindness and confidence," Tamiym said. "The tablets don't honor your people justly. Whereas they depict the Zuzim as unmistakably lovely," Tamiym murmured.

"A worthless compliment for a cruel breed," Shammah said.

"The Zuzim can't overcome the flaw in their own seed," Mattan said. "They seek to create like their rebellious fathers. But as their fathers learned, they are not Aleph. The crossbreed race they created through the Mikana confounded them."

Peleg cringed. "Who would not be dumbstruck if their babe appeared as half-man and half dog and delighted in mortal flesh? They could never hire a midwife again."

"Did you ever carry their rage against the men of Seth?" Sagi asked.

"Yes. War teaches men harsh truths," Mattan said. "However, I now declare full allegiance to Aleph."

"One day, I want to listen to you tell the story of your path to fidelity," Shammah said.

Peleg hesitated. "Commander Mattan, do you perform their night arts?"

"Darkness entices the strongest of men and the star-born," Mattan said. "With the help of Aleph, I overcame the temptation. I lay down my sword and bow my body before unshakable power."

Uz groaned and said, "The gods possess flaws that expose their weaknesses: egotism, lust, rage, stupidity. The human mind alone demonstrates invincibility throughout the ages."

"Why pitch a tent in the bowels of darkness?" Chazon asked. "Heaven's gates open to the meek."

"If meekness is heaven, I do not aspire to it," Uz said.

The scholar's words fell into a rocky silence. Mattan folded his arms, displeased. The scholar's arrogance was hard to bear.

A soldier rushed into the courtyard, chest heaving. Shammah lifted his hand. "Speak. What news do you have?" Shammah asked.

The scout seemed to talk without breathing. "The Mikana didn't murder Lord Dahv. They captured him."

"How many Mikana are there?" Asahel asked.

"About five to nine thousand. They're riding on flying, double-horned beasts, and they have a formidable arsenal. Right now, they surround the city. They also stomp within it. The Mikana locked human survivors into guarded pens."

Eitan and Mattan exchanged glances. Men who fought the Mikana as mortal men and lost filled the tombs of Seth. Mattan had buried many of them.

"Aikah sustained decades of peace with the Mikana and the Zuzim because his devotion to Livnath gave him extraordinary powers. The night arts," Eitan said. "No doubt the Mikana longed to trample the city of Aikah and Livnath."

"Where did they house Lord Dahv?" Chazon asked.

"He's in the palace," the scout said. They summoned nobles and others to the royal courtyard for sport. Some of them were taken and…"

"Cannibalized?" Eitan asked in a soft voice.

"Yes, Commander," the scout said. He appeared relieved he didn't have to utter the word, given what he had witnessed.

"Your observations benefit us," Shammah said. "Thank you."

"King Shammah," the scout said.

"Go on."

"The Mikana abducted the nobles and other families from the mountains as they fled to Arba under the king's instructions. They were carried back to the City of Kings. But Lady Mahalath…"

"Yes?" Shammah's voice rose.

"Lord Dahv dispatched Lady Mahalath and her party first to Arba. Scouts who followed the path of the nobles as they fled say Arba has also been destroyed, and the Zuzim captured all the women."

"And Lady Mahalath was among those taken?"

"Yes, my lord."

"By all that is good. We have wars on two fronts," Asahel exclaimed. "Where will we get the soldiers we need?"

Shammah's expression was grim. "We will form companies from the men with Commander Mattan. Commander Mattan will act in Chaniya on behalf of the throne and prepare for additional enemies who may seize the chance to attack. The Shamgar will guard Sagi's family and the queen."

Sagi dropped a dish he'd been carrying. Mattan knew why. A man from Rabbah in charge of Chaniya stoked an array of nightmares.

Sagi threw a dubious glance at Mattan. The commander bowed.

Shammah continued. "Tomorrow, we go to Arba. A Zuzim stronghold lies near there. After that, we travel to the City of Knowledge. The journey should last ten days."

"But the City of Kings is where they are now." Peleg stood, offended. "The fight should start there."

Shammah tightened his jaw. "Recklessness. I have sailed that doomed vessel before."

"My lord." Peleg offered the king an abrupt bow and left the room.

Mattan understood Peleg's anger but agreed that the king couldn't afford to expend men where there was no immediate hope. "Many may perish in the City of Kings until we arrive," Mattan said.

"A casualty I do not accept but must risk," Shammah said.

Gila, who sat in a corner, looked up from one of Tamiym's tablets. "Shammah, your intention, I believe, is to attack the Mikana at the root. Then, when you return to the City of Kings, you have already destroyed their way of escape.

"Aikah would commend your decision. Kingdoms and thrones fall from their centers; not from their peripheries," she said. "When Aikah defeated the Mikana, he slew their leaders, their throne keepers. Except for Anash. I wager that Anash leads in vengeance. He escaped Aikah's sword and thirsts for Seth's destruction."

"The queen's memory astounds me," Eitan said. "Aikah killed every Mikana commander he could. He knew Anash would return."

"The City of Knowledge is where they strengthen themselves with their star-born parents," Mattan said. "To destroy the city weakens them. It's their center, as the queen said."

Mattan saw Uz flush with irritation. The scholar couldn't follow Shammah's reasoning. Instead of listening, Uz challenged. He wanted a debate because it was something he could do and win.

Over the years, Mattan encountered this type of rebellion in the barracks and in the fields of war. Distrust poisoned military missions and undermined the commander. Again, he wondered how the young king would manage the doubts Uz expressed.

Uz folded his arms. "With all respect to our dead king, Lord Aikah, was nothing learned in Aleph's desert ruin? What are our odds?"

"Twenty to one." Peleg bounced back into the courtyard, the anger on his face diffused. "I gave those odds to the king once before, and we survived. I pledge to follow him, Uz. You should, too."

Mattan saw the rigid lines in Shammah's face soften. But just as the tension eased, Uz instigated more conflict.

"Your odds mean nothing," Uz said. "The histories also speak of times when we bartered and compromised with the Mikana and then defeated them after winning them over. We have a few of the commander's kind who sometimes enter Chaniya. There is no trouble. Perhaps we can negotiate peace?"

"Those times weren't as blissful as you depict Uz. I lived through some of them with Aikah and Aleph expanded my learning," Chazon said. "With the Mikana there is no genuine peace, no true friendship."

"What Chazon speaks is truth," Mattan said. "Some of my kin may mean well, but most don't. They are marked by the ways of their Zuzim forefathers and either can't or refuse to repent."

Shammah pulled out his dagger and stroked its blade. Mattan could tell that the instinct by Uz to trust the Mikana and seek a false peace annoyed him. Those who survived death, like Shammah, would quickly recognize an enemy intent on carrying them back to the grave.

"As King Aikah often told me, not every truth lies in the knowledge of men," Shammah said. He plunged the dagger into a barley loaf on the table.

"Your experiences falter in the face of Aleph's commands," Shammah continued. "Uz, will you not learn this, or shall the king search for another way to instruct you?"

Uz, Mattan noted, had the grace to blush.

Tamiym tapped her fingers on a trellis, watching Shammah study the wild onions growing in a corner of the courtyard.

He turned to face her. "Your parents could teach me how they cultivate vegetables," he said.

Tamiym wanted to scream. In hours, the company would be going to Arba, and the king was examining vegetables.

"To harvest, they sacrifice, my lord," Tamiym said.

"Do they share their skills?"

"Their discipline, but not their gifts, my lord. Please tell me where the sky chariots came from? The gods ride them. Not mortals."

"Onions don't interest you?"

"Chariots soaring from Aryeh. Lion-faced horses. They are impossible visions for mortals."

"Your lack of knowledge about them does not mean they do not exist."

"You promised me an answer."

"I am unable to explain how we rode past the stars."

Tamiym gasped. "You encountered stars?"

"Would you believe me if I did?"

"Riddles will not satisfy me."

"Perhaps a ride will please you."

"It doesn't take much to please me, but it takes much to explain how the understanding of our world was expanded."

"I do not believe that."

"I am not a difficult woman."

"Did I say that?"

"Do you hesitate to explain because of what you saw on Aleph?"

"A sapphire throne bemuses me," Shammah said. "Of course, kings would be filled with wonder. We scramble to dominate the world."

"That could not have affected you, my lord," Tamiym said. "You have not been king for long."

"But I have lived and walked among them."

"Lived where?" asked Peleg, entering the courtyard with his mouth full of dates. "I was with you a good part of it."

Shammah and Tamiym laughed until Peleg frowned them into silence.

The moment felt heady for Tamiym. "I intend to immortalize this journey in an epic for the scholars of Chaniya," she said. "It will sit on the shelves of our library."

"The attack will not be simple. Danger lurks like foxes. I will honor your family if they refuse to let you go," Shammah said.

"They will."

"You could perish."

"We could all die," Peleg said. "But, my lord, your night arts and that appalling mountain will keep us safe."

Abelia patted Sagi's hand as Tamiym and Shammah's company rode toward the north. "Wish her well, husband."

"This journey isn't for women," Sagi said.

"This journey isn't for men or women who don't have a thirst for it," Abelia replied. "Tamiym's nights and days of learning have led her to this. You trained her as your first-born son. If you're worried about the crops and the farm animals, the boys are big enough to assume chores, too."

Their two young boys, hanging above on the trellis, groaned.

"You are wise to submit," Dahv heard Anash say. The Mikana warrior may have immortal powers, Dahv thought, but his greedy, vengeful ambitions originated from the ways of earth.

The warrior ordered Dahv, Qayin, and Lehabim to be bound, leaving them stumbling in childlike steps. Dahv saw Lehabim twitch his fingers; the commander missed his whip. The king wished he could scourge the Mikana warriors, although they overshadowed the tallest of Dahv's company.

But the warriors demonstrated that they did have weaknesses, he observed. Their eyesight was limited. They turned at awkward angles to view something behind them. Their hooves revealed tender spots of flesh.

As the Mikana entered the City of Kings, dragging their captives, the odor of the warriors' burning flesh soured the air.

Sniffing with confidence, Anash and his prisoners marched through the ruined streets and crammed survivors in pens.

Farmer, merchant, scholar, and noble huddled together. Dahv's efforts to evacuate the city before dawn had failed. Anash had anticipated an early evacuation from the city and sent warriors as the evacuees fled to Arba.

Dahv wished he were blind. Viewing the devastated kingdom drenched him in helplessness. He scanned the pens with fear, wondering whether Mahalath and her slaves reached safety in Arba, or if the Mikana had killed them along the way.

He didn't see her, but in one crowded pen, he glimpsed Mahalath's parents and sister. Once E-ven caught sight of Dahv, the noble turned his back on him.

Anash separated Dahv from the others and escorted him to the summit of the charred temple tower.

"People of Seth, you are now Mikana. Your savior-king is now my governor," Anash said, smacking Dahv's shoulders. "By his personal submission, lasting peace has come to Seth."

When night had fallen, Lehabim seized his chance. The Mikana had imprisoned him, Qayin, and the others near the palace. The commander paraded Dahv among his warriors for amusement. During their three-day period of captivity, the commander and his soldiers managed to loosen their bonds, although they pretended they were still captive.

The Mikana warriors guarding them rested near a fire. They rubbed their hooves and complained about the rocky trip from Yaphah. The lieutenant assigned to oversee the company was alone, napping against the wall of a burned house.

Lehabim knew it was time to strike, but he carried no weapons to disable the aching Mikana soldiers. He needed help.

He slid toward Qayin. He loathed conferring with the priest, but he was a citizen of Seth, and this was about saving their country.

"Priest," Lehabim said. "I have calculated a plan to escape. Employ your night arts to help us overcome the Mikana."

Qayin nodded, closed his eyes and muttered. He reopened them and reached into his robes. He pulled out a fistful of roots and slipped them to Lehabim.

"Take the roots and dust them on the head of the leader," Qayin said. "Act now. The potion has a temporary effect."

Lehabim waited to sprinkle roots on the lieutenant's head when he slumped on the wall. The lieutenant's light snoring turned into a wheezing slumber. Then Lehabim grabbed the lieutenant's sword and sliced off the warrior's head. He signaled to his soldiers, and they overtook the remaining warriors, decapitating them all.

Through the night, Lehabim and his men moved northward from pen to pen, killing other Mikana and gathering soldiers who had survived the initial onslaught.

By dawn, Commander Lehabim led six hundred soldiers of Seth. He had slaughtered more than five hundred Mikana. Silence was Lehabim's greatest defense. But he was uneasy; his tasks seemed too easily accomplished.

He was right.

Anash and several thousand soldiers arrived at the pens where the men from Seth had gathered.

"Commander," Anash said as he stomped toward him. "Tactically inventive, but you miscalculated."

Anash nodded at a sneering Qayin beside him. The priest bowed with vulgar arrogance.

Mikana soldiers dragged Dahv forward. He looked drugged. Nevertheless, Lehabim noted Dahv's expert grip on a rough Mikana sword.

No alliances last forever in war, Lehabim thought with the regret of a philosopher, bristling at the thought of entering the underworld with Qayin's smirk being the last bit of mortal life he witnessed. *I should have thrashed him.*

Anash nodded at Dahv, who clutched the sword and stumbled toward Lehabim, who tossed a longish curl of his blond hair as the sword in Dahv's hands cleaved into him.

CHAPTER TWENTY-SIX

CHILDREN OF ALEPH

The City of Arba lay in ash and cracked bricks. Some of Shammah's men shed tears as they combed the rubble for survivors, especially Asahel. Although his family was long dead, and he no longer lived in Arba, the attack devastated him.

When they reached a district where Asahel once lived, he discovered a father who died protecting his children. Shammah pulled the youngsters from the arms of their father to allow Asahel a few moments to steady himself.

They found more children and injured soldiers. The women and older girls were either dead or captured. Shammah didn't share what he knew about the Zuzim and their fixation on the women of Seth. Shammah suspected Tamiym knew of the tales about the Zuzim as she gathered children in her arms before Mattan's soldiers placed them on carts and carried them to Chaniya.

"Oh, loved one, come here," Tamiym said to a girl of three or four years standing in the shadows of a house distinguished by pastel-colored doors and elaborate carvings. "Who made your jewelry?"

"My older sister," the girl said, rubbing the copper bracelets against her arm. "She had planned to help my father make more before the goat-men with wings snatched her away."

"Where is your father?" Tamiym signaled Asahel to follow the girl's outstretched finger.

"In there. Asleep," the girl said as Tamiym rocked her. Asahel, his face streaked with tears, nodded and went inside. When he returned to Tamiym, he shook his head.

The destruction brought by the Zuzim dominated the conversations among Shammah's soldiers after they left the city and reached a group of triangular structures jutting from the plains outside of Arba. Shammah knew that his men, grim and crouched among the tamarisk trees, craved revenge, and he implored Aleph to watch over them. Anger left them vulnerable.

When daylight turned to dusk, the triangular stones lifted and flowered into a translucent palace. Rotating quartz cylinders revealed steps emerging from the earth. Droplets of light fell to the crystal stairways, and as the soldiers watched, children in hooded cloaks crossed the plain to them, and circled the moving structure.

On his side of the plain, Shammah and his men gasped, their hands on their weapons. A blond-haired child approached.

"King Shammah, we're here to help you," said the child, with a voice like the songs of birds in the morning.

"Who are you?" Shammah asked.

"We will guide you along the steps to avoid discovery. On the other side of this plain, one in our troop has alerted Commander Eitan. Will you follow me?"

"You know us. May I ask you your name?"

"Expectant."

"I do not understand."

"That is my name."

The child smiled and waved her hand toward the hundreds of children spread out on both sides of the plain.

"My lord, you do not intend to follow them, do you?" Uz grunted. "Should we not investigate these creatures first?"

Shammah ignored him. He focused all his energy on the child before him.

"Follow me," Expectant said. This time, she spoke like a commander of many battles.

Tamiym thought they would crash against the crystal walls and floors. They didn't. The mysterious children took the hand of each member in Shammah and Eitan's companies. Accompanying Tamiym was a child who identified himself as Truth, whose burnished skin gleamed like copper as they descended the stairs. He smiled with a bashful sweetness, but confidently gripped Tamiym's hand.

"Beautiful," Tamiym whispered.

"But are they true?" Truth said.

Truth followed Expectant, who clutched Shammah's hand. Like the soldiers about him, Shammah appeared bemused by the children guiding his company.

Before they knew it, they had descended into the palace. Expectant paused, and the rest of the children released the adults and pressed themselves against the walls. The children linked hands, and their cloaked bodies became wide tent folds that spun about at the perimeter like a weaving instrument.

"You can enter the chambers unseen," said Expectant, her disembodied voice echoing within the sheer tent. "Do not rescue those touched by the Zuzim. Search for the mark."

The two companies walked into a library. Stacks of tablets littered the room, along with astronomical instruments, swords, spears, and other gleaming weapons carved with a precision Tamiym never saw among metalsmiths in the City of Kings.

The companies passed a large chamber where the Zuzim gathered in garments of gold and purple, their red manes draped across their backs. Their skin tones ranged from the white of snowy mountain peaks to the black glory of fertile earth.

Male and female, they laughed and conversed with intensity, like human nobles at a feast. Excitement and pleasure hung about them. The sensations were so strong that Tamiym felt dejected because she wasn't a part of the gaiety.

Truth's voice interrupted Tamiym's thoughts. "But are they true?"

Tamiym blushed. She felt guilty and anxious. *How did Truth know my thoughts? Why couldn't the Zuzim see us?* One of the Zuzim seemed to stare at her, but he was only reaching for a cup. His face wrinkled. Then he turned again, his red mane clacking where rows of tiny crystals threaded his hair.

"They neither see nor hear you," Truth reassured Tamiym. "We have created an unsullied tent to surround you. Purity blinds them. It protects you."

"Why are the Zuzim blinded?" Tamiym asked.

"They are loyal to darkness," Truth said.

The company reached a large room similar to quarters for a king's concubines. Luxurious curtains and bedding, platters of meat and roasted vegetables, and cups of drink were everywhere. Linen and bracelets of gold and silver swathed each sleeping woman. Their braided styles mirrored those worn by the Zuzim.

Chazon the priest, who stood near Shammah, pointed to the women who would come with them under the tent. The ones with crystals planted on their cheeks stayed. Tamiym felt grief. Crystals adorned so many of the women's faces.

Shocked by the soldiers' arrival, some unmarked women shuffled from them in fear, although the soldiers insisted. When Tamiym reached a corner where girls stretched out on mats, they were all awake and jumped up to accompany them. They didn't have to be encouraged to slip away. Tamiym almost wept with joy when she saw that none of their faces bore the Zuzim crystals.

Shammah left that chamber and entered another. The others followed. In it, they found a woman Tamiym discerned as Lady Mahalath. Tamiym resisted the jealousy that sprang within her, but the accompanying sadness refused to leave. Shammah scanned Mahalath's cheeks, and Tamiym watched him sigh with relief.

He roused Mahalath from sleep. Once she awakened, Tamiym saw that she was a beauty with dusky skin. Her raven hair lay in intricate waves. Tamiym felt the weight of her class as a farmer's daughter, with her robes of flax, and what Uz described as her masculine desire for knowledge.

She watched Mahalath purse her lips with the simper of someone who had supped on honey. When the woman realized it was Shammah before her, she gasped, and Shammah motioned for her to be quiet as he helped her from the bed.

Tamiym forced her mind to cling to reality. *This is his betrothed.*

The soldiers helped the women to their carts. Tamiym assisted them, hounded by the thought of abduction by the Zuzim. What she didn't want to consider was what the women they left behind had sacrificed to receive Zuzim crystals.

She and her mother had talked often about the dangers of women mingling with the star-born or their descendants. Some families in Chaniya had sold their daughters to pay debts or save land. Thankfully, Tamiym's family struggles hadn't led them to such a brutal decision.

They wrapped the women in heavy blankets and fed them nuts and water. The last woman Tamiym helped into a horse-drawn cart was Mahalath. She smiled at her, and Mahalath nodded, but Tamiym was conscious of her rough hands that had harvested crops and handled a dagger while Mahalath appeared to have never held a spoon.

Tamiym returned to her horse as rain fell. She was losing track of time after spending weeks with Shammah's company. Usually, she was harvesting with her family, hoping that unexpected rains wouldn't flood their fields. All of that seemed eons away.

In that moment, Truth was beside her, in his initial form of a child. Tamiym sensed he understood her astonishment. Events that defied mortal laws were becoming commonplace, so Truth's transforming himself at will was expected. Almost.

He clutched her hand. "Bind truth near you. The king will need your wisdom. Never deny him."

"He will not need me," Tamiym said. "He will have her."

Truth's grip made her wince. Tamiym tried to pull away. His features and shape were childlike, but he clenched her hand like a seasoned soldier.

"Never deny him truth," Truth urged.

Truth left to join Expectant and the others who were instructing Shammah and Eitan to tell their soldiers to fall back among the tamarisk trees and away from the crystal steps.

"The Zuzim will not follow you," Expectant said.

Expectant, Truth, and the other children circled the Zuzim structure. Tamiym rubbed her hand. It burned as she watched the children stretch their hands toward the building.

"Aleph!" the children cried.

As lightning cascaded from the sky, the ground covered the stairs, the underground chambers, and the triangular monuments.

Nothing remained but a grassy plain.

The soldiers lit fires and started simple meals of roasted meat and barley soup. Shammah and Chazon joined the camp and sat, warming themselves before a huge blaze. Mahalath watched them from her cocooned position on the horse cart, trying to calculate the days since the abduction at Arba.

She wrapped her arms about her body, chilled and glad the rain had ceased. Memories of Zuzim faces, wreathed by their heavy, red manes, swarmed before her eyes, but she ignored them.

She studied Chazon and recalled the night at the feast. It was one of the last normal events she had experienced before King Aikah's death, before the sacking of the City of Kings, and before her capture by the Zuzim. She felt ages older.

Mahalath uncurled from the corner of the horse cart. She stepped over the other sleeping women. When she reached Shammah and Chazon, they stood. She gestured for them to return to their seats as she sat down on a rock. Shammah's hand guided her.

"Did they hurt you, my lady?"

Mahalath heard the concern in his voice and trembled. His voice possessed no guile, and it startled her because her aristocratic social circles required she deceive and manipulate. But intrigue didn't matter anymore. She didn't know where her family was, whether Dahv had lived, or whether she had a country.

"No, my lord, I am uninjured."

She sipped hot liquid from the cup Chazon handed her. "What brew is this? It burns the throat."

"It also heals. Lady Tamiym made it and served us earlier," Chazon said.

She drank the liquid. Despite the blanket a soldier gave her, every joint felt frozen. "Who is Lady Tamiym? I did not know you rescued other noblewomen from the City of Kings with us."

Chazon glanced at Shammah, whose lips thinned as he threw a twig in the fire.

"Lady Tamiym is from Chaniya and came with us on the journey to rescue you and the other women," the priest said.

Mahalath tried to remedy her offense. "Please identify her for me, so that I may meet her. I may know her family."

Chazon nodded toward Tamiym, who sat in a patch of wood with several soldiers, telling stories. Tamiym's hair was bound at the neck, and she looked tired, but every soldier near her listened.

"Thank you. I will make certain we meet. I am sure she is an extraordinary woman. Any woman would have to be to make this journey. Lord Shammah, I saw you snatched by the hawks of Livnath. How do you live?"

"By the power of Aleph," he replied.

"Ah. The mystery deity of Yaphah. I must present an offering. At what shrine should I express devotion?"

"There are no altars on earth that would satisfy."

Mahalath felt a wall between them, but she refused to take offense. She could hear her mother teaching her every form of politeness. Sometimes her mother taught in kindness. At other times, she had berated Mahalath day and night that she would be queen one day, and that she must practice self-control. The entire family line counted on her, her mother would say as she and Rina visited relatives or studied a family history.

Rina. How Mahalath missed her. Her sister took their mother's teachings on how to live as an aristocrat in stride, while each lesson wounded Mahalath.

She took another sip. Her voice carried the detachment of a traveler musing about a country she was exploring. "Do you have any word from the City of Kings? From my family?"

"The Mikana destroyed the city, and captured Dahv. And I do not wish to cause you more pain, but am sorry, we had not heard about your family. Can you tell us anything about your ordeal?"

"My mind still grasps the idea of freedom. My perspective is dim. May we talk at another time?"

"Of course," Shammah said.

Chazon frowned. He could feel the growing tension in Shammah because of war and a loveless union. A man should not face managing these massive twin challenges at the same time. Both were thieves.

"Mahalath is a typical noblewoman, and one who knows her role as your intended wife," Chazon said. "More than likely, she feels more comfortable talking with the women about what happened in the Zuzim palace."

"Perhaps you discern rightly." Shammah broke more twigs and tossed them into the fire.

"I never desired her as my queen," he continued. "But I felt compelled—obligated—to keep the marriage contract. I felt love would spring someday between us."

"And where is your heart now?"

"Imprisoned by a marriage that may never know love," Shammah said as the fire crackled. "If I had been there to protect Mahalath, if I had listened to you, she may have escaped."

"Could it be she seems detached because she has shifted her affections?" Chazon asked. "After your disappearance, it was becoming clear that Dahv intended to claim her. He always associated with her family. He joined their feasts, their times with the scribes. Does this offend you?"

"A union between Dahv and Mahalath—or anyone else—would change things."

Shammah threw more twigs into the fire. This time, the flames leaped high.

CHAPTER TWENTY-SEVEN

HIGHER GROUND

"The carts are leaving," the soldier said. Tamiym ignored him as he moved away. She refused to go with Mahalath and the other women. With defiance, she faced Shammah. She had expected such moments when she would have to debate men about how they could cooperate with women. What she hadn't prepared for was challenging the king of Seth himself about the role of women, and she was disappointed that she had to.

"You need me," she said to Shammah as he prepared his horse.

"I need you protected." Shammah's words shot into the air.

"I can help."

"By serving me soup?"

She grimaced. "Insults will not work, my lord. I think you look forward to the hours when I bring your rations and retell epics to your men. I was not tutored by the magnificent Chazon. I was not reared in Yaphah. I did not travel on military campaigns with the wise Eitan. I did not know the battle-genius King Aikah, but I studied the histories of Seth. You more than need me, my lord. You want my opinions. And I suspect your Existing One at Aleph wants you to let me stay."

Tamiym exhaled. She added that last sentence for emphasis, and it stretched the truth. She had no understanding of how the Existing One viewed women.

"Have Asahel collect your horse."

"So, I changed your mind?" Tamiym glanced at the carts wobbling along the rough path.

"No," Shammah said. "You follow yours."

Rain drenched Shammah and his men as they traveled toward the Tiras Mountains. When they reached the river Nehara, Shammah hesitated. Commander Eitan pulled his horse alongside him. "Rain and snowmelt have swollen the banks of the Nehara. We should wait."

Shammah nodded in agreement, and Eitan signaled to the men. As he did, water rushed from the river's mouth toward them.

"To higher ground!" Shammah yelled.

The company and their carts moved toward elevated, rockier areas. Several carts overturned.

Peleg's horse tripped over a boulder. Water charged in his direction.

Tamiym maneuvered her horse toward him before anyone else could reach the fallen sailor. "Your hand!"

She helped Peleg swing himself up behind her on her horse. It relieved Shammah to see Tamiyn and Peleg out of danger.

"And I instructed Tamiym that Asahel could help with her horse," Shammah mused. "Sagi was mistaken about Tamiym's skills. So was I."

Eitan and Javan grinned with admiration. Then the magistrate slapped a glum-faced Uz on the back.

Six days had passed since Mahalath and the other women traveled to Chaniya. Shammah and his companies had stopped to camp in the mountains.

The king of Seth caught Tamiym watching him. He guessed that because he almost sent her home, she remained aggravated with him. Along their journey, she and Peleg teased each other. The gloomy Chazon invited her to help make his concoctions, and Eitan doted on her like a daughter and often rode near her as protection. She and Asahel also took turns sharing stories, but Shammah felt she had pulled away from him.

This night was her turn to tell a story, and the men settled down from the day's ride and ate their soup, eager to hear Tamiym.

Shammah stood away from the camp but within earshot.

"No one had seen bears, but on this starry night, a bear appeared at the magistrate's doorstep and demanded payment," she said.

"But we have a small pack of wolves stalking us," Peleg said.

"This epic is not about wolves, wherever they may be," Tamiym said.

"Why is there a magistrate in your story?" Javan said.

"There is always a magistrate in trouble somewhere," Uz said.

"My hand did not bear the stylus to write this story, Javan," Tamiym said. "The bear demanded barley and emmer wheat. He also demanded the magistrate's daughter in marriage."

"And if he refused?" Peleg asked.

"The bear would destroy the city by killing every citizen," Tamiym said. "The bear had already slain a priest, a farmer, and a merchant who possessed too much money."

"What did the magistrate do? Tax the bear?" Uz asked.

"He did try that, but the bear ignored him," Tamiym said. "The wise magistrate made a decision instead."

Javan beamed.

"Don't get too excited, Javan; magistrates are always searching for riches or on their way to meet people who have it," Peleg said.

Shammah knew why he had said that. Peleg often told him about how many magistrates took bribes or contorted the laws to increase their wealth and protect their position. Aikah must have overlooked many unjust acts to enrich the throne. Otherwise, they couldn't have been so prevalent in the clandestine rungs of life in the City of Kings.

"The magistrate devised another plan. He employed a soldier who did not fear bears. Then he paid him to trap the beast," Tamiym continued.

"Did the magistrate get his money's worth?" Peleg asked.

"I will tell you that tomorrow night," Tamiym said. "But here is a hint: why would the bear want the magistrate's daughter?"

Tamiym was one of the reasons Shammah relied on Aleph. Their campaign had to work. She and so many others had to be protected. The plan was to set traps in the Mikana's City of Knowledge, the infamous region fortified by rock walls, but he didn't yet know what traps to set.

"You have not eaten, my lord," Tamiym said. She joined him on the mound of rocks where he sat, carrying a steaming bowl. "Peleg made it. He outdid himself tonight."

Despite her storytelling, and although she was irritated with him, she didn't neglect her evening ritual to bring him food after the rank and file had eaten.

"Our meat is gone, but there is plenty of barley," she said. "Peleg offered to slaughter wolves for meat. No one wanted wolf in their soup—not yet."

The king nodded his thanks. She caught him at a moment of vulnerability and worry, and he didn't want to alarm her. He neither asked her to sit nor encouraged her to leave. Perhaps the coolness between them was ending. And maybe the successful bear story helped.

Tamiym fanned her hands before the fire to warm them. "In one epic, the saying goes that when branches of date palms blow, help is coming."

She paused for effect, allowing them to listen as branches on nearby palms bending in the cold, night breeze.

"I sense a storyteller's imagination." Shammah sipped his soup. "You are aware of my worry. We are deep in the mountains. The Mikana threaten all of Seth, and, despite my strategic plan, this campaign seems, well, misguided and foolhardy."

"Instructions from Aleph are baffling," Tamiym said. "The scholars in Chaniya debate the merits of Livnath, the other gods, and Aleph. They hate the chatter about deities, but all acknowledge that Aleph is its own master, champion of its own mystery."

"You speak truth, my lady. Maybe your epic about the bear is true."

Tamiym brushed a loose braid away from her cheek. "It is not. But help is coming."

"Are you starting to believe in the power of Aleph, scholar of all things?"

"You mock my studies. But Aleph is indisputable as an attractive ruling deity."

"You make belief in Aleph as simple as studying calculations or peeling fruit," Shammah said, putting down his bowl.

"Who can prove that our lives concern the gods? Aleph's affections are no more verifiable than our observations about other deities attached to the stars. I prefer…the tangible."

"But do you not concern yourself about the afterlife or the underworld?"

"I do when I think of my parents and brothers —but we are born, we exist, and hopefully we die old and fruitful. It is all any thoughtful person can wish for. That is why I wanted to come on this journey. There is meaning in it."

"Do you mean destiny?" he asked.

"Destiny. Its presence excites me. I live my epic." Tamiym paused. "Forgive me for interrupting your solitude with such things."

"Never apologize for sorting out truth, Tamiym," Shammah said, reaching over to touch her hand. "You're trying to understand the heights where wisdom dwells."

CHAPTER TWENTY-EIGHT

FORBIDDEN KNOWLEDGE

Winds brought forth a soft, cold rain. Shammah assigned soldiers to guard the perimeter of the camp and keep the fires hot. No one slept. Shammah stayed at his perch on the rocks, shuddering in the chill, imploring the Existing One of Aleph to hear his petition.

He didn't know what to do. None of Aikah's military training provided answers. Unlike his father's clashes with the Mikana, stories Aikah recited to Shammah hundreds of times, Shammah's view of war veered from his father's audacious appetite for violence.

Aikah served Livnath, the goddess ruled by petulance, not wisdom, so Shammah recognized why Chazon urged him to tarry for Aleph's direction on how to attack.

But to wait left Shammah anguished. His soldiers were cold and hungry. He heard their coughs and moans as many of them fell sick because of the damp. The sense of helplessness ushered in the faces of the thirteen soldiers who died in his care. He didn't want to lose any more men because of a foolish decision.

The small stretch of cloth that covered Shammah between the rocks whipped away from him. The winds had returned. As he backed further into a curve of rock to protect himself, he remembered Tamiym telling him that the company had no more meat. Then he recalled the soldier's horror in Chaniya when he mentioned the cannibalism of the Mikana in the City of Kings. The Mikana were carefree meat eaters, consuming animals—and sometimes people—if their bellies ached enough.

Stories of their cannibalism ignited panic in many soldiers when they followed Seth's kings in military campaigns. The Mikana humiliated their victims with late-night rituals of singing and earth-shaking dancing before feasting.

"Ah." Shammah sighed. Aleph had granted him a plan.

The next morning, the king instructed his soldiers to kill the wolves that had haunted their steps since Arba and to bundle them in blankets like corpses. Then he told Chazon to create a brew.

"Sweet venom," Shammah said.

"Not a single Mikana will be immune," the priest said.

An hour before they left camp, Chazon walked among the soaking carcasses and sprinkled them with a coarse liquid.

"What's that?" Peleg warbled. His face wrinkled at the odor.

"Spices." Chazon's tone dared Peleg to ask another question.

Peleg dared. "Not the kind of spices I would use in my pot," he said. "Sailors would fling you into the sea if you fed them that."

When the priest's dark brows furrowed, Peleg walked away, shuddering. A smile tickled Shammah's lips because Tamiym's face registered the same disgust as Peleg's.

"You will thank me later," Chazon said as he poured the last drops.

"I smell more refreshed after neglecting the courtyard cistern for weeks," roared Asahel, prompting the rest of the company to chortle with him. He pinched his nose when he mounted his horse and descended into the valley.

Mahalath and Gila sorted several bolts of cloth. Gila sensed the younger woman's preoccupation, but she tried to ease the distance between them. After all, once the war was over, Mahalath would be the new queen.

"This will cheer the women—especially Abelia—who have been gracious to us," Gila said.

Mahalath offered a tepid smile. Gila felt the frost. The young woman whose family trained her as an aristocrat, who greeted her betrothal with warmth and uncertainty, was now cold and confident. It was as if Mahalath's mind circled thoughts that no one could share or understand.

"I grieve for what you have lost," Gila said. "After the war, we will rebuild."

"Yes."

"Your face shifts like shadows. Did the Zuzim harm you more than we have understood? Do you mourn something else? Do you mourn the women who attended you?"

"I didn't experience injury like the others. I saw my slaves… once. Then, never again. I plead your forgiveness. I do not remember more. Perhaps you sense my worry about King Shammah."

"I will not press you. Why not wait for me with Guriel?"

Gila's worried eyes trailed Mahalath as the Shamgar helped to seat the young woman in the cart.

Shammah's scouts could spot the glinting towers of the City of Knowledge after traveling for a short time. They also could hear the raucous Mikana, their thundering yelps and screeches echoed over its walls.

Luxury coexisted with foulness in the city. Precious stones embellished the walls, and the city wrapped around a golden temple tower that boasted thirteen platforms, its summit protruding skyward like an outstretched hand.

The temple held tablets coveted throughout the known world, but no one dared face the Mikana on their ground. Their brutality and advanced weaponry were famous in the East. Despite those obstacles, scholars everywhere longed to know what the Mikana knew, to feed from the well of knowledge they had gained from their star-born parents.

Meditating on the famed city triggered Shammah's curiosity. The more he thought about the knowledge he would gain, the more excited he became. He imagined evenings studying works with Chazon and Tamiym. Much was to be known about seafaring, building monuments that would last epochs, and creating weapons that would deter kingdoms from battle. To conquer the Mikana extended a chance to capture the known world.

A stele appeared before him. Shammah stopped his horse and heard a voice say to him: "What Aikah maimed and killed to possess, you are given without effort. Remember, as told you in the cave, do not grasp and pine for what Aikah coveted. Receive."

Shammah looked around. No one else heard the voice. Then, before his eyes, the words "Take nothing" appeared on the rotating stele. Shammah's heart pounded as the stele slowly faded. Aleph had spoken to him.

"We will be victorious!" Shammah shouted to the company. "Take nothing from the city, no matter how exquisite."

He could hear the men carping among themselves, a growing annoyance for Shammah because they didn't trust his words. He repeated himself, this time with an imperious tone: "Take nothing."

Shammah motioned to Asahel, who rode up to him. "Go to Eitan's company. Tell him the same."

Asahel rode away.

"You saw the gift from the caves of the Desert Akran, did you not?" Chazon said to Shammah.

"The stele. And I heard the voice again. The voice of Aleph."

Once Shammah's company reached the southeastern wall of the City of Knowledge, they pulled the carcasses from their carts and positioned them atop boulders like sacrifices. They waited for Eitan's signal. When his company reached a designated section of the stone wall, the soldiers lit fires beneath the carcasses. The smoky aroma of roasting meat and fuel filled the air.

In both camps, Shammah and Eitan instructed the men not to touch the carcasses once lit and to retreat to the nearby cliffs.

As the carcasses caught fire, the potion Chazon sprinkled on them created the fragrances of a feast.

The scent wooed desire from the Mikana. One by one, the warriors spilled forth from their fortified houses, some running through the gate and others climbing over the walls.

Saliva splashed from their jaws. They bounced on their hind legs and reached for the smoking meat. Mikana lunged at the carcasses that had the shape, clothing, and movements of females and small children, but gained no preferred status. Each Mikana fought for a portion.

Peleg, crouched near Tamiym, winced and said, "I've never seen such greed."

When one discovered a carcass, a fellow Mikana fought for a piece. Once they consumed the meat, they fell upon each other and ripped each other apart. The carnage lasted for hours. Even the bravest of Shammah's soldiers shook their heads in a flash of sickness.

At last, every Mikana was dead, either dismembered or frothing from a flesh lust that triggered their inner embers to incinerate them.

"Your potion did not douse their stench," Tamiym said to Chazon as they emerged from their hiding places.

"Their embers and stench reveal their shame. No potion can cover that," Chazon said. "They're manifestations of their evil. The Mikana are a cursed race, a crossbreed spawned in rebellion."

The irony that struck Shammah was being in the kingdom of the creatures that slaughtered his men in the marshes so many moons ago. That defeat estranged him from Aikah and changed the course of his adulthood. Anger tumbled within his heart. He shook himself back to the present when he heard Tamiym's voice.

"What about their wisdom?" she said.

Looking ragged, Chazon replied. "The Zuzim taught the Mikana about politics, war, poverty, strategy, commerce, and beauty. They showed them how to craft weapons and cause disease. The Mikana became such scholars because of their forebears that they became known for the learning they had stored in their great city."

Shammah blinked, anger giving way to curiosity. He remembered how ill-timed questions left him and his men vulnerable in the marsh, and endangered Gila when the Zuzim arrived after Aikah died.

I must resist. Every limb wanted to reach for a crystal, study it, or enter a door and explore what lay behind it. Shammah could see the others, particularly Chazon, Tamiym, Eitan, and Uz, facing the same struggle as their faces clouded. They pursued knowledge, and the mysteries of the Mikana allured them to the point of pain.

At Shammah's command, the companies torched each gleaming street altar. When they reached the glittering temple in the center of the city, the two companies encircled the base.

"Do not touch or save anything!" Shammah shouted to the companies as they faced the structure. "What we see will make us ache for more but remember Aleph forbids it. Heed me and save your life."

They entered an opening at the base of the temple. Inside, thousands of tablets rose from the floor to the ceiling, about thirty feet above them. The tablets seemed to whisper at them.

Shammah saw Tamiym and Uz jerk their heads in surprise. Muttered lines from epics and hymns, theories about astronomy, mathematics, geography, and excerpts from the philosophies shrilled and groaned. Beside the tablets, jeweled orbs circled the room. The orbs possessed faces with lips that moved.

At the center of the temple, light rose upward through an opening in a great platform. Symbols flowed from the ceiling within the beam of light, along with voices that whispered mysteries to the soldiers as they gazed in wonder.

Peleg passed under a shimmering orb. He turned, and the orb released images of his beloved City of Kings: the market, the courtyards where he drank beer, and the men who sailed with him appeared in a vision before him.

"Keep moving!" shouted Eitan on the opposite side of the light.

One of the voices cried, "Gila…Queen Gila."

"Do not stop!" Eitan shouted to the men near him, while Shammah and Chazon exchanged surprised expressions. Did Eitan have feelings for the queen? The chambers both enticed and bared desires.

Shammah attempted to move closer to them, but the twirling orbs blocked him, flickering visions of Mahalath and Aikah in happier times. He strained to reach Tamiym, who attempted to persuade Uz to keep moving.

"Tamiym, do not summon the fears of a woman now," Uz said. "This is the tongue of desert families east of Chaniya. We believed that the tongue died out with the last speaker fifty years ago when Rabbah ransacked it. How would this spectacle know it?"

He reached out to the orb that kept speaking and sparkling. "Do not touch it," Tamiym said.

Uz pleaded with her. "I must see inside. We could advance the civilization of Seth. We would be superior to our enemies. All of my study is for this…to learn, to understand."

"No, Uz," Tamiym said, tears falling on her cheeks. "It is not revelation, but temptation. It seduces. Do not succumb."

Javan yanked Uz away from the orb. "Control yourself."

"Keep moving. Now!" Shammah commanded, veering from the orbs surrounding him. He had to reach Uz and Tamiym. "Uz, obey your king and live."

Uz jerked away from Javan. His stubby fingers caressed the orb as his dark face flushed with delight.

"Tamiym! Javan! The orb describes the origins of our world, the gods, and the masters who created us, and the stars and planets," Uz said. "They want to share their wisdom and befriend us. They want to give us power. They say we can retrieve eternal sustenance from our bodies…"

In the next few moments, the orb melted in ribbons of smoke. With it, Uz's body dissolved into a filmy liquid on the stone floor.

Tamiym dropped to her knees. She reached out to touch the substance while one hand was on her lips.

Shammah, finally reaching her, pulled her to him. "Do not."

He threw his torch to the base of platform and drove her forward. The orbs above hit the floor and sizzled. Flames erupted throughout the chambers. Shammah took one last look and saw the Four Faces towering over the orbs, destroying them with swords of amber flame.

Once outside the City of Knowledge, Shammah and his company fell to the ground in exhaustion. Breathing hard, Shammah was trying to rise when he caught sight of an injured Mikana stirring from the piles of smoldering carcasses. The warrior had escaped death and stumbled toward Chazon.

The priest sat with his head in his arms, not realizing the danger.

Shammah leaped to his feet, snatched a torch handle, and rammed it into the creature's chest. Asahel followed behind Shammah and decapitated the Mikana with his sword.

Chazon trembled before Shammah. The king sat on his haunches, breathing hard, soaked with blood. The two men said nothing.

Then the priest bowed.

CHAPTER TWENTY-NINE

COMPANIONS

Geona found a corner and drew her children to her in the overcrowded pen. She tried not to think of her husband, Eron, as she watched the soldiers loyal to the Mikana patrolling the perimeter. Loneliness was too heavy to bear.

The two soldiers who found her and her children in the abandoned house left with glee after learning they would get extra rations tonight because of their discovery.

The pen smelled awful. Louder than the cries for food was the fear that creased the prisoners' faces. Geona tried to ignore it so she could think. As she fed her infant milk, she wondered when she would find food for her daughter.

A woman with a drawn, sallow face shuffled toward Geona. She wore the robes of a priestess, but without the jewelry, which the Mikana stole from her. The woman pulled out a piece of slightly moldy bread and thrust it at Geona, nodding at her daughter.

Geona hesitated. She didn't know why the woman was being kind, but she accepted the gift.

"Thank you," Geona murmured as she took the bread and handed it to Hada, who bit into it.

"They feed us around twilight." The woman slid back into her corner. "I try to save a little food every day."

The next morning, Geona looked at her young son, who slept among the rags she had collected for bedding. Mites gnawed at him as he slept, but Geona thanked Livnath they weren't lying in the dirt.

She panicked when she noticed her daughter had wandered from her. Geona scanned the pen, looking for her. She saw a young woman emerge from one area of the pen, with Geona's daughter beside her.

"I am sorry," said the woman with torn, dirty, but well-made clothing. Geona knew that the woman came from one of the noble houses because a friend of hers designed the fringe. Geona recognized the pattern. That friendship, along with weaving, seemed so long ago.

"She saw my mother braiding my hair and sat down to watch," the woman said.

"Hada, come here," Geona said to her daughter. "Don't run off again. Do you understand me?"

Disconcerted by her mother's scolding, the child lowered her head. It was not often that Geona reproved her, but when she did, the mothering voice that so often rose and fell with the peace of lullabies became stern.

"Mother," Hada said. "Rina's hair is beautiful. I couldn't help it. Please forgive me."

Hada hugged her mother about the waist. Geona stroked her child's hair as she gave a faint smile to Rina. "Thank you."

"My mother and father are over there," Rina said, pointing at a couple who clustered with other prisoners as the soldiers served bread and a milky soup that had a few beans. "I would love to play with Hada. When I saw her, she reminded me of my sister."

"Is your sister here? Is she imprisoned with us?" Geona asked.

Rina frowned. "We haven't seen her since the Mikana attacked."

"May the soldiers of Seth find her," Geona said.

"I must return to my parents," Rina said. She bent down to speak to Hada. "If your mother permits us, we'll braid hair again."

A day later, a Mikana warrior noticed Rina playing with Hada. He craned his neck to take in her smile as she taught Hada to weave with straw fragments. Rina's thick curls fell below her shoulders, and her olive-colored skin bore a burnished sheen. She tried not to show fear, but she nudged Hada toward E-ven and his wife, Mara, for protection.

The warrior stomped to the pen and motioned to Rina with a crooked, hairy finger.

"Come with me." The warrior growled and Rina followed him.

"Sir, may I ask where you are taking my daughter?" E-ven tried to tamp down the grave concern in his voice.

"She pleases me," said the Mikana warrior, leering at Rina, who hung her head.

"My lord—" E-ven protested. "This is our daughter."

"Be quiet," the warrior said, his knobby fingers grabbing Rina's wrist. Rina bit her lip as her father reached out for her until the warrior slapped him to the ground with his other hand.

"Now be still," the warrior said, saliva dripping from his gums and teeth.

Hada called out to Rina as the warrior pulled the woman past the other prisoners. Geona heard Hada's cry and turned around from a far corner in the pen where she talked with several women. They hadn't noticed the warrior enter the pen.

"My lord!" cried Geona, rushing toward Rina and the warrior.

Something in her tone halted him. Geona sounded like the wives who cackled in the market, arguing with merchants and spanking and kissing children at the same time, Rina thought.

They were the loudest and, as everyone knew, the shrewdest.

"What do you want?" the warrior said.

"I need to give her my herbs and roots. She has the sickness, you know. She can't rest at night. When darkness comes, she scratches her stomach and legs sore. She scratches and scratches. The healer says she's afflicted by a spirit who won't release her. But these herbs we've been using…"

The Mikana warrior dropped Rina's wrist. "What sickness?"

"Is it true? I don't see anything on you."

Rina played along with Geona. "I hide the welts. It comes and goes. But it starts with an itch. I've had it since my weaning, my lord. The itching. The howling. When the spirit that haunts me gets restless, I get boils. Hives."

"It's contagious, my lord, so these herbs—" said Geona, appearing her most earnest.

The warrior snarled and shoved Rina further away from him. "Take her back. I don't fancy sickness. Or evil spirits." He stomped from the pen.

When he was out of sight, Rina bowed before Geona. "I am in your debt, Geona."

"Forgive me, my lady, for not being more delicate," Geona said.

"Not at all," Rina replied, grasping Geona's callused hands. "You kept me alive."

Gila halted near a date palm. She glimpsed Mahalath in the courtyard. The younger woman's lush, dark curls fell to her shoulders, except for braided tresses at the crown of her head. She hadn't spoken to Mahalath since their visit to the market.

The younger woman found solitary chores to keep herself detached from the other women.

As Gila watched, Mahalath lifted her arms upward and prayed toward the sky. Gila could not discern the language, but the sounds rose and fell in an awkward melody.

Mahalath's dusky skin bore a yellowish pallor, and her features radiated resignation and agony. Disturbed, Gila placed her hands to her mouth, and the tip of her foot kicked several pebbles. Mahalath stirred. She tied up her hair, gathered her robes, and slipped back inside the quarters where she and other women captured by the Zuzim stayed.

CHAPTER THIRTY

TRUSTING ALEPH

Tamiym found Shammah alone on a cluster of rocks, hunched and gazing at the cliffs below. Even without diadem, royal robes, or jewelry, every act or expression bore the fingerprints of a king. She looked at the bowl of barley soup. While he claimed it was his favorite—especially when there was lamb—how could that be when he grew up in the palace eating Seth's best dishes?

She looked over her shoulder at the campfire where the soldiers laughed at Peleg's banter. Perhaps she should prepare something else for Shammah. But what? She bit her lip. They were two days from the City of Kings and from battle. Maybe serving soup, and not the finest of breads, meats, and wines, fit the moment. If they survived, Shammah would remember these days with only watery soup as sustenance. The gentler ways he possessed would dull the memories of Aikah's brutality and the Mikana's violence.

She walked toward him, and without a word, handed him the soup. He wrapped his hands around the clay vessel to warm them.

"Thank you," he said. "Something is wrong, but I can't plumb its depths."

"Is it the strategy we're pursuing?" Tamiym asked.

"I am confident it is the right approach to bring Commander Zaqen up from the south with reinforcements. Commander Mattan and his men will protect us from the east."

"We all mourn the death of Uz," she offered. "I know it grieves you that we lost him. You know it hurts me. I never witnessed anyone dying like that. I thank you for helping me. Had I touched that liquid—"

"Knowledge can make us foolish," Shammah said.

"Warring in the way of Aleph requires depths of trust I do not yet have," Tamiym said. "Eternal truths are not fully understood in mastering mathematics or poring over the epics and the king lists. They—they must be lived. Touched. Explored. Do you believe this?"

"Tamiym, I do. In fact, more than ever, I know it is. Trusting the unseen unravels every scholar. Aleph left me undone, and my heart continues to bend. I am wet earth molded by hands I cannot see."

The conviction in his voice unsettled Tamiym. She wasn't ready to abandon her questions. They had become a part of her.

"The lions and their chariots will come. You will witness their arrival," Shammah said. He sighed when her face brightened. "But something in the future waits for us. The warning already has come."

Chazon toted his menagerie of potions and oils throughout their journey, and this morning was no different. Tamiym had watched him for hours and gleaned knowledge about the natural power of herbs, fruit extracts, and the practical teachings of Aleph.

"You are a remarkable student, Tamiym. Eager to learn. Not like the king."

He gestured toward Shammah, who, with Javan and Peleg, tended to the horses.

"You flatter me, but you know I'm not docile. We're both unruly learners," Tamiym said. "And you are stealthy, my lord. You have not revealed this concoction's essence."

He motioned for her to pass him a vial from his cart. "You're right. Peleg would have sent me into the mountains for refuge."

"If Peleg had his way, we would all flee to the mountains." Tamiym said.

They chuckled, catching Peleg's attention. Tamiym attempted to conceal her snickering.

"If your amusement is about me, it's unbecoming," Peleg yelled before returning to examining the horses.

Laughter settled into smiles all around.

"We're ready," Chazon said, packing the last of his powders and liquids.

"How will Lord Shammah make his claim to the throne?" Tamiym asked.

"With love and humility, I hope," Chazon said. "Seth will need those characteristics to rebuild."

"The king could face resistance," she said. "Dahv will contest his right to the throne. Do you think Dahv still lives?"

"Yes, but the question is, in what state did the Mikana allow him to survive?" Chazon said.

The assumption presented a host of options, but Tamiym refused to explore them. She had learned since her time with the company to be pragmatic, but not fearful. Imagining an array of manipulations inflicted on Dahv made Tamiym tighten her throat, so she changed the subject.

"It is late for me to mention it, but you never said a word about my joining the company," Tamiym said.

"Do you feel you belong with us?" Chazon asked.

"Yes, but I wanted to know what you think...or thought."

"Would it have stopped you from coming?"

She paused. "No."

"That is why I welcomed you. You are a woman of conviction, Lady Tamiym," Chazon said. He wiped his hands on his robes before bowing. "Do not soil your conviction with self-doubt."

The words stung, but she recovered. The priest's straightforwardness displayed his respect.

"Chazon, did you ever claim someone's heart, and she yours?" she asked.

"Once and long ago," the priest said.

"What happened?" Tamiym pressed. Chazon sometimes behaved as if he possessed no normal human past except as Aikah's counselor and Shammah's tutor.

"I made a choice. Aikah needed me, and I left her to serve him."

"Do you regret it?"

"On nights when stars crowd the sky, I long for her voice," Chazon said. "She wanted us to marry that year, but I joined Aikah in one of his battles, convinced that Aleph wanted me to advise him. She refused to wait. When I returned, I learned that she had become the wife of a rich merchant who begged for her hand. Her mother needed comforts because she was an invalid. My love married to care for her mother. Six months later, she died in childbirth."

"Your mourning must have been without comfort," Tamiym said.

"I have imagined that Shammah is the son we would have had."

"I can see that."

"Love is a narrow passageway," Chazon said. "Don't miss your rendezvous with it."

The scout Shur identified Emit and Rabbah warriors to Commander Mattan, who strode the room as Shur detailed what he had seen.

"How many of them?" the commander asked.

"Several thousand."

"Seth's enemies considered it an opportune time to plunder us," Mattan said.

Seth was a battleground for the star-born to make a point, Mattan knew. Within weeks, decades of overall peace had reverted to the erratic pace of war Seth knew under King Kish.

"How do you want to confront them?" Commander Eron asked.

"We will evacuate the citizens to the north, at the military encampment where we are," Mattan said. "We will then place men in the Temple of the Moon to draw the Emit and Rabbah there. We will place the rest of our men on the edge of the desert for an ambush."

Eron frowned. "How will we draw them to the temple?"

"Star-borns and their descendants love worship—and the opportunity to mock each other," Mattan said. "They mock Livnath, so they will take the chance to desecrate her temple to see how she responds."

"But we will be there instead."

"Right."

"Commanders, the evacuation will have to be done within twenty-four hours," Shur said. "They're conducting a disciplined march."

"I will ask for the winds of Aleph," Mattan said.

"I'm not sure what to say about mocking Livnath. I don't want to invite her rage," Eron said to Mattan, who did not change his expression.

"I grew up in the City of Kings, and she is our patroness," Eron continued. "But I don't want to give up territory for our enemies. I also refuse to dishonor the night arts you used to rescue us from the Mikana. My men will follow your lead."

"Not mine, Aleph's," Mattan said. "You will not regret your decision."

Qever and the people of Rabbah yearned for glory. They appeared as tame, peace-loving warriors by the barbaric standards of the Mikana, but conflict yielded occasions for commerce, and they were opportunistic.

Because the Mikana had breached the City of Kings, the Rabbah could snatch spoils. Of course, Qever wasn't surprised that Lashon of the Emit wanted to ally with the Rabbah. Lashon lusted for Seth's southern borders, where he could ransack the wealthy city of Everlasting at the Cove of Revealing.

Qever persuaded the Emit to march on Chaniya first, the apparent stronghold of the king's heir. Rumors emerged everywhere that the heir hadn't died at Livnath's hand. Qever also enticed Lashon with the promise of being able to boast about slaying Aikah's rightful heir instead of amusing himself with the son of his concubine, as the Mikana were doing in the City of Kings.

"The boundaries of Chaniya are in view," said Lashon, whose screeching terrorized humans to the edge of insanity. La-shon twisted the gold reins on his jackal. "I long for plunder and slaughter."

At noonday, they reached the southern borders of Chaniya, but the farmers had abandoned their fields and carried away their livestock. The Rabbah and the Emit kept marching, their jackals snarling as they cut through trees and homes, en route to the heart of the city where the Temple of the Moon stood.

"The people play games with us," roared Lashon. "They hide."

"We like games," Qever said.

Outside of the tower, stray livestock roamed, and hooded priests moved vegetables and fruit in ox carts. Some priests roasted goat and lamb.

"Count on Livnath's priests never to go hungry." Qever grinned.

"Their goddess is demanding," Lashon said. "I wouldn't mind taking down her temple to bait her. I mean, do I have a temple?"

"Satisfy yourself as the plague descending on Chaniya," Qever crowed.

The Rabbah and Emit warriors stormed toward the hooded priests, shrieking as they rode their jackals, long in limb, like ancient trees, and more agile than horses. Before they reached the temple grounds, the land rumbled.

Many of the Rabbah and Emit warriors tried to steer their jackals away from the opening in the ground, which became a gigantic cliff that led deep into the Earth, but they failed. Lashon, Qever, and some warriors near them escaped the earthquake and leaped to the land around the tower.

The soldiers of Seth shook off their hoods and shouted as they pulled out spears and flung them at the jackals leaping over them. Behind the tower, Commander Eron signaled his men to lob boulders to stop the jackals fleeing the spears.

From a cluster of date palms, Mattan emerged, towering over his men on the elephant he rode. His presence stunned Lashon and Qever, who tossed dozens of Mattan's men to their deaths. They paused when they saw Mattan.

"Champion, why do you not fight with us?" Qever demanded. "You are one of our people."

"I am not. I am fifth-generation free," Mattan said.

Qever snarled and pulled a dagger the width of a small tree trunk from his pocket and flung it into Mattan's shoulder, but the commander and his beast stalked forward.

"You disgrace us!" Lashon's shriek caused many Sethite soldiers to fall from their horses.

Mattan shot an arrow into Qever's chest, the thrust of the arrow forcing Qever to topple. A rock cut into Qever's shoulder as he fell, causing him to yelp in pain. His head spun. He gasped for air.

He pulled himself up on the boulder to see Mattan approaching Lashon, who screeched curses as Mattan threw his sword. The weapon sliced Lashon's neck, and the Emit warrior still yelled for moments when his head rolled from his body.

Qever fell backward, his chest heaving. Above him, a soldier pressed a sword to his neck.

Rabbah and Emit warriors who evaded Shammah's soldiers wailed as the ground opened and swallowed them. Mattan sighed. The Rabbah and the Emit thirsted for profit and blood and refused to honor the Existing One, so to the darkness, they belonged. How grateful Mattan was for the revelation of the Existing One that freed him from the curse of his family bloodline.

Self-seduction could have led him to battle Seth and demand allegiance and even worship. Mattan could be like the Rabbah and the Emit, consigned to the bowels of the abyss, rebellious even at the threshold of destruction.

Mattan surveyed his companies. The soldiers tended to their injuries, counted the dead, and gathered weapons left by the Rabbah and Emit. Blood seeped from his side. He had survived more serious wounds, but this one seemed difficult to reach. Until he dismounted from his elephant, he wouldn't know for certain whether his thick hands would be dexterous enough to cover the gash.

He lifted his bulk from the elephant and groaned. The act of bending agitated his gaping flesh. As Mattan tried to reach the injury, Shur approached him with cloth and a vial. The scout wore an expression of understanding.

Shur opened the wound and cleaned it. "My father owned an apothecary. We lived in the southern sector of the City of Kings. Poor families came to us, but now and then a noble, even a priest of Livnath would seek our care. The priests, if they came, always came at night and paid my father handsomely if he agreed to tell no one that they had been there. Father didn't use the night arts, like some of the healers. He insisted that I learn how to make poultices and sleeping draughts. You see, my service extends beyond scouting and assassinations."

"I am grateful that you possess such knowledge and compassion." Mattan winced when Shur tightened the bandage. "A soldier who seeks understanding and abides with compassion will command armies."

"If I can imitate your kindness, I would be grateful," Shur said.

When the men returned to the barracks, Mattan ascended to his place where he had petitioned Aleph for the soldiers' rescue from the City of Kings. Instead of sitting, the commander hauled himself to the rocks and kneeled in gratitude.

Shammah's men found safe places for their horses and positioned themselves in the hills north of the City of Kings. They watched the Mikana's beasts carry cedar wood and other building materials. Shammah couldn't determine what they were constructing, but their activity didn't surprise him—the Mikana had besieged the city about two weeks.

He packed the thought away in his mind as he stood on a high rock. He lifted his face skyward, and shouted, "Most High of Aleph, please send lions from your throne!"

Golden lions, as if catapulted from their cages, shot from the sky in droves and landed before the double-horned beasts of the Mikana. The lions tore at the feet of the foul creatures, leaving them in agony. One by one, the double-horned beasts tumbled.

Shammah's soldiers slipped from their places and cut off the heads of the surprised Mikana as they hit the ground.

The lions of Aleph soared above the city walls and tunneled below them. Once inside, they attacked the remaining beasts of the Mikana that guarded the city.

Four hulking lions remained outside to accompany Shammah as he, Eitan, Asahel, Javan, and Peleg marched through the Seventh Gate.

Qayin and Haran, flamboyant in their robes, stood behind Anash. Dahv was nearest to the Mikana leader, his handsome face mapped with wrinkles. The Mikana sheared his locks and beard, and the days of battle stained his once-opulent garments.

"Shammah, back from the dead." Anash cackled like multiple hens laying eggs.

"Surrender!" Shammah said.

"Why should I? You're not Livnath's anointed king. He is here," Anash said, waving to the immobile Dahv with a flourish. "He welcomed me. We are one."

"You are a usurper. Relinquish the city," Shammah said. The four lions surrounding him roared and bared their teeth.

"Are these your pets?" Anash pointed a jagged, teasing finger to the lions. "Impressive."

"Relinquish the city."

"I will not. Your father rots. And I have every right, according to the blood oath he made. His death frees us to trample Seth."

From behind the palace and throughout the city, hordes of Mikana rushed at Shammah and his men. Shammah calculated. Most of his soldiers were outside of the city walls. He had underestimated the number of Mikana inside the city.

"Did you think you could anticipate more than me, the dead heir of Aikah? You should've clung to safety in your grave," Anash said.

Aikah's former rival stretched out his hand. Within the city walls, daylight evaporated into darkness.

Shammah heard the people in nearby pens cry out. The Mikana warriors had treated his people like animals. Now

Anash frightened them with the night arts. Shammah decided to pounce. His heart raced with rage.

Shammah's fingers stroked his sword with pride. He and his men could slash Anash's legs. The lions could crush the rest of his body. However, he would risk the lives of his men, and they could perish while slaughtering an enemy.

He turned to signal Eitan, but one lion tipped his head and growled at the king and bared his enormous teeth. Fear rocked through Shammah, and insight flooded his thoughts. He understood the sign from the lion. The temptation to strike Anash passed. Aleph alone claimed the Mikana commander as the prey of the Existing One.

CHAPTER THIRTY-ONE

THE FOUR FACES

Chazon and Tamiym huddled near a cart outside the city walls. A small grove of trees hid them from view. Chazon dropped a few containers and muttered as he prepared his potions. His actions grew intense when darkness began to fall within the City of Kings.

"Are you all right?" Tamiym kept her voice gentle because she was almost certain Chazon's brows were about to jump from his forehead in worry. "We were prepared. You said so before we reached the city walls."

"Zaqen's men should be here at any moment," Chazon said.

Tamiym decided not to push and tried to ignore the thumping of Mikana hooves and shouts from within the city walls. They didn't know what was happening inside the city and what could happen to them where they were.

Two Mikana on their double-horned beasts spotted them. One of them pulled out his bow and started firing heavy arrows. The blows overturned the cart.

Commander Zaqen and his men studied the northern horizon. They saw the shadow hover over the city.

"What is this strange darkness?" Zaqen muttered. "It's noonday."

Anash bared his spiked teeth and flicked his knobby wrist. Lightning crashed around the throne, causing people to scream.

"The power of men is limited to the abilities of children," he said. "No one can withstand us. Darkness will overpower the light."

"Your foolish wish," Shammah said.

The lions transformed into amber flames and flew skyward, illuminating the darkness.

"Where are your thousands of men to protect you from me?" Anash asked. "You came armed only with disappearing pets and light tricks."

"Relinquish the city," Shammah repeated.

Zaqen mounted his horse when his top lieutenant yelled, "Commander, the sign of the king!"

Amber flames soared in the darkened sky just over the city. The face of a lion appeared in the shooting flames. The lion seemed to say the word: *Attack.*

"On your horses!" Zaqen yelled. "We advance on the city, now! Chazon should be on the southern wall. Waiting for us."

As they rode, the darkness faded.

Javan, the magistrate from Chaniya, stepped closer to Asahel. Anash jutted his head upward, sensing his fear. He stomped down the palace steps to Javan. The magistrate trembled at the heat emanating from the Mikana's body.

"It's useless to fight us, isn't it? King Dahv joined us… and the priests. Hail us as Seth's salvation, lest we smite you. We are Seth's savior-kings, the Proud Lords of the Seven Gates."

"Cling to peace, Javan," Shammah said.

The king thought of Uz and his death in the chamber filled with orbs. He refused to let another man in his company die because he refused to follow orders.

Anash jerked his head to Shammah. "Peace? There is no peace for you, heir-without-a-throne. Unless you surrender, you have nothing to say to me."

"Relinquish the city." Shammah drew out each word.

"So, you said. Now, let's see. How should you die once and for all?"

Tamiym and Chazon crawled behind the heavy cart and tried to save the glazed clay containers that held their precious ingredients. She shifted to her side when an arrow struck a pot standing near them, then another. Most of the pots collapsed in the dust.

Another arrow shot past her leg and snared her robe. Tamiym protected a pot with one hand while trying to free herself.

Chazon grimaced. "Where is Zaqen?"

The Mikana toyed with them. With one enormous foot, a Mikana warrior pushed the overturned cart back onto its wheels, forcing Chazon and Tamiym to scramble.

"Whom do you serve, priest?" yelled one of the Mikana, noting the silver hem on Chazon's gray robes.

"The Greater," Chazon said, holding the clay pots in his arms tighter.

The Mikana warrior barked with laughter.

"Greater than me? It would be wiser to worship someone more dependable. The 'Greater' deserted you and the woman to grant you solitude. Perhaps for an afternoon of futile petitions? Oh, and the 'Greater' left you clay pots. Do they shoot arrows? Do they drip with hot oil? I will explain this riddle for you. The Greater seeks your destruction."

Tamiym found the strength to ignore the warrior. She turned her face to the southern horizon.

"The commander is here," she whispered.

Zaqen yanked a bow and arrows from the basket of weapons carried on his horse. A soldier riding to the left of him drew his bow, and both men shot the Mikana, leaving them slumped on their beasts, their bodies burning.

"Kill them!" Zaqen shouted.

Soldiers sped up and decapitated the Mikana soldiers and crippled their animals.

Zaqen dismounted. "My lord," he said.

Chazon frowned. "We must be precise in our attack, Zaqen. Throw these clay pots in the air at the exact moment I indicate."

The priest glanced into the cart at the remaining pots. Zaqen instructed front-line lieutenants to distribute the intact clay pots and throw them upward at his signal.

"Will there be enough?" Zaqen asked.

"There is no power in the pots themselves," Chazon said.

Once the intact pots were in the soldiers' hands, Zaqen waited for Chazon's signal.

The priest held up one hand, his fingers extended outward. When the last finger contracted into his fist, Zaqen called out to his men. They threw the pots into the air and each burst apart.

The sky parted.

Chariots with lion-faced steeds—like the ones Shammah guided that night when he appeared from the sky before Tamiym—stood next to them. The scents of almond oil, myrrh, and flowers filled the air. The air smelled like a garden.

Zaqen caught his breath in awe. He motioned to the men, and one by one they left their horses and stepped inside the chariots tentatively.

Chazon pushed Tamiym forward, but she hesitated.

"You wanted to ride a sky chariot, Lady Tamiym. Shammah has arranged it for you," Chazon said.

"In the middle of battle, he did not forget," Tamiym murmured.

The priest smiled. "Neither did Aleph."

"Dahv, will you not come down to us?" Anash spoke with the arrogance of a noble hosting a feast. His face as stiff as the trunk of a tree, Dahv walked from the palace platform.

"The city is in our hands, Dahv," Anash said. "You have nothing to fear."

Dahv wanted to respond, but Anash, commander of the Mikana, had forced him to drink a potion that left him mute and unable to move unless summoned. His eyes revealed his feelings of horror. Anash outraged him; anger sprang from his pores as he gazed at Shammah. How Shammah survived the hawks of Livnath didn't matter. Dahv wanted to kill Shammah himself.

"Do you see that, Lord Shammah? Your sovereign wants you to join your cursed father in the grave." Anash snarled. "I can't help but oblige him."

Anash motioned to his warriors. "Take their weapons and separate them from the heir."

Javan, Eitan, Peleg, and Asahel struggled as the Mikana pulled them away from Shammah.

Anash stood close to Shammah and opened the top of his robes. The stench of sizzling flesh pierced Shammah's nostrils. Sweat poured from his skin. He held his hand to his mouth to keep from retching.

Dahv watched with glee, begging Livnath to torch Shammah on the ground where his adopted brother stood.

"A fainting king. A disappearing king," Anash said. "You cannot serve as the savior-king can you, Shammah?"

"Woeful indeed. I know enough to hail you as you are: foul flesh, a corruption of man and beast, living, but dead forever, destined for dust, darkness and nothingness. Your crown will fade with you. The mere men you slander will reign where you fall."

Anash roared and bore down on Shammah with his body heat.

Dahv's mind flared with rage, but he remained immobile. He coveted a sword. The City of Kings was his, and it always was meant to be. He knew the sweltering atmosphere Anash created weakened Shammah.

Shammah's face flushed. "Relinquish the city."

Anash frowned and flicked his finger. The two warriors surrounding him pulled out their daggers and placed the blades on Shammah's throat. Drops of blood appeared on the side of Shammah's neck.

Just then, drops fell from the sky, covering the Mikana in amber beads.

"Who are you?" shrieked Anash as the unexpected shower coated his body.

Shammah didn't speak. He swooned as the heat blasted from Anash's body.

Die, adopted son of Aikah, Dahv thought.

The four lions reappeared in midair over Shammah. In an instant, the lions became the Four Faces. Unhooded, their quartet of faces—lion, ox, eagle, and man—shifted with speed, fury washing over each visage as they loomed over Anash.

Shammah tried to catch Peleg's attention. There was no need. Peleg stared open-mouthed as the creatures flexed their bodies with a power that rocked the ground beneath them.

"You trespass in this city, Anash," the Four Faces said in unison.

"You're wrong. Aikah is dead," Anash shouted. "We kept the blood oath Aikah made with Livnath. We didn't attack the City of Kings. Now that he's dead, the city is ours. It is you who trespass!"

"Aikah killed the prophet in Nifla as Livnath demanded in her blood oath. But Aikah did not kill the prophet's son," the Four Faces said.

The hulking Anash trembled beneath the amber beads coating his body like tiny pearls. His eyes widened with horror as he stared at Shammah, who fought to stand.

"Shammah's father, the prophet, held the power of Aleph to defeat you, and his son possesses that same power—in greater measure. Because of this, you trespass."

One of Shammah's shoulders slumped, yet he mustered the strength to say, "Relinquish the city."

The Four Faces brightened at his words and sang:

> *For destiny we serve,*
>
> *For life we die,*
>
> *For thee, we seek.*

The singing emboldened Shammah, but Dahv longed to place his hands over his ears because the melody sung by the four figures ripped through his body.

The Four Faces rose into the air, surrounding Shammah before they disappeared in a funnel of air.

Howling, Anash scurried on the ground, barking. The drops covering his body like a glistening cloak extinguished the embers of his body and caused Anash to groan.

"I'm pierced with swords!" he yelled to his warriors, reaching out a hand to them.

The warriors, themselves covered in the bits of amber, looked at him with horror and fled.

Anash crawled to Dahv, who couldn't move to help him. The Mikana commander then climbed the palace steps to Qayin and Haran near the throne. He burst into a puddle before them, and the hypnotic power he used to subdue the three men broke.

Haran fell to his knees. "Livnath, Livnath, Livnath…"

Dahv longed to kick him. *Haran had a chance to escape, and he was just moaning,* Dahv thought. He started to utter a reproof, but neither could Haran's own subordinate, embarrassed by the high priest's weakness, bear it.

"Be quiet, old man!" Qayin screamed.

Dahv and Qayin fled from the platform. After hesitating for a few seconds, Haran, too, ran.

Chazon and Tamiym's chariots, shielded by clouds, landed near the spot where Shammah collapsed, unconscious. Blood trailed from his neck, and he lay on the ground, heaving. Tamiym witnessed Shammah's courage while Aleph suspended her chariot over the city. *He must not die. Not again.*

"He will live," Chazon said.

"But why did we wait in our sky chariots?" she asked. "The whole point was for us to attack. What if we could have saved him from this?"

"Rest your mind, Tamiym. Focus on caring for him now."

Zaqen assigned several of his soldiers to help carry the wounded savior-king to the Gardens of Destiny. Tamiym had never been inside them, but she knew how their fragrance scented the northern boundaries of the City of Kings.

Shammah had loved the gardens; they were the haven where he had lived most of his life as the king's heir.

Tamiym shuddered at how he would react to the scorched foliage. She felt a bittersweet closeness to him as they placed his soaking body on the bed, and she couldn't keep from murmuring in anxiety when she and Chazon tended blistered patches on Shammah's hands and chest where Anash's heat had broiled his skin.

"He will live, Tamiym," Chazon repeated when the finished cleaning his body and caring for his wounds.

Zaqen's men freed Eitan, Asahel, Javan, and Peleg. They regained their weapons and went after Dahv and the priests. Zaqen commanded his troops to round up remaining Mikana who clung to the walls and stomped through the city and slew them with swords.

When the last of the Mikana perished within the City of Kings, the golden pens disappeared. Shouts erupted from the liberated citizens.

Zaqen's men escorted the people from the holding areas and cared for them. People accepted fresh food and water with gratitude.

The commander's face softened when he arrived at the area where a young woman had lost her infant son when the strange darkness fell on the city. His men had told him that the baby had ached for milk for days. The starving mother couldn't feed him because the Mikana had suspended their rations.

"What is your name?" Zaqen asked to the woman who sat on a stool, holding her baby wrapped in rags, and caressing her dirty hair.

"Geona," she said.

CHAPTER THIRTY-TWO

THE GATE OF ALEPH

Twelve days after facing the Mikana, Shammah's fever broke. He rubbed his fingers against his jaw; his nostrils still burned with the musty stench of fire. From where he lay on the couch, he could see the decimated Gardens of Destiny below. Flames had shredded the abundant foliage into charred stumps. He blinked away tears.

Across the room, Tamiym poured water into a cup. Chazon had once tutored him in these quarters. Year after year, Shammah pored over tablets, asked questions, posed theories, and dreamed. The one person who treasured that kind of mortal life was caring for him, wearing that thoughtful expression that welcomed him with more warmth than a procession of kings.

Tamiym turned toward the bed. "My lord, you are awake," she said, coming to his side. She sat down on a stool.

He grasped her hand, his eyes pleading. "Was the city saved?"

"Your plan worked. The Mikana are destroyed. Unfortunately, your healing took a long time. Chazon created a concoction to heal the burns and another one to remove the poison."

Shammah frowned. "Poison?"

"The blades they used on your neck bore a strange substance. Chazon sat for hours seeking Aleph for the remedy."

"In my dreams, I tried to overcome the enemy, but could not."

"But that's not truth. You did," Tamiym reassured him. "Your words held power. You kept saying, 'Relinquish the city,' and they did."

"Of course, the Four Faces were extremely helpful," he said in a dry tone as Chazon entered the room.

"Aleph chooses the highest moment of battle to issue the greatest of aid," Chazon said, his face the calmest Shammah had ever seen it. Shammah wondered whether he had a glimpse. of the young Chazon before the turbulent decades with Aikah.

"Is that the Shamgar at the door?" Shammah asked.

"Yes, my lord," Tamiym replied. "We asked them to return once we secured the City of Kings and Chaniya. As you anticipated, Commander Mattan's men did see a skirmish with the Rabbah and the Emit."

Shammah sat up from the pillows and faced Tamiym. "But all is well? Are the queen and your family safe? If my soldiers left them vulnerable, they are accountable to me."

"They are all safe," she said, her hand tightening on his.

He slipped back into the pillows. "At last, I know what you meant about something else," Shammah said to Chazon.

Chazon chuckled. "Which lesson are you referring to?"

"You often said, 'When you understand who you are, you will turn away from the roads that do not reach the gate of Aleph.'"

Chazon sat on a nearby bench and hung his head for moments before saying, "Now is the time."

"What do you mean?" Shammah asked.

"My lord, I have concealed something from you. I hope you understand my reasons," Chazon said. "I knew your father; he was a prophet of Aleph. I don't know if you heard the Four Faces say this to Anash during the battle. According to Eitan, they revealed what I kept from you."

He took a deep breath. "When I heard Aikah had murdered your father as a blood oath to Livnath—to ensure his right to the throne—in secret I encouraged Gila to keep you when Aikah brought you to the palace. Aikah didn't deserve any gifts from her because of his harsh treatment, but she agreed. In the end, you became a gift to us all."

Shammah refused to release Tamiym's hand, although she attempted to excuse herself.

"My father was a prophet of Aleph," Shammah said. "And I was the son who rebelled against the gods, even the Existing One."

"Yes," Chazon said. "He was known in Nifla for his devotion to the Existing One. He spoke with an authority that angered the star-born, who manipulated Aikah into taking his life. What the star-born didn't know was that Aleph would use that tragedy to make the prophet's son Seth's savior-king."

"Why was this hidden from me? It would have explained so many things. And what I saw on Aleph would have made sense. Why…?" Shammah asked. "You should have told me my ancestry decades ago. What happened to my mother?"

"She was also my friend. She died in Nifla after sickness hit the city, but she lived many years in peace knowing I cared for you in the palace," Chazon said. "The wisdom of Aleph was that you would discover the truth by living it."

"Did King Aikah know about Aleph's intentions?" Shammah asked.

"Perhaps he only knew what I told him."

"But if you weren't at the battle in Nifla, how do you know why he chose me?"

"Aikah spoke of this to you at his death. He wanted to place someone on the throne untouched by the Zuzim curse. Most of all, you touched his heart," the priest said, wiping his face.

"He attributed this to Livnath, but it was the will of Aleph," Chazon continued. "The Existing One can work through all men. Even a savior-king who bent his knees to Livnath."

Both of Shammah's hands now cupped Tamiym's. Holding onto Tamiym helped him steady himself in this new place; the place where he would have to rule; a place of false and unknown fathers.

He forced himself to speak. "I also dreamed of Mount Aleph, that it was no longer dark and hidden, that it was bright as midday, filled with huge flowers—a garden opening its gates in the West. Strange words. I cannot determine their meaning."

Shammah gazed at Tamiym. "Is it an excerpt from some epic or poem, Tamiym? I thought you would know," he continued. "I have spent more time learning astronomy and architecture. Is it an obscure line in an epic?"

Tamiym released her hands and moved away from the king. "Peleg wanted to visit you when you rose," she said. "And Commander Eitan."

"We were not discussing Peleg or the commander," Shammah said. "What is wrong? Tell me."

"Peleg is eager to see you. But you can eat first."

"Are you offended because I asked you about epics?"

"Not at all," she said. "The kingdom has waited many days for you to awake."

Tamiym locked the door to her thoughts again, but Shammah was confused as to why.

"Your answer evades me, and you know it," Shammah said. "We will revisit my question later. I will not forget."

"We must get you food," Tamiym said in a stiff voice. He arched an eyebrow in rebuke and rose from where he lay. The thought of eating made him feel as if he were riding the seas without a vessel.

Peleg entered the room. "The dead return, but you bear the face of the grave."

"Tell me a mystery. Not what I already know," Shammah said as he stumbled to the doorway.

Tamiym and Peleg both rushed to support him. The king allowed them to assist him, but the grimace on his face revealed his desire for independence. They helped him walk to the other side of the palace where Eitan and Asahel waited. But with every step, the king became more irritated.

He grumbled orders at Peleg and glowered at Tamiym. The Shamgar and Chazon followed.

"Maybe he's pretending to be ill," Tamiym murmured to Peleg.

"Or maybe his blood was mixed with the Mikana's," Peleg said. "The blades they used to prick his neck they probably dipped in Mikana mouth foam."

"Maybe he imitates Aikah on one of his sweeter days," Chazon said.

"Enough!" Shammah said, pulling away from them and going alone into the courtyard where Eitan and Asahel sat. They expressed surprise when Shammah wobbled toward them. Tamiym and Peleg found him a place to stand because Shammah refused to sit.

"More war is to come," Eitan said.

"What is happening?" Shammah asked, leaning on a stone courtyard pillar.

"Dahv and Qayin the priest are infected with the curse that killed King Aikah," the commander said.

"Dahv inherited it from Aikah," Chazon said. "But how was Qayin exposed? Did he follow me into the tomb after we disposed of the king's body? Even the ashes the Shamgar and I buried had the power to kill. The scent was that potent. The Existing One's mercy protected us."

Eitan chewed his lip. "I'm not sure how…"

"I shouldn't be surprised; I sensed the presence of the curse when we overtook the city," Chazon said. "That explains why Anash held them without outright killing them. Death already marked them."

"What else?" Shammah asked.

"Qayin thought he was immune to the curse because he made an agreement with the Mikana and the Zuzim before your coronation," Eitan said. "It seems the priest offered you up in exchange for kingship for Dahv."

"How do you know all this?" Shammah asked.

"Our men found a wild-eyed slave," Eitan said.

"Dathan," Chazon said. "Aikah's scribe."

"Yes," Eitan continued. "According to him, he was present when Qayin met with the Mikana. We're holding him because I think he knows more."

"He does," Chazon said.

"Did Dahv make an agreement with the Mikana?" Shammah asked.

Eitan paused. "He had reason, but I don't know that for sure. We do know from the soldiers who were in the city that Commander Lehabim bribed many soldiers in a conspiracy to make Dahv king. For all that treachery, Dahv rewarded Lehabim with death."

"Did Dahv feel that Lehabim betrayed him?" Asahel asked. "Soldiers from the City of Kings say the two men were once inseparable."

"The Mikana drugged Dahv and ordered him to slay Commander Lehabim," Eitan said. "Unfortunately, we don't know more. We learned from Dathan that the Zuzim spirited Dahv, Qayin, and Haran away from our prison."

Eron wept with his wife, Geona. He caressed her hands, muttering thanks to Livnath that she and Hada had survived. He bowed his head when she explained what happened to their son.

Shadows creased her face from the ordeal. She had survived, but she had suffered. "He was such a little thing, and I was not getting enough food to keep him fed."

"My love, my brave one, you showered him with affection during every moment of his life. You and Hada are with me."

He motioned to the child who stood away from them, twisting the edges of her robe as if she no longer knew her place.

"Hada, I am proud of you, too," Eron said, stroking strands of her golden hair. "You helped your mother and cared for your brother."

She clung to his leg. "Can we return home now?"

"Our house is gone, Hada. The city needs to build everything again. We go to our family."

"To my brother's farm," Geona said.

Artisans throughout Seth came to the City of Kings to rebuild. Nobles and merchants reclaimed their property, but Shammah issued an order prohibiting them from practicing the usury that was once common in the city. Seth's priests couldn't impose temple taxes on those who didn't worship at Livnath's temple or shrines, but they could charge whatever they liked for goods they sold.

Shammah sensed the outrage among the priests, but they kept quiet, grateful they still possessed wealth and resentful that they almost lost it all.

The followers of Livnath installed a new high priest as they built a small temple on a ridge. The structure wasn't as lavish as its predecessor and fewer people worshipped there.

As Shammah toured the reconstruction areas one afternoon with Mahalath, a cluster of priests nodded as they traded in the market. They didn't engage the king in any deeper conversation, and Shammah felt their brooding irritation about the changes he'd made.

"It will take time to win them over, my lord," Mahalath said.

"Perhaps," Shammah replied. "I have not wooed them by my choices since I became king."

Mahalath lifted her curls to cool her neck. "You have changed protocol, my lord. No other king has dedicated his reign to Aleph. Or to the City of Kings. Your name will stand out on the Ten Pillars in the Gardens of Destiny."

"Then they must respect the throne or face the consequences of rebelling against it."

They passed laborers lifting stones from a caravan. Then, just beyond the Gardens of Destiny where the slaves cleared a canal, a new building made from cedar wood emerged.

"What will it be?" Mahalath asked.

"A royal library, for the people," Shammah said. He hoped the project would ignite warmth between them; he hoped she would be like Tamiym and embrace the idea of bringing literacy to those who longed to read and learn Seth's histories.

"What a generous gesture for the nobility. However, we have recovered many of our private collections, so there is no need for this," Mahalath said.

"The library is not for the nobles alone. In this place, everyone can gain understanding."

"Seth will rebuild itself, in time. Shouldn't we preserve our resources so that no one lacks what they need?"

Shammah cleared his throat. "False foundations weaken and fall. Should we preserve the nobility and allow everyone else to perish?"

"Of course. We should not," she said.

When they climbed the steps of the new building, Tamiym was coming from the entrance with one of the craftsmen.

"My lord, Lady Mahalath," Tamiym said, bowing with the craftsman, a portly man with freckles.

"Welcome," the craftsman said.

Fine dust flecked Tamiym's shiny hair. Shammah imagined her trailing the builder throughout the structure. *How beautiful she looks.*

"We were talking about the angles of the ceiling," Tamiym said, brushing her garments. "I think you will approve of what the workers have completed, my lord."

"I wanted Lady Mahalath to see our progress," Shammah said. He turned to Mahalath, who scanned the structure. "Is it not splendid?"

Mahalath smiled at him but said nothing. *Well, at least she offered me that,* Shammah thought. The small building was his first civic contribution as king.

The craftsman caught sight of a worker mishandling a load of cedar.

"Stop!" the craftsman said, nearly dropping a tablet in his hand.

He bowed before Shammah and Mahalath. "My king, my lady, please excuse me."

"Of course," Shammah said as the builder left them, bellowing at the worker as he walked.

"An outstanding library," Mahalath said to Shammah before turning to Tamiym. Shammah exhaled as she spoke at last. *Will she commend the work of Tamiym and the craftsman?*

"How many rooms and tablets will it hold?" Mahalath asked.

"Hundreds, my lady," Tamiym said. "It will contain legal contracts, royal decrees, and epics. This building will also inspire the poets. How can they resist the chance for their words to be unforgotten, speaking still beneath the dust of time?"

"There is nothing like being remembered," Mahalath said. "Forgive me, please, for not formally meeting you in Arba, Lady Tamiym. I appreciate your efforts to save us from the Zuzim. I didn't know you also were helping the king with the building."

"It has been an honor to be a part of the planning these past months," Tamiym said. "The craftsman is unruly but gifted. He naps to receive inspiration during the day, and that slows down the work."

She and Shammah shared a grin.

"Lady Tamiym is being diplomatic," he said to Mahalath. "The lead craftsman needs to be housed in the desert, but he does construct beautiful buildings."

"How extraordinary that Lady Tamiym is involved," Mahalath said to Shammah. "Our code reserves these duties for men."

"They are. You and I both know that tradition limits the opportunities of women. The king gave me special dispensation, I think, because of my interest in Seth's histories. Scholars from Chaniya are a demanding breed."

Tamiym paused. Shammah frowned. His indecision about his obligation to Mahalath and his feelings for Tamiym had led to this difficult moment unwinding out of his control.

"My lord, if you don't mind, I will rejoin the workers," Tamiym said, recovering. "I want to prepare that information for you regarding the ceilings."

She bowed to him and then to Mahalath. "My lady, I am glad to find you well after your ordeal," Tamiym said.

"More than anyone could imagine," Mahalath said.

Tamiym continued down the steps toward the lead craftsman. Together, they circled to the rear of the building. The craftsman waved his arms with excitement as he walked with Tamiym, and Shammah saw her nodding in approval. The king watched them as long as he could, wishing he strolled beside them.

"Indeed, it is a fine building," Mahalath said, nestling her arm in his.

He patted her arm and took her inside. Words refused to spring from his mouth because every thought within him dried up, forsaken leaves that perished in a drought.

CHAPTER THIRTY-THREE

THE EMMER FIELD

Shammah watched slaves capturing quail with nets in the Gardens of Destiny. He felt just as trapped and remembered the dove in Midvar long ago, unable to settle on the wall. The king buried the thought when he glanced at Gila and Chazon, who sat nearby on a bench, waiting for a moment to ensnare him with their words.

"You are not obligated to her," Gila said. "The betrothal need not stand. The dead cannot enforce it. Aikah commanded you to marry her for his own interests. Her parents are rebuilding and are grateful to be alive. They will not demand we keep this misbegotten pledge."

Shammah placed his hands behind his back. The oath deserved honor.

"My father gave his word. I must keep it," he said.

"What about Tamiym?" Chazon asked.

"Obligations do not fulfill my desires."

"Anxiety attacks me when I am near Mahalath," Gila said. "She does not mourn her ordeal with the Zuzim like the other women. What are her allegiances? She stays to herself although her family is free—as if she meditates before Livnath without stopping. And yet she is not a priestess."

"War with the Mikana hurt her," Shammah explained. "She didn't want to leave her family when the Mikana attacked. Dahv forced her to evacuate. She is an aristocrat trained to be the king's wife. I do not expect her to feel the pain of the poor or of war. Her parents prepared her for excessive privilege."

"She has bewitched you with the cloying arms of guilt," Chazon said. "What is more, her blind privilege guarantees chaos."

"Is this happiness for you, Shammah?" Gila asked. "You have whittled the wedding feast down to nothing on the pretext that the city is recovering. What the country needs is a flash of joy. You care nothing for this union, and it manifests in the shadows on your face. We know it troubles you. Everyone knows. You haven't set an actual date for the feast. You have procrastinated speaking with Tamiym directly. Must we say what you refuse to accept?"

Shammah paced in irritation. "You both overstep."

"My king," Chazon said. "Lady Tamiym left this morning. She predicted you would keep stalling on the wedding feast as long as she remained. She felt now was a good time to return home because the workers have nearly finished the new library."

Tamiym stopped her horse near the emmer field. She told the soldiers Eitan assigned to her to camp for the night. It was a only day's journey from home, but the bittersweet allure of the field she and her father had noticed en route to the City of Kings was difficult to resist. She also wanted time to wrestle with her thoughts alone before facing the scrutiny of her parents, especially her mother's discerning questions.

Tamiym walked alone in the field. The crops weren't fully ready for harvesting. About a year ago, everything started here—when she and her father had met Shammah and Peleg on the road. She remembered the hooded men, and how their words stirred her. That poem she heard that day settled over her heart like a hand that wouldn't release her:

Sing now,

Sing again.

A garden opens its gates in the West.

Shammah had used those exact words when he had awakened after the fall of the Mikana, and she couldn't bear the sound of them from his lips. She felt wooed and unfulfilled, loved and rejected. As she stood there, Shammah strode through the field toward her. The Shamgar stood out of earshot from them, talking with the soldiers who had accompanied her.

"Tamiym."

"Why are you here?" Tamiym asked.

He moved closer. "I rode from the city when I heard you left."

Remembering her place, she bowed before him. "Please, you should not do that. The Shamgar are better occupied guarding you in the city than searching for me."

"What were the words again? A garden opens its gates in the West.' What do they mean?"

She wouldn't see him again, so she didn't evade the truth this time. "The words are lines from a poem I heard in this field as Father and I rode toward the City of Kings. I heard the words as four hooded men stood in the field. They were as tall as trees. I do not know how you knew the words. I do not understand how I heard them. All I know is that I heard them shortly before meeting you."

"The Four Faces," Shammah said. "It must have been them you saw. They left me before that. I wonder if they were announcing our destiny. Our lives flow together like a rushing river, Tamiym."

He shifted toward her again and inhaled deeply. "Tamiym, I do not talk with you as the savior-king and the Proud Lord of the Seven Gates, but as your friend. We have seen war together. You fed me soup."

"But you are the king."

"I could not have won a victory without you. You are a woman of more worth than my armies. You represent the heart of our country."

"My lord, thank you, but I read too many epics," Tamiym said, shrugging. "I imitate them in life. I also want to please my father. He wanted a firstborn son. My mother bore me."

Tamiym felt as she did that night when he burst from the sky, making her giddy that he hadn't perished at the coronation. Every part of her wanted to weep on his shoulder.

She bit her lip, sensing Shammah's longing, and remembering Truth, the child of Aleph who guarded her. She wished Truth could grip her hand now because the knowledge that Shammah cared for her was too much to bear.

"I have much to say," Shammah said. "My heart bubbles with words, but my lips stumble to utter them."

"You cannot say them."

"I have responsibilities," Shammah said. "Please forgive me for my indecision in carrying them out. I had hoped…"

He ran his fingers through his heavy coils of hair, and Tamiym wanted to entwine her hands with his. To distract herself, she focused on a stray blade of grass on her robes.

"Thank you for the adventure, my lord," she said. "Every woman in Seth envies me. Maybe the elders in Chaniya will let me teach at the school, and maybe I will agree."

"Tamiym…"

Stop saying my name. While his drawn face implored her, Tamiym stepped backward because she refused to throw herself on his chest, although she longed for the comfort she would find there.

"Honor is the responsibility of privileged men, but it can curse their dreams," Tamiym said.

She bowed again, hoping Aleph would block Shammah from seeing her tears. She wanted to mourn alone.

No longer tentative, Shammah reached for her.

"Tamiym," he said in her ear. He kissed her braided hair, her cheek.

"How I have waited to hold you," he said. "Did you not know it? All I have wanted to do is to keep my word to my father and marry Mahalath. But that word crushes me like stones every time I see you. I am in bondage. I am in love."

She thought of Truth again. She rebelled. She resisted. It was she who enraptured the king, not Mahalath; a daughter of Chaniya, a poor man's surrogate son, was the king's beloved, and she should take her place.

Gasping for air, Tamiym pulled away from Shammah. At that moment, as painful as it was, she felt nearer to Aleph.

"Every happiness, my lord." Her voice broke.

"You love me," he said. "Why leave?"

Tamiym felt her heart burst in pieces across the emmer field. "The code allows the king to have a queen as well as concubines, but I cannot be that for you, my lord. And I respect your willingness to uphold your father's wishes. I must return home."

"Did you think I would ask you to be my concubine?" Shammah thundered, causing the horses to stir. Startled, Shamgar and the soldiers walked farther away.

"That is not how I feel about you. I am King Aikah's adopted son, but I do not follow his corruption."

"But he obligated you to Lady Mahalath, so do not express your feelings." Breathlessness rose within Tamiym. "Let us be friends who can remember that we fought together."

Shammah's face stiffened. Tamiym felt his love and his anger and his pride warring within him. She chose harshness, denying water to the flowering affection between them.

"The king cannot alter the path his dead, short-sighted father has set before him, can he?"

CHAPTER THIRTY-FOUR

BROKEN VOWS

Rina adorned Mahalath's body with powders and her lips with henna. Since the fall of Seth, Rina a growing, mysterious rift with her sister. Mahalath was attentive, and she claimed no offense against Rina, but she was a lyre without strings.

The war had sobered their parents, and caused Rina to drop most of her frivolity, and they were rebounding from their losses. But Mahalath shut herself up, a barricaded wall no one could trespass. Rina longed to know how her sister had sustained the will to survive when she was with the Zuzim. The thought of enduring abduction by the star-born filled her with terror; Mahalath's courage filled her with admiration. But Mahalath, polite and reserved, resisted every effort from Rina to learn more.

She wasn't helping her sister now, either. When Rina suggested the pink and blue robes her sister once adored to enhance her dusky skin, Mahalath instead selected robes of gold embroidered with purple flowers. Rina didn't know where she had purchased the garment—it did not look like the clothing of Seth. When Rina tried to braid her hair, Mahalath chose to do it, keeping it piled on her head in the style she had worn since being rescued from the Zuzim.

Instead of a demure bride, Shammah would receive an audacious one.

"You don't have to marry him," Rina offered. "You wanted Dahv."

"Dahv isn't king. Dahv is gone," Mahalath said. "Lord Shammah is my betrothed. He honors me by keeping the promise of King Aikah."

"But things have changed. Father is taking us to the south. Why not come with us and start over? You love the sea."

"That is not important now."

Rina's voice rose. "Why is it not? Why do we not talk anymore? I speak to a shell."

"I am the same."

Rina felt the coldness and surrendered to it at last.

Mahalath was dressed when a slave brought the royal wedding pendant of lapis lazuli encircled by gold. According to kingdom tradition in Seth, the bride received the jewel before the feast, the culmination of the bridal ceremony. The Mikana hadn't pillaged the treasures that had been stored below the palace when they sacked the city.

Glittering in the sunlight that flooded the queen's chambers, the stone, a metaphor of a city starting again, didn't attract Mahalath's attention like the braids and curls she tucked in place.

Rina urged her to notice the pendant. "Mahalath, you are favored. The jewel is without peer. Queens have received it since the founding of the City of Kings. How proud our ancestors would be!"

"It is a wonderful gift to cherish," Mahalath said, twirling locks of hair before leaving the room.

Mahalath knew she had deflated her sister's spirits, but it didn't matter. She entered the makeshift room created for the occasion, far from the elaborate feasts conducted for generations in Seth.

Nobles, lacking much of their traditional finery, mingled with merchants, laborers, farmers, and slaves. People poured into the room through the courtyard.

Shammah insisted the feast be open to any survivor in the city who wanted to witness a formal return to Seth's social order. As Mahalath walked toward the platform where Shammah and Chazon stood, the crowd cheered and bowed.

When Mahalath reached Chazon, he appeared more an officiator at a royal burial than a priest about to perform the king's wedding. His brows clustered like storm clouds.

Shammah appeared stunning in blue and white robes lined with silver. Friendship warmed his face as Mahalath walked toward him.

Mahalath found the practice of arranged marriages and women's roles backward, and she had often challenged her father on it. He indulged her debates, but they all knew he supported upholding the tradition. Livnath may be the country's patroness, but men ruled Seth.

Mahalath smiled at her father as she passed him and walked toward the king. Perhaps how he and other men viewed women was about to change.

She held out her hand to Shammah and parted her lips seductively. The king fumbled to grasp her fingers, and she sensed his confusion. She was revealing a Mahalath no one knew.

Peleg tapped his dagger. He felt the urge to cut someone's throat. Nothing was right. Shammah longed for Tamiym, Peleg knew, but felt obligated to Mahalath, who, in her tawdry robes, appeared ready to hound the seaports.

The Shamgar, Eitan, Asahel, and Mattan wore shuttered expressions as they observed the marriage ritual, but Peleg refused.

His sour face shouted his rejection of Mahalath as queen. In the streets of the City of Kings, people didn't sidestep the truth.

Chazon was grimmer than ever, and Peleg was glad that at least the priest wasn't pretending.

"To all of Seth: Welcome to the union of King Shammah and his long betrothed, Lady Mahalath," Chazon said. "This was the wish of King Aikah. Lord Shammah honors his father's will, and we declare it so."

Chazon finished with a stumble as if gravel roughened his tongue. "Do you pledge to honor each other in fidelity, in happiness, in trouble, in death?"

"I pledge to honor, by the power of the Existing One at Aleph." Shammah said.

Shammah sounded more thrilled when he described the city's irrigation channels, Peleg thought.

"I pledge to honor," Mahalath replied.

"Seth, behold the Proud Lord of the Seven Gates and his queen," Chazon said.

Shammah's lips grazed Mahalath's cheek. She kissed him with a touch of wildness. Peleg almost roared when Shammah snapped back from her, angry fire igniting his face.

But the ceremony wasn't over. Rina came forward, and Shammah retrieved the wedding pendant from the pillow she held. He placed the pendant around Mahalath's neck and led her into another courtyard for a simple meal of soups, smoked meats, and bread.

The new queen bobbed her head and guffawed as she chatted with guests. Peleg sensed Shammah's annoyance. He winced when slaves served the soup, and Peleg snorted from his place at the table. He suspected Shammah remembered Tamiym's ritual of serving him soup during their journey.

Peleg gulped when Mahalath's robe slipped from her right shoulder. Both of her shoulders were now bare. The robe hung above her bosom, and Mahalath eyed it, but did nothing.

When he saw her dangling robes, Shammah moved toward her protectively. As he did, a twisting snake emerged on Mahalath's right arm.

"What is that?" Shammah demanded.

"A gift from Livnath," she said.

"It moves. What night arts are these? What oath did you make with the goddess?" Shammah shouted, overturning cups and plates as he rose.

Peleg stood with him as the room grew still. Chazon, who was speaking with Eitan, Mattan, and Asahel, turned with alarm.

"Does it matter?" Mahalath asked.

Shammah grasped her arms.

"Do not touch me!"

"Were you marked by the Zuzim?"

Mahalath untangled herself from Shammah. Then she shook her head, and her braids and curls became undone. Tiny crystals twinkled at the crown.

"I made a blood oath with Livnath, for your return. To be your wife," Mahalath said. "In exchange, I became the perfect bride for the Zuzim. In my womb, Husband, is Zuzim seed. A descendant of the star-born will come from this body and sit on this throne now that I am queen."

Queen Gila cried out and stepped toward her. She pulled out her dagger. "Beast! Come down! You betrayed all of Seth."

Mahalath caressed her stomach. "Hush, hag. I bear the son you never could bring your king."

The throbbing serpent slithered from Mahalath's arm and increased in size. Peleg climbed over a few nobles, ready to defend his friend.

The Shamgar reached Shammah first as the serpent lunged with viciousness at the king. The serpent dodged the Shamgar, then entwined Mahalath until she disappeared. The creature flung itself on the floor, slithered to the balcony, and vanished.

"She will not be found," Chazon said to Shammah. "The night arts have captured Mahalath."

A crashing, stomping sound roared from the city. Peleg edged closer to Shammah, along with the Shamgar. Asahel, Eitan, and Mattan ran to discover the cause.

Chazon rushed to the balcony. "My king! Look!"

The giant statue of Livnath emerged from the wreckage of the temple tower, which had remained in ruins from the rampage of the Mikana. As the statue strode from the city, it reassembled its singed and broken body, while crashing through walls and slinging bricks. A few priests shrieked and waved their arms at the statue, whose eyes were molten black.

Peleg, who had learned devotion to the goddess as a child scrambling for life in the City of Kings, was dumbfounded that Livnath was abandoning the city. Her statue, animated with life, marched toward the City of Knowledge. Wound around her throat as a necklace was the serpent from Mahalath's arm.

Peleg whispered as they stood on the balcony. "This is her city. Who will protect us now?"

He glanced at Shammah, who gripped the balcony rail, his face rigid. Peleg felt ashamed. Not only had Livnath thrown the City of Kings into confusion, Shammah's betrothed had humiliated him.

"I'm sorry, my lord," Peleg said.

He paused. "Mahalath committed a horrific act. Perhaps she has also favored the king by freeing him from an equally horrible marriage contract."

Asahel, Eitan, and Mattan returned and told Shammah that palace slaves said the statue of Livnath in Aikah's palace shrine lay face down on the floor, in pieces.

"War will return to Seth one day as Livnath tries to reclaim her sacred city," Mattan said. "We thought we knew war before, but to have battles with all the star-born and their offspring attacking Seth will test our ability to follow the will of Aleph."

Peleg shuddered. More battles with the star-born? He had hoped Shammah's reign would inaugurate lasting peace; he had planned to use his earnings to buy property in the City of Kings, but he wondered now if he would ever get the chance to settle down and become a respectable merchant in the city where he once lived like a thief.

"Mahalath's child gives her every reason to think she can reclaim the throne," Chazon said to Shammah, who appeared numb.

Mahalath's mother Mara, who stood within earshot, collapsed. E-ven rushed to pick her up as their daughter Rina rocked herself in grief. Peleg couldn't imagine how agonized they must feel.

After guiding Mara to a seat, E-ven approached Shammah and bowed. His face was ashen.

"My king, I confess the transgressions of my daughter for violating the marriage contract," the noble said. "I confess my blindness, my ignorance, and my refusal to see how she had changed. I was too proud to see the clues. We will return the forty shekels of silver King Aikah gave us for the bride price and the gifts you gave for the day of your marriage."

"There is no need," Shammah said, gripping the man's slumping shoulders.

"The throne and the council agreed to annul the marriage, Tamiym," Abelia said as they prepared dinner in the courtyard of their home in Chaniya. Desert breezes tossed their hair, and Tamiym tried to lose herself in the breezes, but her mother insisted on discussing Shammah.

"True," Tamiym agreed. "But that has nothing to do with me. Six months have passed since the wedding. He has not come to me, so his feelings must have changed. Kings do that, you know. His father proved himself unpredictable. King Aikah could show rare kindness and within hours become brutal."

"This sounds like the Tamiym who had never seen war and only read about it on tablets," Abelia said. "Is bitterness all you gained from your adventure?"

"It did not end well. Besides, you and Father sometimes make me joyous to be unwed." Tamiym placed a bowl on the table with such force that it almost tumbled to the floor.

Gently, Abelia motioned for her to sit down on a stool. "Tamiym, your father and I love each other; remember that. The difficult times become our chances to cultivate that love. We have argued about how we will sustain our family. We have had days when I wish he would journey to the desert and take you and the boys with him and allow me to rest. But do I still love him? I do. Are we not together? We are. And are we in covenant with each other and our children? He is. I am. Either allow love to be seasoned by trouble or destroyed by it."

"You are wise, Mother. For the circumstances you and Father's endure. Mine are incredible."

Abelia placed an arm around her daughter's rigid soldiers. "Tamiym, do not let hopelessness close your heart to your future, or even your expectation of it. Lord Shammah stirs springs of joy within you. I am a witness."

"Springs?"

"Yes, springs of tenderness once buried beneath tablets and shadowed by solitude. Lord Shammah has a way of unveiling your beauty so that you—and the world—can see it," Abelia said. "And you do the same for him. He may not know it, but he will not reign at full strength until you are his queen."

Ciycera waited for the Zuzim in the Aijalon Valley. A caravan appeared out of nowhere on the southern plain below the Tiras Mountains. The Zuzim arrived with their usual burst of flamboyance. Instead of avenging the deaths of their Mikana sons in the City of Kings, the Zuzim protected their interests. They took Dahv and the priests with them, but they were too late to rescue Commander Anash.

Ciycera scowled as he leaned on his beast. After the Mikana secured the City of Kings, Anash sent him to the mountains with a contingent of troops. Anash sought to revel alone in the Mikana victory. He also wanted warriors to relieve him if the siege didn't go according to plan. Anash's selfish ambition led to the Mikana's survival.

But the commander hadn't expected King Shammah and his companies to gut the City of Knowledge and destroy its treasures. Anash also hadn't expected to be defeated by the Four Faces from Aleph. Every single Mikana warrior perished, either by the will of the Four Faces or by the hands of Shammah's men.

The last of the Mikana now sought Ciycera's protection, including warriors, Mikana females, and their young. Ciycera and the remaining Mikana depended on their star-born parents. They needed them to prepare a refuge and help them rebuild.

Gold and green textiles flapped in the air as the caravan approached Ciycera and his company of about two thousand. The leader of the caravan brought his elephant up to Ciycera, his red hair loose; his ears pierced with huge, gold earrings; his robes a grassy shade of green.

"Lord Sa'ar," Ciycera said, as he stepped down from his beast and bowed.

"Commander."

"Our losses were many. We thank you for protecting our mutual interests."

Sa'ar lifted his fingers and snapped them as if pulling language from the air. "Our interests? Does the alliance between the Mikana and the Zuzim still hold? Your childish attack of the City of Kings served more ego than the interests of the Zuzim. A prophet-priest-king now rules Seth. He surprises us.

He fights the star-born with greater capabilities than our arch-enemy, Aikah, because the Four Faces align with him.

"I longed to witness Aikah defeated by our curse. I craved an opportunity to see him wander in the underworld. I now wish he ruled Seth again because he's a more satisfying competitor than his adopted heir. Fighting Livnath's slave was sport. Fighting a king of Aleph demands harsher measures. As you can see, Ciycera, we will have to revisit our relationship."

Ciycera bowed his head again, forcing rebellious thoughts from his mind in case Sa'ar could read them. The Zuzim were notorious for tormenting their offspring in that way. "My warriors and my people are at your service, my lord."

"We will summon you. We must rebuild a new army to terrorize this new king and his people. Until then, I will send my warriors to protect you."

FROM THE BEGINNING

E itan didn't know what Shammah had planned. The king had asked him to escort his mother back to her people in Everlasting. Eitan dreaded the assignment. If the king suspected how he felt about Gila, why did he ask the commander to accompany her? Did the king want him humiliated after decades of service to the throne? The queen never showed she cared for him. She greeted him with graciousness, but she never made an overture.

He longed for the return of those days in Chaniya when he could delight in her presence without her knowing. In Yaphah, he could try to forget her and resume his role as the detached commander, without spouse or child, but a father to two generations of soldiers.

Traveling with the queen, with no guise to hide his feelings, increased his misery. Love eluded Eitan, but it didn't have to destroy him.

On the day of their departure from the City of Kings, Eitan remained aloof but kind. It had been more than three years since Aikah's death, and Eitan knew Gila had loved him, despite his flaws and cruelty. She had come to Aikah as a young woman, and he was the only man she had known. In her older years, Eitan longed to surround her with peace.

When he helped Gila into her cart, she broke the silence. "Commander, is all well? Have we not become friends after all we have gone through together?"

"We have, my lady."

"Then why place distance between us?"

"No distance, my lady. Shall we go now?"

"Of course," Gila said.

Throughout their journey south to Everlasting, Eitan was quiet but courteous. Aleph showed him kindness; Gila didn't probe.

When they reached their destination and strolled the sand-dusted streets of Everlasting and passed the colorful porches that faced the sea, he savored the soothing pace of the city. It wasn't bustling and earthy like Yaphah, with its merchants and farmers crowding every corner.

Everlasting was a sailor's haven, filled with the squeals of gulls and the swirl of clear, peaceful waters. The queen's birth-place mirrored how Eitan saw Gila—constant and at rest.

No one survived from Gila's family line, but the owners of her ancestral land invited her to visit. Many residents recognized the queen and greeted her with affection. She touched everyone who wanted to be close to her.

They stayed in quarters near the Cove of Revealing. Every morning, she walked alone, and he followed at a short distance, allowing her privacy. He knew she was purging tragedies from long ago when she lost her parents, her brothers, her sister, and her way of life.

One morning, he brought salted fish and bread for them to eat at the shore. She broke her somber mood and shared a wide smile when he unpacked the meal from a roll of fabric.

Eitan couldn't savor the gesture because he felt clumsy. He had insisted on preparing the meal himself. Plain food was a feast for soldiers, but an unworthy meal for a queen.

"Commander, you honor me. We often ate like this as a family. We supped on the shore and then searched for dolphins dancing in the waters of the cove."

"Has remembering been too difficult?" Eitan asked.

She sank her heels into the sand. "At first. We were unhappy before Aikah and his men stormed the city. His arrival soured a life dissolving because of sickness and discord. My mother was dying. In his grief, my father became thoughtless and cruel.

"But it was so long ago, and Aleph has given me many gifts since then," Gila said. "Today I simply enjoy remembering my family in sweeter times. My sister would have loved Shammah. I long for him to marry in happiness."

Gila rose with the eagerness of a young girl bursting with an idea. "One request I do have. Would you take me to Mount Aleph? I do not fully understand, but I feel drawn to the Existing One. Maybe Aleph woos me because I sense the kindness my heart has yearned for so long."

Eitan smiled. His weary dove tasted joy.

When they reached Aleph, Gila knew the mountain stunned Eitan. Instead of the morose place he had described, almost in apology, before them stood a mountain of abundant lawns and multicolored blooms. Gila wanted to run from Eitan's side and slide barefoot into the grasses and nap among the flowers. She wanted to chase a dragonfly or admire the flight of a bird. Just as she shifted from Eitan's side, they spotted a hooded shepherd singing to his grazing sheep.

They approached the shepherd, and Eitan greeted him cordially. "My friend, may I ask you for insight?"

The shepherd leaned on his staff. Gila noticed his large, laborer hands. The shepherd also stood several inches above the tall Eitan. His skin glinted from light to darker shades as the sun darted between the clouds. Cheerful light swam in his eyes like swirling seas.

Gila glanced over at Eitan, who seemed intrigued by the same effect because he straightened his shoulders. Neither of them said a word about the shepherd's appearance, however. But, Gila observed, Eitan didn't reach for his sword.

"Ask me," the shepherd said.

"My home is in Yaphah. But I have battled in the recent war with the Mikana. I have not traveled to Aleph for nearly three years. I feel lost in my region. What altered this mountain?"

"Everyone wants to know," the shepherd said. "One night at sundown, lightning struck the peak. Thunder rolled, rattling the heavens, and the Earth shook. Some shepherds thought the Earth opened its mouth. The next morning, the shepherds saw this peaceful place. It is like a garden opening its gates in the West, is it not?"

"How long ago was that?" Eitan asked.

"Everyone asks that question, too. Some calculate that it happened when the Mikana fell to King Shammah."

"Why was Aleph affected by that?" Gila asked, slipping her hand into Eitan's.

The shepherd smiled as she grasped Eitan's fingers. "Aleph rejoices when false thrones fall."

He waved at Eitan and Gila and sang to the lambs that wobbled behind him as he strode upward on the mountain. Then the shepherd sang:

For destiny we serve,

For life we die,

For thee, we seek.

Eitan cocked his head at the words. "I have heard that melody before. Where was it?"

"Perhaps during your travels?" Gila said.

"I am a babe trying to sing his father's lullaby," Eitan said. "I wish I could remember. I should remember."

"I am glad that the first time I saw Aleph, it was like this," Gila murmured to Eitan. "I envy the sheep. They meander in a place that bears no heaviness."

"When will you go to her?" Chazon asked. "Another young man, who knows how to seize the opportunity to woo her, may be vying for Tamiym's attention."

Shammah studied a pile of tablets. "My responsibility is to rebuild the City of Kings. I have filled the library with architectural drawings of the elaborate city Aikah envisioned."

Chazon groaned. "You are rebuilding, yes. But Aleph resurrected the city from the flames of the Mikana. It is no longer Aikah's city to rule. It is yours."

Shammah pulled out a tablet. "I also want to be certain Mahalath does not return. Her presence must not affect

Tamiym's life with me. Tamiym deserves more than the spectacle and shame Mahalath brings through her allegiance to Livnath and the Zuzim."

"Mahalath's whereabouts will haunt you until you face her again," Chazon said. "And you will face her again. My guess is that she lives with the Zuzim and the Water People, as are Dahv, Qayin, and Haran."

"I have suspected the same," Shammah said. "Livnath seeks to resume her reign as the patron goddess of Seth and seeks allies. My allegiance to the Existing One at Aleph disrupts her control."

"But until she rises up against Seth—and she will—you must move forward," Chazon said. "Stagnation does not please Aleph. Begin your life as king and rule with Tamiym. The people of Seth need the stability of your union. They need to know that you fully possess the Seven Gates of the kingdom. Most of all, you need her."

Shammah folded his arms. "Always the tutor."

Chazon bowed. "Always the friend."

Shammah waited until twilight. Tamiym was in the courtyard, surrounded by tablets and several oil lamps. The bright ribbons tying her braids waved gently as the evening breezes from the desert flowed against them. He ached to twist the ribbons between his fingers and loosen her hair until it fell on her shoulders as it did when he and the Shamgar swung from the clouds in sky chariots.

He stepped behind her, bent, and kissed her neck, his heart on fire at the chance to touch her. As she trembled in bewilderment, he gazed at her with longing. Countless times he had relived being with Tamiym in the emmer field and holding her for the first and last time before his marriage to Mahalath.

"My love, the city is ready for your arrival," Shammah said. She didn't turn.

His voice dropped to a whisper. "The king offers you all that he is on Earth. Other than Aleph, no one holds him more closely than you."

Tamiym still didn't move.

Shammah frowned. *Have I misread her?* Tamiym may have decided that the throne was too demanding and too public. The City of Kings was not Chaniya. To become his queen, she would forfeit a restful scholar's life. He also wondered if the wait had buried any affection she had for him. His silence as he tackled rebuilding the City of Kings and preparing for possible reprisals from Mahalath must've been terrible to bear. He hoped she understood the responsibilities he carried, and that somehow, across the distance between them, she felt the sighs of his heart.

The old shadows from his wandering years dogged the fringes of his mind. He had lived with loneliness before, and he could do so again. Although he was Seth's king, Tamiym had every right to deny him. Aikah had captured Gila and compelled her to share his throne, but Shammah wouldn't demand anything from Tamiym. If he couldn't persuade her, he wouldn't wed her. Shammah stepped back and waited.

"Does this mean that the next time Seth faces war, we ride in a sky chariot together?" she asked.

Shammah caught a hint of warmth underlying her words; how he missed their conversations. Tamiym won his heart and wooed his mind. So that he wouldn't reach for her too soon, he linked his arms behind him.

"Yes, but my queen receives such privileges."

"Then it shall be."

"Will you not look at me, my beautiful Tamiym?"

She ignored him and reached for a flattened piece of clay. Hunching over the tablet to hide her markings, she etched something in the soft clay.

Shammah shook his head when she handed him the tablet. "From the beginning?"

Tamiym turned from the table to cup his face. Bits of clay clung to her fingertips.

"From the beginning, my heart was yours. In every epic I read, in every hymn I taught my brothers, I ached for the scholar and the king I loved. I hoped he would remember me," she said. "Then my hopes dimmed. I felt blinded by darkness. I began to believe that I dreamed you loved me. Then my dreams faded into darkness, too."

Shammah wrapped his arms around her. Tamiym brought his lips to hers. Wells ruptured within him. Above them, the constellation of Aryeh slipped from the sky like droplets on a blanket and wrapped Sagi's desert home in shimmering glory.

If you enjoyed The Gate of Aleph,
please post a review.

**Will secrets hidden in the sea force
a scoundrel to save a kingdom?**

THE LOST TABLETS OF IYAR

SEVEN GATES OF THE KINGDOM BOOK 2

Coming Fall 2022

In the meantime, to show my appreciation for all
the loyal readers of this series, please visit the link below
for a **_FREE_ short story** that links *The Gate of Aleph*
to the next book, *The Lost Tablets of Iyar*.

THE AMBER WHIRLWIND

A Seven Gates of the Kingdom Short Story

Download your free copy with this link:
https://BookHip.com/CBFCRXM

ABOUT THE AUTHOR

A former newspaper journalist, J. H. Ellis enjoys ancient history, chai, and walks with her husband Oscar and their Jack-Chi Shakespeare. You can chat with J.H. Ellis on Instagram or on Twitter at jhellismusingsandbooks and @JudyHowardEllis.

SEVEN GATES
OF THE KINGDOM SERIES:

The Gate of Aleph (Seven Gates of the Kingdom Book 1)

The Amber Whirlwind (Seven Gates of the Kingdom Book 1.5)

The Lost Tablets of Iyar (Seven Gates of the Kingdom Book 2) – Coming Fall 2022

www.ingramcontent.com/pod-product-compliance
Lightning Source LLC
Chambersburg PA
CBHW020005140726
47904CB00018B/1825